The Secret's in the Sauce

A Two Broomsticks Gas & Grill Witch Cozy Mystery Book Seven

Amanda M. Lee

WinchesterShaw Publications

PROLOGUE

Krankle stood at the bottom of the rickety stairs that led to the apartment balcony above Two Broomsticks Gas & Grill and watched the silhouettes move on the other side of the glass. Stormy Morgan and Hunter Ryan were dancing—at least it looked like that to him—and he was annoyed. Since he was a cat, at least for the time being, nobody could read his mood. But he was definitely irritated.

"Is that some sort of ritual I'm not familiar with?" someone asked from the shadows next to the storage shed.

Slowly, Krankle slid his eyes to the figure. He didn't recognize the man, but it was impossible to ignore the magic flowing around him. "Who are you?"

"You know who I am." The man didn't emerge from the shadows, instead clutching tighter to the coat he wore. "Why is it so cold here?"

Krankle snorted. "You're obviously not familiar with this plane. It will get colder. We're rolling into fall. Starting now, the temperatures steadily plummet."

"You don't sound happy about that."

"I'm not." Krankle narrowed his eyes. "You won't be either. Trust me. When did you get here?"

"It's not important."

"What's your name?"

"That's not important either."

Krankle hissed his impatience. "I need something to call you. We're supposed to work together, right?"

The man sighed heavily. "You can call me West."

"As in the Wicked Witch of the West?" Krankle sneered.

"As in I go the direction the wind blows," West replied. "I need your report."

"There's nothing to report." Krankle glanced up at the window again.

Hunter and Stormy were definitely dancing. Knowing them, music wasn't even playing. They just wanted an excuse to grope each other.

"The girl is getting a handle on her powers. She's still learning."

"You're growing, though," West pointed out. "You wouldn't be growing if she were stagnating."

Krankle hated—*absolutely hated*—that Stormy's progress as a witch controlled his development. That didn't mean he wanted to give the man fodder. He didn't know West. He didn't *want* to know West. That meant he was more than happy to keep him at tail's length. "I didn't say she's stagnating. I said she's learning. There's a difference."

"Perhaps she should be learning faster than she currently is." The man's tone held an air of menace.

"She might not be learning at an acceptable rate to you, but she's learning faster than anybody else would be in her predicament," Krankle argued. "You forget, at her core, she's still human. She didn't even know what she was until a few months ago. You can't force her to learn at your rate."

"You would be surprised what I can and can't force her to do," West countered. "She needs to embrace her destiny, and sooner is better than later."

"Well, she's learning at her own pace." Agitated, Krankle hated standing up for the witch, but he couldn't help himself. He had started to grow fond of her, which was not part of his mandate. There was no stopping it, though. The girl regularly touched him, and she got under his skin in a way he hadn't anticipated. "I won't allow you to swoop in and derail her. I know her better than you do. She needs to do this on her own timetable."

"Is that a fact?" West's eyes gleamed as he fixed them on Krankle. "Are you growing soft? I thought you were specifically picked for this assignment because you're not the warm-and-fuzzy type."

"Don't worry about me." Krankle's agitation came out to play. "You don't even know me. I'm doing my job."

"Is that so?" West inclined his head toward the silhouettes visible through the window.

Instead of dancing, Hunter had decided to tickle Stormy as he chased her around the kitchen. Krankle could hear her giggles from a full floor away.

"That doesn't look like you're doing your job."

"I can't control the cop." Krankle scowled at Hunter. "He's part of the package."

"You could get rid of him."

"If you think I'm killing him, you've got another thing coming. He's well aware of what I am. Well, he's as aware as he can be with the information I've provided them. He doesn't trust me."

"Perhaps that was an error on your part."

"Maybe it was." Krankle was at the end of his rope. "But for practical reasons, you can't kill him. Stormy would never recover if something happened to him. She would fall apart, and even if she did eventually come out of it, it would be years down the line."

"I didn't say he had to die," West countered. "You can break them up."

Krankle snorted. "Nothing will break them up."

"They're humans. Their ties are tenuous at best."

"No." Krankle shook his head. "That's not true. Some humans mate knowing that their ties won't hold, but the ties between those two will never break. They lost each other once. They won't risk it again. They're a package deal."

"I still think you could break them up."

"I'll be ousted from that apartment long before he is." Krankle wasn't the type to delude himself. "Besides, they plan to buy a house together. They're looking forward to the future. The witch even talks about writing again ... though she hems and haws about that. She's not quite there."

West was quiet for a beat. When he spoke again, frustration laced every word. "You were supposed to gain control of the girl early. That's why you arrived in this form." He cast a disdainful look toward the cat. "You were supposed to lure her in, make her trust you. Most importantly, you were supposed to guide her to a different path. She's not on the right path."

"Well, I'm doing my best." Krankle didn't want to hear a word of complaint. "It's not my fault she keeps running into different opponents. Those fights help her development, but they also make her stronger in a different way. You won't be able to mold her the way you think you will."

"I will if I isolate her."

Krankle emitted a disdainful chirp. "You can't isolate her. Let's say you did manage to cut Hunter off at the knees and get her to break up with him. That's not going to happen, but let's say you manage it. You would still have to get through her family, and they're tighter than you might think when looking in from the outside. Then there are the other witches."

West jerked up his chin. "What other witches?"

"Are you kidding me?" Krankle lashed his tail. "She met up with the Winchesters almost immediately. They've essentially adopted her now. They're the reason her powers are progressing as quickly as they are."

"*Tillie.*" West growled deep in his throat. "I'd hoped to avoid her."

"Yes, well, good luck with that." Krankle turned smug. "She's drawn to Stormy's fire. She likes chaos. This town is full of turmoil right now. She's not even your biggest concern, though. Her great-niece, Bay, is the one you should worry about."

"Why? Is Bay a demon in witch's clothing too?" West demanded.

"No. She's stronger than Tillie though. She doesn't yet realize it, but her powers are growing. She and Stormy have been taking lessons from Tillie together."

"And what can the Winchester witch do? She won't have access to all of Tillie's powers. She's not a daughter or granddaughter."

"It doesn't matter in the Winchester family. They don't pass down their powers in a single line, like you're used to. Bay is a necromancer. She can do things ... well, let's just say they're not good. She could call an entire army of the dead to her side in an instant, and we couldn't do a thing to fight it."

"Huh." West rolled his neck. "That's not what I wanted to hear."

"I'm sure. The Winchesters aren't the only ones Stormy has bonded with either. There's another who's even more of a worry than Bay and Tillie combined."

"Who?" West spat, his face contorting. "Who else could she be spending her time with?"

"Another witch resides in Hawthorne Hollow." Krankle assumed a far-off look. "She's part witch and part pixie, and she constantly causes ripples in this area."

"Hawthorne Hollow has a nexus," West argued. "Perhaps that's what you sense."

"No, it's the witch. I've met her. She's a child of the stars. God, she's got a mouth on her." Krankle almost smiled, but it came across as a sneer. "If Stormy needs help, the pixie witch will come running."

"That could ruin everything," West complained.

"It could. That's why I want to tell Stormy." Krankle had made up his mind days before. He'd just been waiting for their meeting to express his opinion. "We need to tell her everything. I don't think we can wait, as was the original plan. It's better to tell her now."

West shook his head. "No."

"We have to. If Stormy keeps developing without direction, we'll have no say in the outcome, which will come back to bite us."

"I said no." West was firm. "She's not ready."

"She *is* ready." Krankle's voice was soft as he watched Hunter and Stormy make out on the second floor.

"Good grief. How often do they mindlessly mate?" West sounded horrified.

"Constantly. It's like they're in heat." Krankle was right there with him. Stormy and Hunter's continuous pawing made him nauseous. "It makes me want to wretch." Thankfully, his current guise was a cat. That meant nobody was surprised when he puked on a shoe.

"And you're certain we can't break them apart?"

"They're bonded for life," Krankle replied. "It's a waste of time and will just piss her off. That's why we have to tell her. All your plans—all *their* plans—won't work. We need to plot a new course."

"The girl isn't ready to know the truth," West argued. "She won't accept everything coming her way."

"She will," Krankle argued. "She's stronger than we anticipated."

"She's still human. She will crumble if we don't do this the exact right way."

"You're wrong. She's strong, and her bonds with the other witches ... and even that stupid idiot up there ... make her stronger. You need to adjust."

"I'm not adjusting anything," West fired back. "We'll tell her when I deem it's necessary, not a moment before."

"You'll regret it."

"Says you. I happen to think I know better. That's why you're the cat, and I'm not."

"Then I guess we'll have to wait and see." Krankle lashed his tail again. "When I'm right, though, I will expect an apology."

"When I'm right, I'll expect a lot more than that. Just keep doing what you're doing for now. The girl will be informed when it's time."

"You'll realize after the fact that you missed the right time," Krankle argued. "When that happens, you won't like where we'll find ourselves."

"And where will that be?"

"On the outside looking in."

"You let me worry about that. Just follow your orders. Otherwise, we're going to have a problem."

"I know my mission." Irritation reared up and grabbed Krankle by the throat. "I won't fail."

"See that you don't. We have a lot riding on this mission, on her. We need it to go smoothly."

Krankle didn't say what he wanted to say. If he'd learned one thing since binding himself to Stormy, though, it was that nothing in her life went smoothly. Their mission wouldn't suddenly be the exception to the already-established rule.

"I'll keep watching her," Krankle said, resigned. "You should adjust your timetable though. Trust me."

"I'll do what I want. I'm in charge here. You just do what you're told."

"If you say so."

"Yes, I say so. You're not the boss of this operation. Going forward, all the big decisions go through me."

ONE

"That's a lot of boxes."

I used my forearm to wipe the sweat from my forehead and marveled at the neat stacks of boxes my boyfriend, Hunter Ryan, had lined up in my grandfather's second garage. The space was often empty—my grandfather didn't use it much—and Hunter's belongings had taken over the bulk of the building.

I was officially exhausted—and maybe a little giddy. "Is that everything?" I looked around.

"Everything but the furniture," Hunter replied. "Since we agreed to get everything new except my bed and couch, I've already lined up buyers for most of the other stuff. They're coming tomorrow to pick it up. Landon said he would help me move the couch and bed this weekend."

I nodded. Landon Michaels was a local FBI agent whom we'd met through another witch. Bay Winchester and Landon had been married for months, and they'd become a second family to me. I spent an inordinate amount of time with them. Landon, while sarcastic and sometimes full of himself, had a heart of gold. He'd positioned himself as an important touchstone for Hunter. They were both in similar situations, law enforcement representatives devoted to witches, and they talked on a regular basis. I was growing increasingly fond of the man.

"Okay." I managed a smile, though I suddenly felt overwhelmed. "That's good."

Hunter slid his eyes to me. Worry lingered there. "What's with that 'good'? That sounded like a loaded 'good.'"

"It's not," I assured him quickly, shaking my head. "It really is good."

Hunter didn't look convinced. "Are you having second thoughts?" He almost seemed resigned.

"No." I stepped toward him, my palms out. "I'm not having second thoughts."

He'd asked me that at least ten times over the past few weeks. We'd known each other our entire lives, but we'd only been back together for several months. He was constantly worried he was pushing me too fast, that I wasn't ready. He couldn't understand that I'd been ready since the moment we'd laid eyes on each other after a decade apart.

"Please stop thinking I don't want this." Frustration suddenly grabbed my throat and squeezed. "It's just happening so fast. It feels like a dream."

"A good dream I hope." Hunter sidled over the last few steps and wrapped his arms around my waist. "I don't want to overwhelm you."

"You won't." I meant that. We had a plan to move forward, and it was a good one. "I'm ready for you to move in," I assured him. "Heck, we've practically been living together for the past few months anyway."

"That's true." He stroked his hand over my hair and rested his cheek against my forehead. "It's all finally happening."

I didn't have to ask what "all" he referred to. "Yeah. It is."

Hunter held tight for another few seconds then pulled back far enough to study my face. "I love you, Stormy Breeze."

I scowled. "You know I hate my middle name." My mother had fancied herself a hippie at one time and had named me with that in mind. She'd left her hippie ways in the dust, but the name had persisted.

"I do know that." He grinned. "I happen to love it though."

"You would."

He gave me a soft kiss, then his shoulders jerked as the door at the other end of the garage opened to allow my grandfather entrance. Hunter quickly released me. My grandfather made him nervous at the oddest moments. Clearly, it was one of those times.

"Hello. Thank you again for letting me use your garage for the winter, sir."

Grandpa, who was dressed in trousers and an unbuttoned flannel over a white T-shirt, cast Hunter an annoyed look. "Oh, don't be weird," he groused, then looked around. "I already told you I was fine with it. Once the snow falls, I won't even enter this garage. You won't either, so make sure you get everything you want in here by the end of the month. Once January rolls around, this building will be out of reach without snowshoes until the beginning of March."

"I'm pretty much done." Hunter dragged a hand through his dark hair. "I still have the couch and bed. Landon will help me with those."

"And you're moving into the apartment above the restaurant tonight?" Grandpa queried. Since he owned the restaurant and had been letting me stay there for minimal rent after I'd gotten myself into a bit of financial trouble and moved home, he was understandably curious.

"I am," Hunter confirmed. "I have all my clothes in the backseat of my truck. I also have the first rent check for you. It's in my notebook, though, packed in a box. I'll get it to you by the end of the day."

Hunter had insisted on paying twice the rent my grandfather received from me. I'd told him it wasn't necessary, but Hunter had disagreed. He'd said he wouldn't feel good about himself if he didn't pay for the privilege of living with me. That was such a Hunter thing to say.

Grandpa waved off the statement. "I trust you. Don't worry about it. Get the moving done first. That's time sensitive." His eyes moved to me. "Stormy can bring the check down tomorrow when she works her shift with me."

I scowled at the thought. I wasn't a morning person by nature, but I'd agreed to stay on the morning shift with my grandfather, even though I was finished with my probationary period. I'd worked at the restaurant when I was a teenager, so I knew the ins and outs of restaurant work, but he'd put me on probation despite that when I'd been forced to move back to Michigan. My initial plan had been to move to the dinner shift when I could—it offered better tips—but that hadn't come to fruition for multiple reasons. The biggest of which was that I would never see Hunter if I opted to work nights. As a police officer, he started his shift early. If I didn't do the same, we become two ships passing in the night, and nobody wanted that.

"I'll make sure you get it regardless," Hunter promised as he glanced around. "I'll put the couch and bed over there and cover them with tarps." He pointed toward the far end of the garage. "That should be it."

"And you're putting your house on the market this month?" Grandpa asked.

"I will put it on the market as soon as the cleaners get in there and spruce it up," Hunter replied. "I'm not sure it'll sell in December, but I see no reason not to have it ready."

"You probably won't have a lot of people looking until after Christmas," Grandpa acknowledged. "Is your plan still to buy the McDonald house?"

Hunter nodded, his hand landing on my back. "It is."

The McDonald house had always been my dream home. It was located on the other side of Shadow Hills—which didn't say much because I could drive from one side of town to the other in three minutes flat—and I'd always been enamored with the space. When Hunter had heard that Nora McDonald was thinking of selling, he'd swooped in to snap up the house for us—well, for me actually. He would've been happy staying in his current house, but since he'd bought and decorated it when I'd been away, he'd decided that a new house for a new beginning was the way to go. I'd told him I would be fine moving into his house, but he didn't want that. He wanted us to build a life together, and that was one of the reasons I loved him.

"Nora won't even put her house on the market," Hunter explained. "We've already agreed on a price. When she's ready to move, we're ready to fill out the paperwork. It's not happening until spring, though, so we need to get our finances in order before then."

I cringed at the mention of finances. Hunter's were perfectly fine.

Heck, they were pristine. Mine, however, were a bit of a mess. When I'd left Shadow Hills, my goal had been to become a famous author. I'd managed it for a bit. Okay, maybe I wasn't famous. I'd gotten a solid book deal as a first-time author, however, and my first book had sold well. Unfortunately, my second book had been a dud, and my finances had fallen off a cliff along with the book's sales. If I'd been smart, I would've come home then. Instead, I'd believed I could turn things around and had started living off credit cards. I was in dire straits by the time I returned home in the spring. Hunter had yet to see everything I was dealing with, though he'd started making noise about me showing him the damage. I dreaded the day.

"I think you guys will be happy there." It was rare for Grandpa to be so easygoing. Mostly, he liked messing with his children and grandchildren. On that particular subject, however, he'd been nothing but delightful. "It sounds like a good plan to me. Stormy will get her dream house. You'll get your dream woman. Everybody will be happy."

"And you'll get us out of the apartment above the restaurant," I added. "So you can take your afternoon constitutional there without being bothered."

"Yes, I look forward to that." Grandpa pinned me with a serious look. "You're taking that cat with you, right?"

At the mention of Krankle, my stomach tightened. I'd adopted him when I'd thought he was a helpless kitten lost in an alley. I'd fed him, loved him, invited him to curl up on a pillow in my bed. That had all been before I'd found out he was a gnome shifter from another plane. I couldn't look at him the same way anymore.

"We're taking him," I replied stiffly. *Really, what else can we do?* We couldn't leave him behind. We were the only ones who knew his true origins. If I abandoned him, even though he was capable of taking care of himself, I would look like a monster.

"Yes, and we're thrilled about it," Hunter agreed sarcastically.

His relationship with Krankle was tempestuous at best. They were constantly pushing one another's buttons. Hunter wanted answers, something Krankle was reluctant to give, and when Hunter gave him grief, Krankle retaliated by crapping in his shoes. It had turned into a thing.

Grandpa chuckled. "As long as you're taking him, that's all that matters. What about writing?"

As far as transitions went, that wasn't his finest offering. I feigned ignorance. "What do you mean?" I didn't meet his heavy gaze.

"Oh, don't do that." Grandpa wagged a finger. "Let's pretend for a second that we're both adults."

I turned away from him and focused on the boxes. "These won't fall over, right? I don't want your stuff to get broken." I felt Hunter and Grandpa staring at my back but didn't turn around. I could imagine the expressions on their faces—not something I wanted to see up close and personal.

"We're not going to push her on the writing," Hunter explained to Grandpa. "She'll do it when she's ready."

"I think I'm done with writing," I argued. I waffled back and forth on the subject, sometimes from minute to minute. It had always been my dream, but somewhere along the way, I'd lost it. I had found a different dream. Only sometimes did it involve writing.

"You're not done writing," Grandpa scoffed. "You're just ... in a mood."

"Or I'm not nearly as good at writing as I thought." My hands fisted at my sides as I swiveled back. Talking about writing inevitably made me itchy. "Have you ever considered that?"

"No," Grandpa replied, not missing a beat. "You're a great writer. You get it from me. How could you be anything other than great?"

I had to bite back a laugh. It was so like him to believe he was the source of everything good in our family. He also took credit for my cousin Hannah's double-jointed knees. Why that was something to be proud of, I couldn't say. "I don't know what will happen with the writing." I chose my words carefully. "I just ... don't know. I guess we'll see in a year or two."

"Or you could get back on the horse and put those fears to rest right now," Grandpa argued. "There's no reason you can't try."

I could think of a million reasons. The biggest one, the one that made me sick whenever I thought too hard about writing, was the only one I couldn't give voice to. *What if I only had one good book in me?*

"I think you should give it a rest," Hunter interjected. "She's doing the best she can. If she doesn't want to write right now, she doesn't have to."

Grandpa shot Hunter an incredulous look. "I thought you wanted her to write."

"I want her to do what makes her happy," Hunter countered. "If she's not ready yet, forcing her to write won't make her enjoy it. Drop it."

"No." Grandpa shook his head. "I agreed to keep my opinion to myself when she first came back. She's settled now though. You're moving in together. She's getting her life on track. That means it's time for her to start writing again."

I didn't want to be trapped in the conversation. It made me itchy and uncomfortable. When I darted a look toward the wide double doors, however, behind which Hunter's truck was parked, Hunter shook his head.

"No, there's no reason to run," he chided. "It's fine. You'll start writing again when you're ready."

What if I'm never ready? That was another fear constantly plaguing me. *What if I somehow had this wonderful ability to spew words onto the page and turn them into magic, but I've lost it? What if it never comes back?*

As if reading my mind, Hunter slipped his arm around my waist. "Don't listen to him," he said in a low voice. "He's not trying to upset you. He just doesn't understand how hard it is for you."

"What I don't understand is why you're coddling her," Grandpa shot back. "She's my granddaughter. I think I know better than most what she is and isn't capable of. She's always been a good writer. That was part of her dream life. She should be chasing her dream."

Hunter looked exasperated. "You're just too much sometimes. Has anybody ever told you that?"

"Nobody who counts." Grandpa was firm. "She needs to at least think about writing again. She doesn't need to hammer out a book by the end of the year or anything, but she could start jotting ideas in those notebooks she used to carry around with her constantly or something. I never thought I would miss those notebooks, but I do."

He wasn't the only one. I hadn't carried a notebook in years. It was as if I'd run out of ideas at some point—another reason I couldn't even think about writing. I had no ideas. When once I'd had so many I couldn't write them all down, my mind had become a blank.

"Knock it off," Hunter growled. "You're pushing her too hard. She's just going to dig in her heels if you keep insisting. She'll start writing when she's ready."

"Oh, you baby her." Grandpa scuffed his unlaced boots against the garage floor. "She's got talent. She got it from me. Do you know anybody who tells a better story than I do? She should be embracing it."

I had no more patience to spare. "Let's get going." I tugged Hunter's shirt sleeve. He'd taken his coat off when moving the boxes, but we were done with that. It was time to go. "We can unpack your stuff tonight, then celebrate."

Hunter's eyes gleamed. "That sounds fun."

"Oh, gross." Grandpa made a face. "Don't be making a bunch of noise with people eating downstairs. I run a nice, clean family establishment. I don't want to explain strange noises."

"Yet you yelling every time someone orders poached eggs is allowable," I muttered.

"I heard that." Grandpa only had trouble hearing when my grandmother wanted something from him. "Only a psychopath wants poached eggs. That's been proven in a court of law."

Ah, there was another instance of him telling stories. "Listen—"

Before I could finish, a scream rang out from the other side of the garage door. It came from the street, and it didn't sound like kids playing. I jerked my eyes in that direction, confused. I couldn't see anybody on the street behind Hunter's truck, but obviously, somebody was out there.

I started to suggest we check out the noise—it would make for an easy escape—but another scream erupted, louder than the first. Something was definitely going on.

"To be continued," Grandpa groused as he headed toward the double doors. "This conversation isn't over. Obviously, the neighbors need my attention, however, so we'll deal with that first."

I was more than happy to switch my attention to the neighbors.

Whatever horror they faced had to be better than what we were dealing with in the garage.

"Yeah, let's see what's going on." Hunter took my hand. "It's probably just the neighbors fighting again. It's a regular occurrence in this neighborhood. We should check it out though."

Two

Once we were clear of Hunter's truck, the source of the screaming became apparent. Absolute bedlam had broken out on Division Street, and women stood around some huge lump in the road as they screamed at one another. To my absolute surprise, my grandmother was one of them.

"Which one of you did this?" Grandma demanded, hands on hips. She wore her housecoat and slippers, which informed me she hadn't planned on a walk outside. "I know it was one of you. We all know what you were doing together, so it had to be one of you."

Confused, I edged to my right to get a better look at what they were arguing over. I didn't know what I had expected—perhaps that a vandal had broken a garden gnome and tossed it in the road or something—but as I grew closer, it became apparent that whatever was on the ground was bigger than a garden gnome.

"Is that...?" I trailed off.

"A body," Hunter said grimly. He increased his pace. "Ladies, what is going on?"

The women—all of whom I recognized—scattered like crazed chickens when they saw him.

"I didn't do it," Grandma announced. "I was inside doing my beauty regimen when I saw all of them milling about. I'm innocent."

Hunter gave her a hard look before kneeling next to the body. He didn't immediately jump in to save the individual on the ground because it was obviously too late. Edmund Hawthorne, the former owner of Shadow Hills's only garage, lay on his back, his eyes wide and unseeing. No heart attack or other ailment had claimed him though. No, that would have been too easy. He had a knife sticking out of his chest.

"Holy crap," I muttered as realization swept over me. "Holy crap!"

"Watch your mouth," Grandma ordered.

My eyebrows drew toward one another. "Since when is crap a dirty word?"

"It's a four-letter word, and I don't like it," Grandma snapped. She did a double take when she saw Grandpa with us. "Just what the hell were the three of you doing in the garage?"

I wanted to ask why "crap" wasn't allowed when she was dropping "hell" in the middle of the conversation, but it didn't seem like an argument worth risking my sanity over.

"What happened here?" Hunter demanded. He pressed his fingers to Edmund's neck to check for a pulse. He appeared long gone, but Hunter had a job to do.

"Ask them." Grandma folded her arms across her chest and lifted her chin toward the four women gathered on the other side of Edmund's body. She looked incensed—a rare occurrence. She was often the calm one in our family, which didn't say much. We were all prone to histrionic fits depending on the day.

"I'm asking *all* of you," Hunter snapped as he pulled out his phone.

Since Shadow Hills was so small, it would take the ambulance at least fifteen minutes to reach us after the call, especially if the driver had decided to stop for a late lunch.

"Hold on." Hunter held up his hand when Grandma opened her mouth again. "Just a second." He placed his call, giving the location of the body, then turned his eyes back to my grandmother. "Go."

"I was just minding my own business," Grandma started.

"Oh, right," one of the other women snapped. "Like you've ever minded your own business."

I recognized her as Florence Chase. She used to be a member of my grandmother's inner circle—it was like the Golden Girls mafia around these parts—but they'd had a falling out when I was in high school and had never repaired the friendship despite being neighbors.

"I'm talking now, *Flo*," Grandma drawled, putting emphasis on the shortened name. "When we want your opinion, we'll bark like dogs to alert you to your turn. One bitch recognizes another, right?"

My eyebrows practically flew off my forehead. My grandmother was often described as "sweet." I'd never heard her talk like that to anybody before—well, anybody who wasn't related to her. She'd never done it in public to my recollection. That was for sure.

"Let's not start this," Hunter snapped, on his knees as he inspected the body. "Just tell me what happened."

"I don't know what happened," Grandma replied primly. "I was moisturizing my face—I do that, so I won't look like Flo over there—when I noticed them all out on the road. Naturally, I came to see what they were looking at. That's when I found this." She gestured toward Edmund. "What a mess. Who will get the blood off the street?"

Of course she would worry about that. "Are you the one who screamed?" I asked.

Grandma shot me a withering look. "I don't scream."

"You do when I'm feeling motivated," Grandpa said out of nowhere. He'd been largely quiet since we'd escaped the garage, which was unusual for him. He typically decided to add his two cents to the conversation when he had an opening to boast about himself.

"Don't be gross." I scowled. "I'm going to have nightmares."

"We're all going to have nightmares." Hunter rolled back on his haunches and surveyed the foursome opposite of us.

They steadily edged away from the body.

"Which one of you found him first?"

Iris St. James slowly raised her hand. She was in her seventies—as was everybody in the group, including the victim, if I remembered correctly—and her platinum-blond hair was like a helmet in the wind. It didn't move. "I did, on my afternoon walk." She shot a challenging look toward Grandma. "That's what I do because I don't want to look like her."

Grandma took a step in her direction, but Hunter swept out an arm to keep her back.

"Don't even think about it," he warned.

I had questions about my grandmother and her former friends, but I thought it best to wait to ask them.

"Do you always walk this route, Iris?" Hunter asked.

She nodded. "I always walk the same route. I take Jefferson to North Limits. Then I swing around to Monroe Street and walk down Division before heading home."

"She makes sure to walk past all our houses," Florence volunteered. "She thinks she's sending us a message."

"The only message I want to send you includes a goodbye," Iris shot back.

"Unbelievable." Hunter pinched the bridge of his nose.

I felt sorry for him. He'd hardly made any headway, and he likely already had a headache.

Hunter regained his focus. "Did you scream when you saw the body?"

"Oh, no." Iris shook her head. "I just stood there and stared, convinced I was having a bad dream."

"That's how we all feel when we're near you, Iris," Grandma drawled.

"Who screamed?" Hunter demanded before the argument could kick up again.

"That would be me." Gwen Gilmore raised her hand. "I was watching out the window and saw Iris. At first, I thought she was walking a dog or something. I heard a rumor she'd given up on dating because the Replens was no longer working, but then I realized the thing in the middle of the road was too big to be a dog. I came out to see what it was, and when I did ... well, I lost my head for a moment." She looked sheepish.

"I don't need Replens," Iris hissed. "I'm not old and dried up like you."

I slapped my hand over my face. The conversation just kept getting worse and worse.

"I don't care who needs ... whatever it is you're talking about," Hunter hissed. He leaned closer to me. "What's Replens?"

"Vaginal lubrication," I whispered.

He made a face. "I need to know what happened here," he barked.

"We don't know what happened here," Blanche Thomas volunteered, speaking for the first time. "That's why we're all so upset. This is a quiet neighborhood. Well, except when Charlie over there decides to go skinny-dipping. At least it's winter, though, so we don't have to worry about that again until June. You have our sympathies for curling up with that every night." She pressed her hand to her heart in a mocking fashion and stared pointedly at my grandmother.

"Was that insult supposed to be aimed at me?" Grandpa demanded.

"This isn't about you," Hunter replied.

"It sounded like she was talking about me. I'll have you know, I'm in prime condition." He ran his hands over his extensive middle. "That's the reason all you harpies like to watch me swim in the summer. You want a piece of this." He swung his hips.

"He's the reason we need the Replens," Florence explained.

"I think I might pass out," I muttered.

Hunter shot me a sympathetic look. He couldn't very well soothe me when he had a dead body to deal with, however. "Basically, if I'm following this conversation, you're saying that none of you actually saw who did this to Edmund. Am I right?"

"He was just out here," Iris said. "He's probably been there all night."

"No, he wasn't." Hunter shook his head. "We've been here about three hours moving stuff to store in the garage. He wasn't in the middle of the road when we arrived. We would've seen him."

"Oh." Iris looked taken aback. "Well, maybe you hit him when you were pulling in. You might not have noticed."

"And what, he was walking around with a knife in his chest out of boredom?" Hunter challenged.

"Oh, right." Iris looked as if she was concentrating, but her forehead didn't move a fraction of an inch.

My grandmother, as if picking up on my unasked question, smiled. "Iris throws regular Botox parties. That's why her face is frozen stiff."

"You're just jealous," Iris fired back. "You could hide raisins in those wrinkles of yours. You wish you looked as young as I do."

"I look ten years younger than you," Grandma fired back. "Are you kidding me?"

"If by ten years younger you mean ten years older, you've got me there." Iris gave a feral smile.

"Un-freaking-believable," Hunter muttered. "Just what did I do to deserve this?"

I felt bad for him. I didn't know how to help him, however. "Where does Edmund even live?" I couldn't remember him in the area at all. I just remembered the garage.

"Over there." Gwen pointed toward the opposite side of Jefferson. "He lives in the corner house there."

"Mrs. Garibaldi's house?"

"She died," Grandma replied. "People say it was a heart attack, but I heard she was taking a stripper pole class."

I was really confused. "A stripper pole class?"

"It was a thing five or six years ago," Hunter volunteered. "That dance studio, the one downtown that's now been turned into a gym? Well, before they closed the doors for good, they tried to bring in more clients. A pole dancing class was one of the offerings."

"Huh." I'd heard of pole dancing classes before. They were a regular thing in some of the cities I'd visited over the years. I simply couldn't imagine anybody in Shadow Hills participating. "Was anybody any good at it?"

"Phoebe," Hunter replied.

Well, that made sense. Phoebe Green wore her sexuality like one wore a scarf in the winter. She'd been horrible to me for as long as I could remember. Somehow, a pole dancing class seemed like something she would do, and not because she wanted exercise.

Slowly, I tracked my eyes back to Hunter. "How do you know Phoebe did well at that class?"

"Because she told anybody who would listen," he replied. "Heck, she told people who had no interest in listening. Let's get back on topic, please. When was the last time anybody saw Edmund?"

"Oh, um, I saw him this morning," Grandma replied. "He went out to get his newspaper in his underwear." Her smile told me she thought that was a good thing.

"I saw him around ten o'clock." Gwen almost acted as if she were trying to one-up Grandma. "He was on his front porch in his robe. It wasn't lashed properly."

Confused, I flicked my eyes to Hunter. He looked as baffled as I felt.

"I saw him at lunch," Florence sang. "I made a pot of chili in my crockpot yesterday and had way too much food. I decided to take him some of my extras. We ate it together."

Hunter nodded, taking it all in. "Anybody else?" He glanced at Blanche.

"I didn't see him today." She almost looked disappointed. "I was busy dealing with my Medicaid prescription plan. They shorted me on a bill."

"For Replens," my grandmother muttered under her breath.

I shot her a quelling look. *What is even happening here?* I'd never seen her like that. Under different circumstances, I might find her reaction to the entire thing funny. Nothing about it was funny.

"Okay." Hunter took control of the scene. "For now, I need you all to go home."

"What are you going to do?" Florence asked.

"Well, since I'm a police officer, I'm going to investigate," Hunter replied. "That's the plan anyway."

"How do we know it's not an accident?" Gwen wrung her hands. "Like ... maybe he was bringing the knife to someone else and accidentally tripped. It's tragic, but that's nothing to investigate."

Grandma shot her a well-duh look. "You think he tripped, somehow fell on his back, and accidentally rammed the knife into his own chest? How stupid are you?"

"You're stupid," Gwen fired back. "It was a legitimate question."

"It was a stupid question." Grandma shook her head. "Seriously, what is wrong with you people? Well, other than the obvious."

"If the word 'Replens' comes out of your mouth one more time, you're in trouble," Hunter warned. "You guys need to head inside too," he said to my grandparents. "I need to focus on my work."

"Well, that's a fine 'thank you for letting me use your garage,'" Grandma sniffed. "I guess I know where we stand. Come on, Stormy." She jerked her chin for me to follow.

Hunter immediately shook his head when I shot him a questioning look. "Stormy will stay with me. I need an assistant."

Iris shifted closer. "I could be your assistant." She peered through lowered lashes that had to be fake.

"I think I'll stick with Stormy." Hunter looked relieved when the ambulance rolled around the corner. "There's Dale. You guys need to head inside. I'll have more questions for you all later, but I need to handle the body first."

"Fine." Grandma's eyes flashed. "Just know I'm not going to forget this." With that, she turned on her heel and flounced toward the house.

When I looked at Grandpa, he was smiling.

"This is pretty far from funny," I chastised.

"What?" Grandpa shook his head, as if emerging from a reverie. "That right there, Stormy, is exactly why I fell in love with your grandmother. She's fiery." The look on his face had my mind going to a place I never wanted to visit.

"Oh, you're going to be gross, aren't you?"

"I'm considered a prime piece of grade-A beef for a reason." Grandpa whistled as he chased after my grandmother.

Thankfully, when I looked back to where the other women had been moments before, they were gone. "What's going on here?" I demanded of Hunter. "What was with all the aggressive women?"

He laughed at my befuddlement. "I forget sometimes that you took a break from the joy that is Shadow Hills." He moved away from the body so Dale could take a look at the situation. "All the women in this neighborhood have been at each other's throats for years."

"I knew that my grandmother had fallen out with Florence," I admitted. "I didn't realize she was at war with the rest of them."

"Oh, this isn't a her-against-them thing. Your grandmother hates all those women, and they hate her, too, but none of them like each other.

Sometimes, they'll call a truce for a few days, but that never lasts long. They all work against each other."

"You're talking about the old lady mob?" Dale removed the rolling gurney from the ambulance. "Yeah, you don't want to get on their bad sides. It's like *The Godfather*, except with old ladies, and you won't find a horse head in your bed."

I was almost afraid to ask. "What will you find?"

"Don't say the word Replens," Hunter warned.

Dale chuckled. "You'll more than likely find a set of bloody knitting needles in your bed. They actively hate one another and promise death whenever they're in a mood ... which is often."

"Huh." I rolled my neck and stared back at my grandparents' house. Given the look on my grandfather's face when he'd chased my grandmother, nothing on Earth could tempt me to go inside. I had questions though. "You don't think any of them are responsible for this, do you?" I asked Hunter, gesturing toward Edmund.

"I don't know," he replied. "I plan to find out though."

THREE

Once Edmund's body was in the ambulance and on its way to the medical examiner's office—Shadow Hills was too small to have its own, so the town contracted with the county—Hunter suggested we check out Edmund's house. I was game, but I felt multiple sets of eyes on us as we walked down the street.

"We're being watched," I mused. "I bet everybody will be asking questions about why I'm involved in this."

Hunter didn't take my hand like he normally would, but he shot me a reassuring smile. "It's fine. If anybody has a problem with it, they can take it up with me."

"Yeah, that's not how it works here." I managed a grin, but it faded fast. "How could he be stabbed in the middle of the street like that, and nobody noticed? It seems everybody in this neighborhood is up on what everybody else is doing. How did they miss a murder?"

"Yes, well, this neighborhood is ... eclectic."

His word choice had me hiding a smile. "Are you including my grandparents in that observation?"

"Yup." He bobbed his head. "Do you know how many complaints I get any given summer regarding your grandfather's need to skinny-dip?"

"No. How many?"

"More than I can count. Apparently, he likes to wander around the yard naked when he's done."

"I heard he likes to climb on the trampoline and dry there."

"Where did you hear that?"

"Him."

Hunter choked on a laugh. "He is open about his nudist tendencies."

"What do you tell people who complain?"

"That as long as he's not walking down the street naked or flashing kids or something, they should mind their own business. They, of course, disagree. They think I'm giving your grandfather a pass because of you."

"Are you?" I was honestly curious.

"No. He's been skinny-dipping for as long as I can remember, and you were gone for a decade. I didn't arrest him during your missing years."

"Yeah, but you were pining for me," I teased, going for levity. "You probably let him do his thing to feel closer to me."

Hunter cast me a sidelong look. I expected him to deny the charge. Instead, he merely shrugged. "I *was* pining for you. I wouldn't have given your grandfather a free pass simply because of that, though. The truth is he's not hurting anybody. He minds his own business when he does ... what he does. Your grandmother is more of a problem."

Like that, he had my full attention. "What do you mean by that?"

"Listen, you know I love your grandmother, right?"

I nodded.

"She's been nothing but good to me. Even when you were gone, she went out of her way to bring me Christmas cookies at the station. She invited me to Thanksgiving. Heck, she dropped off Valentine's Day cookies too. Whenever she stopped by, she told me that it would all work out."

I was taken aback. "What would work out? Us?"

He nodded.

"How could she know that? I was living in denial that entire time."

"She wasn't. She kept saying that you would come home when it was the right time. I didn't want to believe that because I thought false hope would cripple me, but in hindsight, it seems she was right."

I leaned close to whisper, "I was pining for you too. I didn't always realize it, but you were the ache I couldn't quite get rid of."

He snorted. "I'm not sure that's a compliment, baby. I don't want to be an ache."

"You never left me. Not really."

He leaned in and pressed a quick kiss to the side of my head. "I feel the same way. I don't want to talk about your time away, though. I think we've covered that topic as many times as necessary. As for your grandmother, she was always good to me, but she wasn't always good to everybody else."

"You mean the other ladies in the neighborhood," I surmised.

"Pretty much. The women of a certain age in this particular neighborhood are like the Golden Mean Girls."

I pressed my lips together to keep from laughing at the picture he painted. "Is that so?" I asked when I was relatively certain I could speak without laughing. The last thing we needed was the spying neighbors filming us having a good time in the wake of Edmund's death.

"It's true. They're cliquey. They fight with one another, call each other names. They don't declare one day of the week for wearing pink or anything, but they're not far off."

"I want to say it's difficult for me to picture my grandmother acting that way, but it's actually not. I saw a hint of it at the senior center when that whole thing came up with the euchre tournament. She likes being in charge. More than that, she likes when other people aren't in charge."

"It's a power game," Hunter confirmed as we arrived in Edmund's driveway. "All the women in this neighborhood want to be in charge, and they're willing to mess with the other women to claim the crown. It's very frustrating. We get eight or nine nuisance calls a week from this part of town, and it's always the same people."

"Does my grandmother call too?"

He shrugged. "Not as often as some of the others—Blanche, for example, calls three times a week—but your grandmother is not above reporting that Iris didn't put her garbage bags in the bin or that Florence walks by your grandma's windows without wearing a bra."

I couldn't contain myself as we reached the front door. I burst out laughing. "Does she really report that stuff?"

"Yup."

"Well, it's probably good she doesn't bother to hang out behind the restaurant and stare into the apartment at night because I rarely wear a bra once I'm home from my shift."

"Yes, we need to talk about that." Hunter checked the door and found it open.

"You want me to wear a bra?" That wasn't the tack I expected him to take.

"Of course not." He made a face. "It's just, now that we're living together ... I might have one of the guys from the department over occasionally. You tend to leave your bras hanging on top of the lamps and stuff."

"Oh." Realization dawned on me. "You want me to pick up after myself."

"I won't be a nag," he countered. "It's just ... that apartment isn't overly big. I thought maybe we could come up with some rules or something." He looked distinctly uncomfortable.

"What sort of rules?"

"Like ... I won't leave my boxers on the bathroom floor, and you won't leave your bras hanging on the lamps."

"I do that when they're drying."

"I know." He looked pained. "Can't we find a spot in the bedroom for that, though?"

"Sure." I didn't understand his discomfort, but it wasn't worth fighting over. "We can do whatever you want. It's your home now too."

"See, I'm uncomfortable with the entire thing." He grumbled as we let ourselves into the small ranch house. "It's your apartment. You're just letting me live there until we move into the new house. I don't want to be bossy."

"It's not a big deal," I assured him. "I don't even think about the bras. If they bug you, I'll find a spot to hang them in the bedroom."

"We'll talk about it later." Hunter removed two sets of rubber gloves from his coat and handed a pair to me. "Don't touch anything with your bare hands."

I took the gloves and wrinkled my nose. "You just carry these around in your pocket?"

"You never know when you'll need them. It's just a habit." He snapped his into place. "I need to see what we've got here. If I think the attack happened inside the house, I'll have to call for the county's crime team. They have special lab technicians. I really don't want them finding your fingerprints in this house. Then I would have to explain why I brought you with me."

"Got it." I put on the gloves, even though it felt weird to wear them, and headed into the kitchen. "It looks like he was eating dinner." I glanced at the clock on the wall. "It's only five o'clock. Does that mean he was eating dinner at four o'clock?"

"I believe that's a specific joke about aging for a reason." Hunter studied the food. "Looks like spaghetti with meatballs and fresh-baked bread." His brow furrowed. "I wouldn't have pegged Edmund as much of a cook."

I pointed toward the pink Tupperware container on the counter. "I think someone dropped it off." I angled myself so I could better look at the bread. "Also, I'm pretty sure that's one of those loaves you buy frozen. They're amazingly good, but nobody baked the bread from scratch." Something occurred to me. "He's a senior. Does Hawthorn Hollow have a local Meals on Wheels or maybe a meal delivery service through the senior center?"

"Oh, that's an idea." Hunter cocked his head. "I think the senior center has something. I'll have one of my guys ask some questions. I could see Edmund going that route."

"It looks good." I glanced around. "I don't see signs of a struggle, and he was about halfway through his meal. Does that mean something drew him outside?"

"I like how your mind works," Hunter replied. "I very rarely have to explain things to you. I think it's the author in you. You puzzle things out yourself."

"Oh, can we not go there?" I groused, my shoulders hunching. "You're as bad as my grandfather."

"That is a terrible thing to say to the man you love." Hunter looked wounded. "I wasn't trying to push you. I'm prepared to wait years if it means you'll go back to writing because *you* want it. I'm just saying, you have an orderly mind when it comes to stuff like this. It's as if you can see it and plot it in your head."

"Oh." I smiled. "I guess that was a nice thing to say."

"Yes, it was lovely. I expect to be rewarded with kisses at the first opportunity." He playfully bumped his shoulder into mine before walking into the living room. "Nothing is out of place in here."

To me, the room read as sterile. The coffee table didn't even have a coaster. "See, I would've guessed Edmund was the sort of guy who liked to watch football and basketball games regularly," I mused. "This living room doesn't look like a lot of living happens here."

"That's because the back of the house has a Florida room," Hunter replied. "It has a television. He smoked his cigars and drank his beer out there."

"Oh." That made sense. "Should we go there next?"

"Yeah, I just want to check his bedroom first." Hunter headed down the hallway. "Whatever happened, I don't think the fight broke out inside the house. I think it happened outside. All the knives were still in the butcher block."

I hadn't even looked. "I think you're the one with the orderly mind. I wouldn't have thought to check that."

I turned the corner to follow him into Edmund's bedroom and immediately smacked into Hunter's broad back as he froze inside the doorway.

"Ow!" I ruefully rubbed my nose.

Hunter angled his head to look over his shoulder, genuine horror reflected in his eyes. "I don't think you should see this," he said in a low voice.

"Oh, no." The words were akin to waving a red scarf in front of a bull, and I shifted so I could see what had the color draining from his handsome features. I expected to find blood, maybe even another body. Instead, I found something so much worse.

My mouth dropped open, drying the saliva, and I openly gaped at the bedroom. It was not what I expected. In fact, it was unlike anything I'd ever seen. It was—well, words escaped me.

"What a passion pit." My stomach threatened to revolt when I saw what looked to be a huge dildo on the bed. "Oh, my... "

Instinct had me reaching for it, but Hunter slapped back my hand.

"Don't touch that," he hissed. "You don't know where it's been."

He had a point. Still, I couldn't believe what I was seeing. Sex toys occupied every surface of the room. The old-school television on the nightstand came with an attached VCR, and VHS tapes lay scattered in every direction. I picked up one of the tapes so I could read the title, then instantly chastised myself for doing something so idiotic.

"*Village of the Rammed*," I read aloud.

"Oh, this is so bad," Hunter muttered, lowering his head. "I could've gone my entire life without seeing this."

He might've been embarrassed, but I was officially intrigued. "Look at all these tapes. *White Men Can't Hump. Throbin Hood. The Hitchhikers Guide to the G-Spot.*"

"Stop reading those." Hunter shot me a death glare. "I'm going to have nightmares."

"Sorry." I wasn't really. He was a bit of a prude when he wanted to be. I couldn't stop myself from reading the titles. "This one doesn't sound so bad. *The Good, the Bed, and the Snuggly.*"

"After seeing this room, something tells me it isn't wholesome."

"Probably not." I forced myself away from the tapes and looked at the bed. "Are those fuzzy handcuffs up near the headboard?"

"Stop pointing stuff out to me." When I glanced at Hunter, I found his eyes squeezed shut. "I need to wake up. This is just a bad dream. This totally isn't real."

I lightly clapped his shoulder. "I'm really glad you made me wear the gloves now."

"You're enjoying yourself far too much."

"I think that's what this room was designed for." I moved to the chest at the end of the bed. It was open, and the items inside were— well, there were no words. "I don't even know what some of this stuff is," I said in awe. "What's that plug thing?"

"What did I just say?" Hunter was beside himself. "Stop pointing things out to me. My head might explode."

I couldn't help myself. He was so adorable sometimes it made my heart hurt. "We can look it up on the internet later."

I moved to peer inside the closet, but footsteps in the hallway made me jerk my head in that direction. Hunter heard them, too, because he carefully positioned himself between me and the door as a figure filled the open frame.

"Hunter?" a man asked, confused.

"Hey, Marty." Hunter relaxed, if only marginally. "I didn't hear you knock."

"It's my father's house," Marty replied. "I don't generally knock." He made a face as he glanced around the bedroom. "Ugh. Why are you guys in here?"

"Why are you here?" I blurted.

He didn't seem surprised by the bedroom, which had my mind going a million miles a minute.

"I heard that an ambulance was sent here, and I wanted to check on my dad. He's not answering his phone."

Suddenly, I felt sick to my stomach for reasons other than the passion pit.

"I have bad news for you, Marty," Hunter said in an even tone. He'd had to deliver that sort of news before and seemed prepared. "Your father was killed about an hour ago. We were in Stormy's grandfather's garage and heard screaming. He was dead on the street. Somebody had stabbed him. I planned to notify you myself, but I wanted to check inside the house first," he continued. "I need to secure it as a crime scene, though I've yet to find evidence that whatever scuffle happened started here."

Marty blinked several times, clearly confused. "I don't ... understand." His voice turned raspy. "Are you saying my father is dead?"

"I'm sorry." Hunter didn't couch his words. "He's dead. He's on his way to the medical examiner's office right now."

Marty staggered and leaned against the doorframe to keep himself upright. "Oh, geez."

"I'm sorry, man." Hunter's tone was soft. "I wish you didn't have to find out this way."

"It's not your fault." Marty waved his hand and squeezed his eyes shut. "I told him this would happen. He didn't listen to me, of course—he never listened to me—but I told him."

"You knew he was in danger?" Hunter straightened. "What had he gotten himself into?"

"It's more like who did he get himself into," Marty replied grimly. "I think the answer is pretty obvious." He gestured toward the outrageous bedroom. "My father fancied himself a ladies' man for the last two years of his life."

"Meaning what?" Hunter asked incredulously. "Who was he dating?"

"In this neighborhood? The more apt question would be who wasn't he dating? Any woman in the area who was even close to his age made his list. He was dating them all."

Hunter looked staggered. That was nothing compared to what I felt though.

"You've got to be joking," Hunter said finally.

"I wish I were, but it's true. He was sleeping with all of them ... and he was proud of it."

Oh, well, that was the motive we were looking for.

"Yeah, I'm going to need a list." Hunter looked resigned. "I'm also going to have to ... I don't know, close off the house for a little bit." He gestured toward the bed. "This could be evidence. I'll inventory everything."

"Yeah, I don't want any of it after," Marty said. "You can burn the whole thing down as far as I'm concerned."

"Let's start with information," Hunter prodded. "We'll go from there."

FOUR

Marty laid it all out for us, and it wasn't pretty.

"I thought it was just a phase, that he was lonely or something after my mother died," Marty explained. "When it started with two of them at a time, I tried to let it go. He just kept expanding and expanding though."

I had questions—oh, so many questions—but it was Hunter's show. We'd moved into the living room because the bedroom proved too distracting. The memory of the room would be burned into my brain for a very long time, however.

"Did the women ever fight over him?" Hunter asked.

"All the time." Marty pressed the heel of his hand to his forehead. "I haven't come around much the last few months. It was too stressful. We started meeting at the diner for dinner once a week. He would tell me about all his conquests, but I hated the stories. The last time I was here, two of the women got in a fight over him in the front yard. They actually tried to wrestle each other."

"Who was it?"

"I don't remember. I'm telling you, every single woman in this neighborhood visited that bedroom. It was horrifying."

"I can imagine." Hunter slid his eyes to me. He looked as if he had a million questions but was too polite to bury Marty in a salacious retelling of his father's sexploits, given what had happened mere hours before. "Listen, you need to get in touch with the medical examiner's office. I don't think they will release your father's body until tomorrow at the earliest. It will probably be the day after that."

"If you plan to do a funeral, I'm sure Sebastian can help," I volunteered, referring to my best friend, Sebastian Donovan. He owned the local funeral home, and despite his high-strung personality, he was very good at his job. "He'll know what to do."

"Yeah. Thanks." Marty blew out a sigh. "I think I need a bit of time to come to grips with this. I can't believe it happened. I mean, I warned him it could, but he didn't listen. He was having too much fun."

"We need to close off the house now," Hunter supplied. "Do you need something before we do? Paperwork or anything?"

"Oh, um, I don't think so." Marty pushed himself to a stand. "If I need something, I'll let you know. I can't think right now. As for the house, I don't even want to worry about it. It can wait."

"Okay."

We talked for a few more minutes, then Marty made his exit.

When it was just the two of us, Hunter turned his incredulous eyes to me. "Can you believe this?"

Honestly, I could. My visits to the senior center had told me Shadow Hills housed a lot more single women of a certain age than men. I'd seen some of the squabbles firsthand. Edmund's circumstances seemed extreme, but I didn't have trouble believing that the local women would fight over what they considered an eligible bachelor.

"It seems Edmund liked being the center of attention," I mused. "We're assuming that's what got him killed, right?"

"I think that's our best bet." Hunter exhaled heavily. "This is just ... unbelievable."

"What will you do?"

He was quiet for several seconds, then let his shoulders droop. "I'm going to finish searching the rest of the house. Then I'm going to lock it up. You can help me with the police tape. After that, I think I'll have to wait for the autopsy report. Maybe we'll get lucky, and his fingernails will have some skin samples under them to DNA test or something."

"You won't get the autopsy report today, right?"

"No. Tomorrow."

"Okay, well, let's finish up." I tried to be upbeat, but it wasn't easy. "I'll make dinner when we get home."

"Just no spaghetti."

I smirked. "I was thinking I would order takeout from the restaurant."

"Ah, so by 'making dinner,' you meant you would order it."

"Do you have a problem with that?"

"Nope. I'm too tired for anything else."

WE SPENT ANOTHER HOUR AT EDMUND'S HOUSE, and when we left, it was locked up tight. By the time we got to the restaurant, we were too exhausted for anything but ordering burgers and fries and carrying them upstairs.

Krankle the cat—or gnome shifter with attitude—was nowhere to be found. Hunter had installed a cat door so he could come and go on the balcony at his leisure, so it was hardly surprising. The cat had been aloof over the past two weeks. He kept saying he was there for a reason, yet he'd never told us what that reason was. For once, I was glad he wasn't around to make things worse.

"Let's watch some television," I suggested when we'd finished dinner and I'd dumped the empty containers. I grabbed the remote and patted the spot next to me. "We can cuddle."

"Nothing weird," Hunter warned as he got comfortable next to me. "Nothing sexy. I can't deal with anything sexy right now."

"How about *Little House on the Prairie*?" I had to hold back a laugh at his glare.

"We don't have to go that clean. I'm not watching *The Golden Girls* or *Mean Girls* now either. Those two things have been ruined for me."

I had to bite back a laugh. "How about some reruns?" I flipped through our streaming options. "Does *Friends* sound good?"

He nodded as he grabbed a blanket from the back of the couch and settled us both beneath it. "Yeah. I could use something mindless." He cuddled close.

"I know you're bothered by what you saw, but—I don't know—I didn't think it was so bad."

The look he shot me was full of dumbfounded disbelief. "That place had more dildos than pairs of shoes."

I laughed at his outrage. I couldn't help myself. "I don't want to insult you, but you're kind of a prude when it comes to that stuff."

"How is that not insulting?"

"It's just ... most of that stuff was harmless. You can get it at random stores in bigger cities, and it's not a big deal. Sure, I didn't recognize a few things, but I bet there are websites and stuff."

He blinked several times, his gaze firm on my face. "Are you saying that I'm somehow not ... *you know* ... in that department?"

It took me several seconds to realize what he meant. "No, I'm not saying that," I replied hurriedly. "Not even a little. It's just not as big of a deal as you're making it out to be."

"You don't think the fact that he was nailing every senior citizen in the area is a big deal?"

"Well, that's a mindset thing." I hadn't bothered selecting a streaming site, and I figured I likely wouldn't need to since we were mired in a serious conversation. "I'm going to guess, from Edmund's perspective, it was validating to be fought over. As for the women, you said it yourself. They've been at each other's throats for years. I bet their competition over him wasn't even about Edmund."

"If it wasn't about him, what was it about?"

"Winning."

He considered the statement, then nodded. "I guess I can see that. The whole thing is still creepy. That bedroom was one step off from a sex dungeon."

I tried—no, really I did—to keep from laughing, but I couldn't. "Yeah, that was pretty far from a sex dungeon."

"How do you know?"

"I know things. I've been to cities. I watched the news in those cities. Sex dungeons are way darker."

He finally cracked a smile. "Oh, yeah? I would ask you to tell me about them, but I'm still creeped out."

"We could go to bed and maybe wash away the bad with something good?" I suggested pointedly.

He didn't consider the offer long. "Yup. I'm feeling better." He grabbed me around the waist and threw me over his shoulder. "Let's drown out the bad with something good."

I giggled all the way into the bedroom. "I'm glad to see that your rebound rate is still impressive."

"Yeah, *that's* my superpower."

"I can't wait to see it up close and personal."

I CRASHED OUT HARD. I HAD NO DOUBT I would dream about Edmund's passion pit—really, there was no escaping it—but thankfully, the dreams weren't too terrible. To my surprise, something woke me around two o'clock in the morning, and when I emerged from sleep, I was instantly alert.

"Hunter?" I murmured and rolled to check on him.

He was out cold, sprawled on his back, and snoring as if he didn't have a care in the world. On instinct, I pressed my hand to his chest to make sure he was okay—my magic would tell me otherwise, or so I hoped—and his heartbeat felt normal. His breathing was regular. He obviously hadn't woken me. *So, who?*

Slowly, I tracked my eyes to the end of the bed. There I found an ethereal figure watching us—a familiar one. Edmund, or rather his ghost, stood staring down at us. He didn't look as if he were perplexed or having a bad day. No, he looked intrigued.

"Are you real?" I whispered. I didn't want to wake Hunter. If Edmund's appearance was some witch thing, Hunter wouldn't be able to see it anyway.

"I was just about to ask you the same thing," Edmund replied calmly. "You're Stormy Morgan."

"Yeah." I clutched the sheet tighter. Living with Krankle had taught us not to sleep naked, but I was only dressed in tiny sleep shorts and a thin tank top. Given what we'd learned about Edmund, I didn't want to give him any ideas. "You're dead," I blurted with zero finesse.

"So I've learned." Edmund's smile was pleasant enough, but his eyes had a hard edge only visible thanks to the streetlight from the lot filtering through the shades. "It's a sad thing."

I readjusted, checking on Hunter one more time, and kept my voice low. "Do you know who killed you?"

"Not off the top of my head."

"What's the last thing you remember?"

"I was eating dinner. Then I heard something. I went to check it out. Everything after that is fuzzy."

"Yeah." I felt sorry for him. Well, kind of. "We saw your bedroom." I tried to keep the accusation out of my voice. "It's quite the passion pit."

Edmund beamed. "The ladies love it. I'm not surprised you were drawn to my lair."

I narrowed my eyes. "I wasn't drawn to your lair. I went to check out your bedroom with Hunter. He's a police officer, in case you've forgotten."

"No, I haven't forgotten." Edmund's speculative gaze landed on Hunter. "He's always been a good-looking boy."

The statement, thrown out with equal parts affection and reverence, threw me. "Um..."

"Not like that." Edmund shot me a dirty look. "Don't be a weirdo. I'm just saying, I get why you're with him." He straightened and smoothed his ghostly clothing. "I was never blessed in that department. Other departments, I got my fair share. But the looks thing..." He trailed off. "I thought it was a detriment until I got older."

"What changed when you got older?" I was legitimately curious.

"Everybody ages, Stormy, and in a town this size, looks matter less than stamina when you reach a certain age."

My acid reflux picked that moment to react. "Now who's being gross?"

"It's a simple statement." Edmund held out his hands. "The women in this town couldn't get enough of me despite my lack of looks. What does that tell you?"

"That for some reason, there are a lot more single women of a certain age than men. Why do you think that is?"

"Who cares?" Edmund looked exasperated. "All that matters is I'm a star."

"Even if you want to look at it that way, you're nothing now," I argued. "You're dead. In fact ... wait." Something occurred to me. "Why are you a ghost?"

"I don't know. Why are you back in this town?" Edmund challenged. "You were supposed to be one of the rare few who got away."

"That's always how I looked at it too," I conceded. "The thing is, when you're out there, you realize that being here isn't so bad. I got to see the world, so I'm not sorry that I left. I still want to see some things, too, so I expect I'll travel again at some point." I cast another surreptitious look toward Hunter. "I lost more than I gained by leaving though."

"Oh, how sweet." Edmund rolled his eyes. "You two were always joined at the hip as kids. I thought maybe you would escape together, but he remained behind, and you left. Have you considered you weren't supposed to return?"

I didn't like the question, or his tone when delivering it. "No, I didn't consider that. I know where I'm supposed to be."

"And it's here, with him?"

"Yes." No matter how often I questioned my professional future—I didn't want to keep working for my family forever—I no longer doubted my personal one. I couldn't lose Hunter again. Whatever was coming, we would face it together. "What about you? Why are you still here?"

"I have no idea."

Unlike other ghosts I'd interacted with or heard about, thanks to my association with Bay Winchester, a Hemlock Cove necromancer, Edmund didn't seem upset about his plight. He was more energized than anything.

"You're probably still here because you're confused about what happened to you," I mused. "That's what Bay says happens to ghosts sometimes. Your soul is supposed to be absorbed by a reaper, but apparently, we only have one up here, and he or she—I have no idea if it's a he or she—is lazy. That's what Tillie says anyway."

"Who is Tillie?" Edmund slowly drew his eyes away from Hunter and back toward me. "Do you mean that woman from Hemlock Cove?

She is a pip. I totally wanted to romance her, but I could never figure out a way to get close."

"Yeah, she would've chewed you up and spit you out," I said. "Plus, she's older than you by a good ten years or so."

"Age is just a number." Edmund pursed his lips as he went back to looking at Hunter. "Do you think you two will stay together forever?"

"That's the plan." I couldn't understand his fascination with my boyfriend. "Why do you care?"

"Because it's such a waste. With looks like that, the boy should be sowing his wild oats. No offense to you, because you're okay to look at, but he could be sampling from every well in this town."

I was officially horrified. "Hey!"

"I said no offense." Edmund shot me a dubious look. "There's no reason to get worked up. He's just too good looking for you. In fact, if you ask me, he's wasting those looks settling down with one woman. Even when you weren't here, he wasn't using them to his advantage."

"You listen here." I was officially at the end of my rope. I had no idea what to do about my predicament, however.

Before I could figure out what to say—I wanted him out of our room because he was starting to annoy me—he crossed to Hunter's side of the bed and stared down at my boyfriend.

"Someone needs to put those looks to good use," he said, more to himself than me. "Someone needs to give the boy a new lease on life."

Confused, I watched as the soul shimmered then proceeded to climb into Hunter—he didn't hover over him or try to touch him, just clambered right in—and left me flabbergasted.

Hunter murmured something in his sleep and shifted, as if recognizing something was happening, but he couldn't stop it. Edmund muttered to himself from inside Hunter, and it was disturbing, to the point where I knew I had to act. *What can I do, though?*

My witchy instincts kicked into high gear. I grabbed Hunter's arm, magic flowing through me, and did the only thing I could think to do. I pulsed the magic inside him, intent on evicting Edmund.

"*Apage.*" The word was a dark echo as I embraced my magic.

The Winchester witches—Bay and Tillie, mostly—had been

working with me on my magic. I'd come to the game late and was old for lessons, but we were all determined.

Edmund fought the eviction but lost. He was morose when he reappeared outside of Hunter's body. "Just what do you think you're doing?" he demanded. "I deserve a chance to live."

"You already had your chance," I fired back. "That's Hunter's body. You don't get to set up shop in it."

Edmund's eyes narrowed. "What did you do to kick me out?"

"Don't worry about it."

"Is it because it's him? Would you let me be if it were somebody else?"

Frustration reared up and grabbed my throat. "No. Your time is done. You need to vamoose to the other side. You don't belong here any longer."

Edmund's expression darkened. "Who are you to declare that? I'm the one who decides my fate."

"You don't get Hunter's body," I hissed. "I won't allow that to happen. You need to get out of here, cross over, or whatever it is you do, and move on. You're not staying here though."

Edmund drew himself up to his full height, defiance in his eyes. "We'll just see about that."

With those words, he blinked out of existence, returning the room to normal other than my ragged breathing.

What in the hell was that?

FIVE

I didn't sleep well, for obvious reasons. I kept jerking awake. When it was all said and done, I'd managed another hour of solid sleep before I woke to Hunter cuddling close as he shut off my impending alarm.

"Morning." He kissed my forehead.

Even though I was reasonably certain I'd fought Edmund off, I couldn't shake a small niggling worry in the back of my brain. "What's my favorite guilty pleasure food?"

Hunter's eyebrows hiked. "Is this a quiz?"

"Yes, and I'll tell you why when you answer." I refused to give in to his cuddling until I could be certain I was dealing with him and not Edmund.

"I don't know that you have one favorite." He scratched his chin, seemingly dumbfounded and yet game to respond. "I guess I would say that goulash your grandfather used to make on snowy days—the elbow macaroni and beef dish that shouldn't be good but is always delicious. You used to inhale that like you were about to run smack-dab into an apocalypse or something."

I released a pent-up breath. Edmund couldn't know about the

goulash. "It's you." I slipped my arms around his waist and held tight. "It's really you."

Clearly confused, Hunter returned the hug before tilting my chin to look into my eyes. "What's wrong?" He was calm but clearly worried. "Did you have a bad dream?"

"It wasn't a dream." I told him about the ghost's visit, leaving nothing out.

When I got to the part about Edmund hopping into his body, Hunter looked more amused than worried. "Um, I don't want to ignore your feelings here, baby, but that sounds like a dream to me."

"It wasn't a dream." I was firm. "It was like *Invasion of the Body Snatchers*."

"Okay, but ... it sounds like a dream."

Frustration rumbled through my stomach. "It wasn't a dream."

"Stormy, come on." Hunter used his most reasonable tone, which only served to agitate me further. "You saw Edmund's bedroom, heard about his sexual proclivities, and went to bed with me after a bout of romance. It's only natural that you would confuse things in your sleep. That's how dreams work."

I wanted to shake him. "I didn't imagine it."

"But ... I would've woken up." He was earnest. "If you'd held an entire conversation with another guy in our bedroom, I wouldn't have slept through that."

He had a point, still. "You were dead to the world, snoring. We whispered. Plus, I don't think you would've seen or heard him. That's a witch thing." That I hadn't ever experienced before. I saw no reason to point that out, though. "It was real. I need you to believe me."

He looked pained. "I always believe you," he said after a beat, stroking my hair back from my forehead. "If you say it was real, then it was real."

"Just two seconds ago—literally—you told me I imagined it."

"I know, but well, I don't think that now." He attempted a smile, but it didn't touch his eyes. "I believe you. Let's just not panic, okay? You managed to fight him off. That's the important thing."

"What if he comes back?"

"Then you'll fight him off again."

In the grand scheme of things, Edmund hadn't been all that difficult to fight off. Still, I had my doubts. "I need you to text me every hour today." I knew, to Hunter, I probably sounded like a maniac. I didn't care. "Just text me some tidbit only you would know. I'll freak out otherwise."

"Okay." His smile was instantaneous. "Can they be dirty memories?"

"Sure." I had no problem with that. "Most of the stuff we did as teenagers was pretty vanilla though. I still remember the time you thought you touched my boob, and it was really my purse."

He scowled. "You just had to bring that up, didn't you?"

I shrugged. "It was one of the memories I held onto when I wasn't here. It always made me smile."

His expression softened. "Fine, but I'm only texting good memories, where I look like a sexual god."

"Well, that will be fun too."

WE SHOWERED, HAD COFFEE, AND FED the cranky cat before heading downstairs. Krankle had become something of an enigma in the past few weeks, and I had questions. Since the cat never answered them, I'd taken to ignoring his existence for the most part. I'd thought that would force him to come to me. So far, it hadn't worked.

"Try not to get worked up," Hunter admonished me as we said our goodbyes by the back door. "I'll text every hour. I'll be working on the Edmund case all day, so I can text updates too. Just ... don't let this freak you out."

That was easier said than done. Since I'd realized I was a witch, and not only accepted my magic but embraced it, our lives had been thrown into turmoil. Hunter was easygoing, so after the initial shock, he'd settled into our new life with more ease than I had. I tended to get worked up.

"I'll do my best," I promised as I rolled onto the balls of my feet to give him a kiss goodbye. "Just be careful. If you feel a ghost trying to get inside you, fight him off."

Hunter blinked twice, then nodded. "Sure. That's exactly what I'll do."

I waved him off, exasperated. "You still don't believe me."

"I do," he insisted, his eyes taking on an intense glint as he grabbed me around the waist. "Don't ever think I don't believe you, because I do. I'm just ... trying to figure things out. This is above my pay grade. I make jokes when I'm nervous."

That was true. It was also true that he couldn't fathom what I was trying to describe, which meant he was less likely to believe me. "Don't forget the texts. I'll be a crazy woman by the end of my shift if you forget."

"I will not forget the texts." After another kiss, he released me. He looked torn when opening the door, as if he didn't want to leave. "Call if you need me. It's okay, even if you're interrupting something. I'll answer."

That was the sort of burden I didn't want to put on him, but I nodded all the same. "Thanks. I'll see you in a few hours."

Grandpa was already heating up the griddle when I joined him. Familiar with my morning duties at that point, I immediately went to the coffee machine, fired it up, and found the filters.

"You seem quieter than normal," Grandpa noted when I didn't immediately greet him. "Did something happen with Edmund?"

I shot him a suspicious look. "Are you asking because you want to spread gossip?"

"That is a horrible thing to say about your grandfather." His soupçon of hurt didn't fit the circumstances. "I can't believe you would even think that."

"Grandma recruited you, huh?" I surmised. "She wants you to feel me out and come home with something good."

He nodded. "She feels that since you and Hunter live together, we'll have easier access to the gossip. If you hold back, she'll be livid. She's the gossip queen in the neighborhood right now. She won't be happy if she loses her throne."

"Oh, well, I would hate for Grandma not to get what she wants," I replied dryly, my fingers deft as I used the razor to open the bags of grounds and poured them into the filters before stacking them. We would go through coffee at a fantastic rate when the restaurant filled, and it was always best to have the filters ready, so we didn't have to waste time during the rush. "I mean, someone is dead, but by all means, let's worry about Grandma's standing in the neighborhood."

Rather than agree with me, which I expected, Grandpa pinned me with a no-nonsense glare. "Oh, get off your high horse," he chided. "Your grandmother is perfect in almost every way. She likes her gossip. So what? We all like to gossip. If somebody tells you they don't, they're lying."

"You mean you like gossip almost as much as she does," I surmised.

He shrugged. "I wouldn't mind hearing what you've got."

I knew I should keep my mouth shut. I was only in the inner loop when it came to Edmund because I'd happened to be with Hunter when the body was discovered. He wouldn't want me spreading the details. I couldn't help myself, though.

"Did you know that Edmund was sleeping with a bunch of different women in the neighborhood?"

I expected Grandpa to be shocked and demand details. Instead, he nodded, his expression dark. "Yeah, everybody knew that. They say he was hung like an albatross. I never believed it though."

My lips puckered in disbelief. Then something occurred to me. "An albatross is a bird."

"So?"

"So, that means it doesn't have a penis."

"Um, I'll have you know that three percent of birds have penises."

That was a very specific percentage to cite, and I had to grab my phone to check. I wouldn't put it past my grandfather to make something up just to win an argument. To my surprise, he was right. "Huh. It really does say three percent of birds have penises. Chickens can still have penises but barely. Apparently, they're tiny little nubs. Ducks have them too."

Grandpa looked smug.

"Albatrosses don't, though." I matched him smug smile for smug smile.

"It's not really about the albatross," Grandpa replied. "I was trying to think of a big animal. If you want to use an elephant in place of an albatross, I won't argue with you."

Only then did I realize we were arguing about bird penises when we should've been mired in a serious discussion. "Anyway, according to Marty—that's Edmund's son—his father was nailing everybody in the neighborhood."

"I haven't seen Marty in a bit," Grandpa mused. "Supposedly, he came for dinner, but I haven't seen him at his father's house in a long time."

I pictured the passion pit. "Yeah, he said his father's dalliances annoyed him. I think maybe he worried he would walk in on something that would scar him for life."

Grandpa chuckled. "What a baby."

"Nobody wants to see a parent ... doing that." I was horrified at the thought of my parents doing it, even though I knew I wouldn't exist without them performing the deed. "Don't be gross."

"I'm not being gross. You're being a priss. Just because people get older, doesn't mean they don't have sex. Why, just last night, your grandmother and I—"

I cut him off with a loud coughing noise. "Don't go there." I extended a finger. "I will start throwing up, and it's too late for you to call in a replacement."

Grandpa gave a pronounced eye roll. "Good grief. You need to grow up. It's not a big deal."

"So, you're saying that Edmund's proclivities didn't impact the neighborhood, and you were fine living in his, um ... shadow, so to speak?"

Grandpa straightened. "First off, I'm gifted in that department. Ask anybody."

"I think I'll pass."

"All the neighborhood women have seen it. Why do you think they have their coffee on their patios in the morning? They want to see the miracle that is me, even if they pretend otherwise."

That was a horrifying thought. *What if he's right? Is that the reason Hunter gets so many complaints? Were the women hanging outside to get a peek and then calling to complain when they got their fill? Just ... ugh.*

He didn't appear bothered about getting all the chickens clucking on a regular basis. He would get them worked up, then everybody else had to deal with them.

"Secondly," he continued without a care in the world. "Do you know how many times I saw different women hiding in the bushes to peep through Edmund's windows?"

"No, but I'm curious," I admitted. "Which women were peeping the most?"

"It was all of them. Iris. Florence. Blanche. Gwen. They were the regulars. A few more rode the Edmund Train before hopping off at different stops. Some of the ladies weren't willing to put up with his wandering eye. The others, however, dug in and turned it into a competition. They all wanted to win, no matter the cost."

"Yeah, but Edmund was the prize," I argued. "Why fight so hard to win him?"

"That I can't answer." Grandpa held out his palms. "I'll leave the mystery for you to solve."

Part of me didn't want to know. The other part, however, was unbelievably curious. "I'll go check the front and open the door."

"No poached eggs today," he warned. "You tell anybody who tries to order them that they've been recalled."

"Yeah, I don't think that'll work."

"If you don't want a scene, you'd better figure something out."

"Yeah, I'll get right on that."

THE MORNING WENT BY SMOOTHLY, with my cousin Annie handling the restaurant side while I tackled the café alone. It wasn't difficult because breakfast was easy. Half the people who came in just wanted coffee and to gossip with one another. Only one topic of interest circulated that morning, which meant I was dodging questions about Edmund left and right.

"Are you sure you can't tell me something?" Odette Tillerman asked as we stood at the register and I checked her out. "You must know something."

"Sorry, I don't know a thing," I lied as I handed over her change. "Hunter didn't tell me anything."

Odette shoved a dollar at me, her annoyance palpable. "It would've been twice that if you weren't such a bad gossip."

I shoved the dollar in my apron pocket. "Live and learn, I guess."

I glanced up as the bell over the door jangled, my mouth opening to greet whoever entered. Unfortunately, the trio of women invading my quiet morning weren't a welcome sight.

I snagged gazes with Hunter's ex-girlfriend. "Monica." We were never going to be close friends, but we'd managed to forge an uneasy acquaintance. Her friends, however, were another story. "Celeste." My stomach tightened. "Phoebe."

Phoebe Green was my high school nemesis—yes, that sounded dramatic, but I didn't care—and our animosity had spilled over into adulthood. Upon my return to Shadow Hills, she'd picked fights with me left and right. But the tables had turned. She was spending her weekends in jail after being convicted of extortion. She wasn't quite as full of herself as she used to be.

"There's a booth open in the corner." I pointed.

Monica shot me a tight smile. "Thanks. Phoebe really wanted breakfast after ... well, after."

"She means after she had to spend the weekend in jail," Celeste offered helpfully. "It's not going well," she offered behind her hand in a stage whisper everybody could hear.

As far as I could tell, she wasn't true friends with anybody, including Monica and Phoebe. That didn't stop her from following them everywhere they went.

"Oh, knock it off," Phoebe groused. Her hair wasn't as shiny as normal, and her minimal makeup wasn't like her. "I just want some eggs. Is that too much to ask? I want eggs and no judgment." Her dark gaze landed on me. "Do you think you can manage that?"

"Absolutely." I bobbed my head. The last thing I wanted was to get into a public fight with Phoebe when I had other things on my mind. No matter what Hunter believed, I knew beyond a shadow of a doubt that I hadn't dreamed Edmund's visit the previous evening. "I can get you both of those things. Well, unless you want poached eggs."

Monica arched a perfectly manicured eyebrow. "Why not poached eggs?" Since she was often the one who ordered the dish—thus sending my grandfather into the rant to end all rants—I wasn't surprised that I'd gotten her attention.

"They've been recalled," I replied evenly.

"The eggs have been recalled?"

"Just the poached eggs."

"That makes no sense."

"Take it up with the man behind the grill." I inclined my head toward the booth again. "Does everybody want coffee?"

"Yeah." Monica sounded thoughtful. "Coffee would be good."

I filled three mugs and followed the women to their table. "Does everybody know what they want?"

"I want to hear about Phoebe's unfortunate incarceration, but she won't give me the dirty details," Celeste replied. "I think there's been some forced lesbianism."

Before I could blank my face, my mouth fell open. "What?"

"She's making that up," Phoebe growled. "She watched one season of *Orange Is the New Black* and thinks it's the same thing as reporting to the county jail every weekend. She's driving me crazy."

Despite my dislike for Phoebe—and it was immense—I was relieved. "Well, I'm glad to hear that part isn't true. Do you know what you want?"

They placed their orders, for once, without drama.

I thought I was about to get away when Celeste called after me, "Do you think Hunter will be in for breakfast this morning?"

She had a crush on my boyfriend and had made no bones about it since I'd returned. She drove me insane, making me dislike her even more than Phoebe, which shouldn't have been possible.

"Probably not," I said. "He's working on a murder. I don't think he has time for breakfast."

"Oh, that's right." Phoebe immediately perked up. "Maybe, since Edmund was such a pervert, people will start talking about him instead of me."

I had questions. Unfortunately, I wasn't comfortable asking them of Phoebe. "That's something to hope for, huh?"

"Absolutely." Phoebe's eyes gleamed. "That's the best news I've had all week."

"Well, I'm glad Edmund could die to make things better for you."

She clearly didn't pick up on the sarcasm. "That makes two of us."

SIX

I made it through my tedious shift. True to his word, Hunter texted every hour, and some of the texts were fairly raunchy. My grandfather caught me reading one that turned my cheeks pink and demanded I stop doing whatever I was doing. I was more than happy to oblige, though I did peek surreptitiously at my phone for the next hour.

Finished for the day, I ran upstairs to shower. I saw no sign of Krankle, which meant he was out yet again, so I left him to his gnome stuff and headed downtown. Winter in Northern Lower Michigan was brutal, and though we weren't at the bad part just yet, temperatures had turned brisk relatively quickly. I could've driven, but I wanted to think, and I was best at thinking while walking.

I stopped at the coffee shop long enough to grab a fancy latte, then I headed across the street to visit Sebastian. The funeral home lot was empty—it wasn't exactly a hopping business—so I looked forward to an extended gossip session. Sebastian wasn't alone, though. He was with Lorenzo Rossi. They had been spending oodles of time together lately, though I didn't press them on the details. They both seemed nervous since they'd never openly dated in Shadow Hills, but gauging by their smiles and laughs, things were moving along nicely.

"There she is." Sebastian beamed at me. "I was just about to call out the cavalry. I haven't seen you in days. I thought you forgot about me. It hurt."

I flopped onto one of the small settees in the parlor. "I could never forget about you. I've just been busy."

"That's no less hurtful."

"I guess not." I rolled my neck and sighed. "So, did you hear about Edmund Hawthorne?"

"We did." Sebastian's feet rested on the coffee table, something he frowned upon when others did it. "It happened by your grandparents' house, right?"

"Yeah. We were over there dropping off Hunter's stuff to store for the winter when we heard screams."

"That's right." Sebastian's eyes sparked. "You and Hunter are officially living together. How does it feel?"

"We've essentially spent every night together since we first hooked up," I noted. "It's not all that different." *Other than the ghost I'm convinced tried to hop inside my boyfriend last night*, I silently added. "It's fine. I want to talk about Edmund."

Sebastian's forehead creased. "Why? I thought he had a heart attack or something."

"Um, no." I shook my head. "He was stabbed."

Sebastian readjusted, leaning forward on the couch. "Excuse me? That's not the rumor going around. People are saying he was found dead on the side of the road."

"Actually, he was found dead in the middle of the road, and he was definitely stabbed."

"Well, that changes things." Sebastian's expression reflected pure bafflement. "I can't believe I missed that tidbit. Did Hunter make an arrest?"

"No. We have no idea who did it. Apparently, the neighborhood is full of suspects, though."

"Ah, you mean Edmund's harem." Sebastian's horror turned to amusement in the blink of an eye. "Yeah, that's been going on almost two years now I think. It's pretty gross and weird."

"Um, I'll say. Do you have any idea what he had in his bedroom?"

"No, but when you say it like that, I'm all ears." Sebastian waggled his eyebrows. "Let me guess. He had his entire ceiling decked out in mirrors."

"No." I wrinkled my nose. "That's freaky to think about."

"I've always wanted a mirror over my bed." Sebastian's eyes darted to Lorenzo, who looked more amused than horrified.

I had no idea if they'd progressed to sleepovers yet, but I made a mental note to ask Sebastian the next time we were alone. It might not be any of my business, but that didn't stop me from wondering.

"He had some weird stuff in his bedroom," I offered, drawing Sebastian's gaze back to me. "For example, did you know they still had those television-VCR combos? Edmund had one in his bedroom, and the amount of porn that guy had was unbelievable."

"Wait." Sebastian lifted his hand. "He had his porn on VHS tapes? That's so retro."

"He also had this huge trunk full of sex toys, and I didn't even recognize some of them."

"You didn't recognize what the toys were supposed to do or what they were supposed to represent?"

"Both."

"Well, now you have my full attention." Sebastian didn't even bother feigning disinterest. "What else?"

"It was just a lot of toys ... and porn ... and fuzzy handcuffs and stuff. Marty told us that his father has been sleeping with every single woman in his neighborhood."

"Yeah, that doesn't surprise me." Sebastian grimaced. "I heard that, a few weeks ago, he was banging Florence Chase, and Iris St. James threw a rock through his window. Florence said it was an assassination attempt."

"How can you have known all this and not told me?" I demanded. I knew I sounded whiny, but I couldn't help myself.

"I did tell you," Sebastian shot back. "I told you that Edmund was dating all the women in his neighborhood. You weren't interested."

I did not remember that in the least. "Well, I'm interested now. He's dead, and half his admirers were standing around him in the street when we found him."

"Seriously?" Sebastian rubbed his hands together. "Do you think they all got fed up and killed him?"

I hadn't even considered it, but I couldn't help but wonder. "I don't know. Do you think that?"

"I think that's the better story."

I pursed my lips and debated. "I don't know. I can't imagine those women coming together to carry out something like that. I think it's far more likely that one of them killed him in a fit of rage."

"Which one are you leaning toward?"

"As far as I can tell, they all look equally guilty. Out of curiosity, though, do you know how all of this started?"

"Just the rumors," Sebastian replied. "I don't think anybody has *all* the details."

"I'm more than willing to listen to the rumors at this point."

"I hoped you would say that." He beamed. "So, they all have one thing in common. Do you know what that one thing is?"

"It's obviously Edmund's penis. They can't get enough of it, which is the stuff of nightmares if you ask me."

Sebastian chuckled. "That's not it, but I've always liked the way your mind operates. They all play euchre at the senior center."

My heart plummeted. "No."

He nodded.

"What is it with the people of a certain age fighting over men in this town?" I demanded. It wasn't the first time a senior citizen fight had ended with murder. The previous altercation had boasted a magical twist. I could only hope the current incident would be different.

"I don't know." Sebastian chuckled, holding out his palms. "I can't answer that one for you. What I can say is that the seniors in town get randy sometimes. The winters here are long."

"And this town doesn't have nearly as many men as it does women," I said. "Why is that?"

"I don't know." His face went blank. "I've never really considered it, other than a passing thought. You're right though. The senior center has three women to every man."

"Don't women live longer than men?" Lorenzo queried. "I thought I read something like that."

"Yeah, like a couple of years or something," Sebastian replied. "It shouldn't be this noticeable though. Stormy's right. Patty Dobkins and Martha Madison were fighting over a man when things got out of control. Technically, they were fighting over a card game, too, so that gets convoluted. Now, apparently, it's happening again. Maybe it's something in the water."

That is such a Sebastian thing to say, I mused. He saw a conspiracy theory around every corner. I was much more interested in Edmund's harem—and the euchre ties. "So, it started at the senior center?"

"It did," Sebastian confirmed. "I heard that Iris was the first, and Florence swooped in to try and steal her man—or maybe it was the other way around—then the others got involved. I could be wrong, though."

I had questions—so many questions—and didn't know where to start. "It's euchre day at the senior center, right?"

Sebastian nodded. "It is. Every day is euchre day there, but today is tournament day. Why? Do you plan to go and demand answers of the seniors?"

"Actually, I'm curious which ones from that group will show up the day after their shared boyfriend was killed."

"Oh." Realization dawned on Sebastian's face. "That is a dastardly plan. We should totally do that."

Lorenzo stirred. "Are you guys seriously going over there?" He looked horrified at the thought. "I mean ... they're old."

I gave him a dirty look. "That doesn't mean they can't contribute to society."

"Yeah, but they were doing dirty things together. I don't know if I could deal with that. I would be imagining horrible things."

He wasn't the only one. I'd seen the treasure chest. His imagination was nothing compared to reality. "You don't have to go. I can go by myself."

"No way." Sebastian shook his head fervently. "We're totally going over there together."

Somehow, I knew he would say that. "Then let's get to it. I have a lot going on. If the senior center has some sort of murder club, I would like to sniff it out and shut it down by dinner if possible."

Sebastian snorted. "Oh, look at you. I love how you think you're smarter than them. They've been at it a lot longer than you, Stormy. You'll have to work hard to catch up to them."

That was exactly what worried me.

PER USUAL, THE SENIOR CENTER BUSTLED with activity. I waved at one of the volunteers as we cut across the room, but she didn't seem interested in intercepting us. She was too busy monitoring the punch, which wasn't surprising because spiking it had turned into a seemingly endless game.

"Your grandmother is over there." Sebastian pointed when we reached the middle of the room.

I looked in the indicated direction and found my grandmother surrounded by her usual cronies. None of them, thankfully, were women from her neighborhood. "Yeah, let's start there." I moved in that direction.

"It smells like mothballs," Lorenzo complained from somewhere behind us. "Don't you smell that? It can't be normal."

"You're psyching yourself out," Sebastian hissed. "Don't think of the mothballs. Think of the community."

"I can't," Lorenzo lamented. "All I can think about now is what they're doing with the mothballs."

I ignored him and crossed to my grandmother. She was intent on her hand, which looked solid if they were playing clubs or spades. Apparently, hearts was the suit, however, and my grandmother's disdain was evident by her angry eyes.

"What are you doing here?" she asked when I grabbed a chair from the empty table behind her and scooted close.

"You know what I'm doing here," I replied in a low voice, tossing a smile toward her friends before focusing on her. "How come you failed to mention yesterday that your neighbor Edmund had his own harem?"

"You didn't ask." Grandma sounded irritatingly blasé.

"Your neighbor is dead."

"He was a derelict anyway. I'm fairly certain he was spreading chlamydia last year, and he refused to inform his sexual partners, so it kept getting worse."

Oh, well, great. If I didn't think I had enough images swimming through my head, she had to add that one. "You don't think the harem was motivation for murder?"

"Not so much. Obviously, you think that, though."

"Infidelity is always a motive for murder," I insisted.

"Infidelity?" She burst out laughing. "Oh, you're so cute." She clucked her tongue. "I like that you're still young enough to think that any of that matters when you reach a certain age."

I. Was. Horrified. "Are you saying you aren't faithful to Grandpa?" That was a bridge too far. I couldn't handle it.

"Don't be ridiculous." If looks could kill, I would be dead. "Your grandfather and I are committed. None of the people in that little group were committed to one another. You're basing your judgment on your attachment to *Little House on the Prairie*."

An insult lay buried in there. I just knew it. "Hey!"

Grandma's expression softened. "Oh, I love you, Stormy, but you're a bit of a prude."

"I'm worldly," I countered.

"No, you've traveled a lot and think that makes you worldly," Grandma corrected. "You're not worldly, though. You also look at romance through the eyes of an author. In your world, everything is supposed to fit together perfectly. The hero and heroine are supposed to face obstacles but come out stronger on the other side. That doesn't always happen in the real world."

I hated to admit she was deflating my faith a bit. "You don't think it's possible to live happily ever after?"

She chuckled. "I think your idea of happily ever after is different now than it will be when you're my age. Sometimes, happily ever after is watching your favorite television show without your significant other yammering on about golf."

"That's so wise," Sebastian intoned behind me.

I shot him a death glare. "Do you think someone from Edmund's harem could be responsible for killing him? Also, what is it with women at this center fighting over men? Can't you pick a different subject to fight over?"

Grandma chuckled. "Ah, there's that prudish streak of yours again."

"Hunter is the prude," I groused.

"Hunter is a bit rigid, but given who his father is and how he was raised, it doesn't surprise me that he can't think outside the box sometimes. He'll get there. You, however, have an imagination as wide as my mother-in-law's mouth. You shouldn't struggle so mightily."

I sensed censure there and didn't like it. "Let's focus on Edmund. You know those women better than anybody. Could one of them have killed him?"

"Any of them could've killed him at one point or another," she replied. "Edmund was a bit of a troll. I'm guessing he pushed one of them too far."

"Because they loved him and wanted monogamy?" That was the only thing that made sense in my book.

Grandma shot me a pitying look. "Oh, my poor girl." She tsked and shook her head. "You really do want to see the world through rose-colored glasses, don't you?"

My annoyance knew no bounds, but I managed to hold my tongue.

"The thing with Edmund wasn't about him. Perhaps, at one time, one or more of them wanted a relationship. That didn't last long, though."

"So, if they weren't looking for love, what was it?"

"Victory." Grandma's lips curved when she looked at her new hand. "Edmund wasn't the prize. Bragging rights were. In fact, if Edmund had actually committed to one of those women, she wouldn't have kept him for more than a few weeks. It wasn't about him. It was about wearing the crown around the neighborhood."

Grandma wasn't the first to suggest it, but it finally started to sink in. "Do you think Edmund knew he wasn't the prize?"

"Absolutely not." Grandma shook her head firmly. "That idiot had no idea he wasn't at the heart of their competition. He actually fancied himself a ladies' man."

"Grandpa said there was a rumor about his ... you know."

"His what?" Grandma asked blankly.

"You know," I gritted.

"I do," she confirmed. "I just want to hear you say it."

"I think I'll pass."

Grandma called clubs as trump. "I have no idea if Edmund was as well-endowed as they say. That was certainly the rumor. But even if he was, that's not worth killing over. You can always buy the hardware in whatever size you want. The competition was about winning his affections, but that wasn't an actual prize."

I let loose a breath as I sank back in my chair. What she said made sense—in a roundabout way. "Do you think it was a heat-of-the-moment thing?" I asked finally. "I mean ... you don't think whoever did this is a danger to anybody else, do you?"

"I don't know." Grandma looked momentarily perplexed. "I hadn't considered it. I think it's unlikely, but never say never. If one of those women snapped, it's been a long time coming. It's possible they can't put things back together again if Humpty Dumpty has fallen."

She had a way with words. I had to give her that. "You'll be careful, right?" I kept my voice low.

"I'm not competing with any of those women."

"Yeah, but you said it yourself—it might not matter now."

She nodded. "I'm always careful."

I stood and glanced around the room. "They're here." I scanned the tables. "All four of them."

"They are," Grandma confirmed.

"I thought for sure our killer would be somewhere else."

"It's euchre day. Where else would they be?"

While that must seem a legitimate point in her head, it meant little to me. "I think I'll make the rounds. You know, just have a chat with them."

"That sounds lovely." Grandma was completely focused on her game. "Make sure you don't go into *Little House on the Prairie* mode with them. They'll eat you alive."

I scowled. "I don't have a *Little House on the Prairie* mode."

"Of course you don't."

SEVEN

S ebastian wanted to stay and watch me work, but a text from Marty had him shaking his head. "He's coming in to talk to me about his father's arrangements. I have to go."

"It's fine," I assured him. "I'll just ask a few questions while I'm here. No need to worry."

He didn't look convinced. "I can leave Lorenzo." He shot an apologetic look toward his boyfriend. "I mean ... I know you think it smells like mothballs, but maybe you should stick close."

Lorenzo nodded without hesitation. "I can do that."

"No," I said firmly. "It's the senior center. Nothing is going to happen."

"If I remember correctly, you were almost killed by the last senior center director," Sebastian countered.

He had a point, loath as I was to admit it. "Yes, but there's a new director. Richard Something-or-Other."

"Richard Taylor," Sebastian volunteered. "Everyone calls him Dick. He seems fine—nothing murderous about him. But he doesn't worry me."

I flicked my eyes around the room. Only two of the women who had been present for the discovery of Edmund's body occupied the same table. The rest sat separately.

"Even if they did want to hurt me, they wouldn't do it here," I said finally. "They're all far too terrified of my grandmother to even risk it."

Sebastian cocked his head, considering, then nodded. "Okay. Be careful." With that, he tugged on Lorenzo's arm, and they headed out.

Once it was just me, I looked around, debating, then headed for the table where Blanche and Gwen played on opposite teams.

"How are things going over here?" I asked.

Gwen briefly flicked her eyes up to register my presence, then refocused on her cards. "I didn't realize you volunteered here." Her voice held no warmth.

"I don't." I grabbed a chair from an adjacent table and sat, making sure not to position myself behind either woman lest she assume I was spying. "I came to see my grandmother and thought I would check in with you guys."

"Why would you possibly want to check in with us?" If possible, Blanche looked even less thrilled to see me than Gwen had. "Wait ... did your grandmother send you over to spy?"

"My grandmother barely even acknowledges I'm in the room," I replied. "She hates nothing more than having her euchre game interrupted. Trust me. I know that from firsthand experience."

"So, why are you here?" Gwen demanded. "Did your boyfriend send you to interrogate us?"

"Believe it or not, I came to see how you guys were doing." It took everything I had not to snap at her. If she thought I was being aggressive, she would shut down. That was the last thing I wanted. "I mean, seeing Edmund dead like that had to be difficult."

"Why would we care?" Blanche challenged.

"Well, he was your neighbor. Oh, and he was stabbed. I don't know anybody who wouldn't be affected by that."

"Oh, right." Blanche moved her jaw. "We're horrified and sad. When is his funeral? We all want to go. Isn't that right, Gwen?"

For her part, Gwen looked as if the last place she wanted to be was dragged into the conversation. "Is it going to be a Catholic ceremony? I don't like Catholic funerals. Nothing is worse than seeing a body propped up in the middle of a church. And all that singing? All that standing and kneeling? I'm old. My knees can only take so much."

I answered honestly. "I have no idea if it's going to be a Catholic ceremony. Marty is over meeting with Sebastian now. You'll go regardless, though, right?" The question came off a little more pointed than I had intended, but once it was out there, I couldn't take it back.

"If it's not a Catholic ceremony, I'll probably go," Gwen replied. "It depends on what's happening with my stories that day though."

"Your stories?"

She pinned me with a dark look. "Things are getting good on *The Bold and the Beautiful*. That Ridge is an idiot. And Taylor? What a walking doormat. If it's their kids on the show that day, though, I can miss them. They're boring."

"Right." I had no idea how I was supposed to respond. The entire thing was out of control. "Well, um, about Edmund." I hadn't asked any of the questions I wanted answers to yet, so I pushed the conversation in a specific direction. "Do you happen to know who he was with right before he was killed?"

"Why the hell would I know that?" Gwen barked.

"Because I heard, um ... that you were spending time with him." Though distinctly uncomfortable, I pushed forward anyway. "For example, I heard that maybe you were eating dinner with him a few nights a week."

"Is that what you heard?" Gwen challenged.

"I think she's asking how often you boiled the noodle for Edmund," Sissy Conners offered from her spot across the table. She was Gwen's partner, but they didn't seem too close.

"That's nobody's business," Gwen shot back. "Only a vulture would ask about something like that. Are you a vulture?"

"Not last time I checked," I replied dumbly.

"Well, then don't act like one."

I flicked my eyes to Blanche and found her glaring at Gwen. "When was the last time you saw him?" I asked in a soft voice.

Blanche realized after the fact that I'd been watching her and blanked her face, but it was too late. "Oh, who knows?" She waved her hand in a breezy fashion. "I saw him around the neighborhood on a regular basis. I didn't spend much time with him though."

I didn't believe her. Clearly, nobody at the table believed her either. None of the women called her on the lie, however.

"Okay, well, I wondered if somebody might've had a grudge against Edmund."

"I think half the town had a grudge against him," Sissy offered. "I heard he was packing a missile but delivering an asparagus stalk that had been boiled to within an inch of its life."

I pressed my lips together, horrified at the visual she painted. My grandmother might've believed me to be a prude, but it wasn't hard to ascertain what Sissy was implying. "I see."

"If you're looking for someone to point your busybody nose at, you should talk to Flo," Blanche volunteered. "She was the one who slapped Edmund across the face a few days ago."

"She did?" I sat straighter in my chair. "Why would she do that?"

"You'll have to ask her."

Since I had nothing left to talk to Blanche and Gwen about, I headed toward Flo. She was even less welcoming than the other two, and halfway through the conversation, I was wishing for a scarf and gloves to ward off the chill.

"Did they really blame me?" Florence demanded, her eyes darting to the other table. She looked prepared for cold-blooded murder. "I can't believe them. That's just un-freaking-believable."

"Did you slap him?" I asked.

"Of course. He had it coming, though."

"Because he was, um ... spreading the love around?"

The look Florence shot me was incredulous. "Because he marred my fence when he was out there raking. I told him to be careful. That fence was freshly painted. Did he listen? No. Now I have to have it fixed in the spring."

I hadn't expected that response. "So, you were mad about the fence. You weren't mad about Edmund spreading his fertilizer around multiple flower beds."

She blinked twice. "Is that what those harpies said?" With her anger directed toward Gwen and Blanche, Florence had almost no emotion reserved for Edmund, which I didn't understand. "Now you listen here." She gripped her cards and levered herself on an elbow as she leaned closer to me. "Those idiots are the worst of the worst. I mean the *worst of the worst*. They're the ones who were in love with that filthy old man. I just didn't want him messing up my fence."

She was lying. She clearly had the same relationship with Edmund as the others, and yet sitting next to her, I saw no emotion pointed at the dead man. Everything she had in reserve she directed toward her rivals.

"I see." I glanced at the other faces around the table. None of them reacted. "What about Iris?" I asked for lack of another topic. "Did she have a reason to kill Edmund?"

"Oh, absolutely." Florence turned grim. "She was convinced he was the one who rearranged her garden gnomes this summer." She clearly thought she'd explained something.

"What now?" My voice squeaked.

"You heard me," Florence barked. "Iris has a bunch of garden gnomes. They're ugly little cusses. I hate them all. She loves them, though. This summer, someone moved them all into sexually explicit positions. We're talking doggie, the three-legged puppy, the speed bump, and the boa constrictor—all on display for everybody to see."

I slapped a hand over my mouth, unable to decide if I would burst out laughing or start crying.

"It was the speed bump that did it for her," Florence continued without acknowledging my reaction. "That was Edmund's go-to move. Man, she was pissed." Florence's smile stretched across her entire face. "That was a fun day."

It took me a moment to collect myself. "You don't think Iris killed Edmund over garden gnomes, do you? Not really?"

"I think she was mad about those gnomes, and Edmund was often an idiot. I can think of a million reasons people would want to kill him."

"Okay, well, thanks for the information."

Unsteady on my feet, I stopped at the punch bowl long enough to get a drink and ran into my grandmother again.

"How's it going?" She looked perfectly relaxed, which likely meant she was between rounds—and winning.

"Some of these people are horrible," I whispered. "They're all pointing the finger at each other for killing Edmund."

"Of course they are," Grandma replied. "Nobody wants to be the old lady in prison. Give me a break. Whoever did it wants to get away with it."

"It has to be one of them, though," I insisted.

"How do you know?" Grandma's pushback was blasé. "It wasn't just these women playing Hungry Hungry Hippos with Edmund. I know at least three other women on the block who were playing the game."

"How did he manage that?" I demanded. "He was old. Even on Viagra, you can only have so much sex in a day."

Grandma snorted. "It's not about the sex. How many times do I have to tell you that? It was about the game. They all want to win. Edmund wasn't the prize. He was just a means to an end for them. Like ... think about it as a race. All these women wanted to place first in the hurdles race. Edmund was the hurdle they had to get over."

What she said made sense on the surface. Still, I couldn't shake the notion that I was missing something important. When I opened my mouth to say so, I caught a hint of movement at the front door. My initial reaction was to stop and watch whoever came in. Instead, when I realized the individual in question was transparent, I inadvertently grabbed my grandmother's wrist.

"What's wrong with you?" she demanded when I caused her to slosh her punch.

"Do you see him?" I queried in a low voice.

While up on all the witch stuff, my grandmother rarely wanted to talk about it. Only when I was struggling at the beginning did she offer any guidance. The magic came from my grandfather's side of the family, which meant she wanted nothing to do with it. She'd put me in contact with my great-grandmother and called it a day.

She followed my gaze. "What am I supposed to be seeing? Are you talking about Rick? He's done pretty well here since he took over. He's more hands-on than the last one, who was a murderer, but he kind of lets us do our thing however we want to do it. I appreciate that."

"Not Rick," I replied in a low voice. "There's, um ... someone next to him."

Grandma looked again. "I don't see anyone. Who am I supposed to be looking at?"

Rather than explain it to her, I waved off the question. "Never mind." I edged away from her. "I'm probably going to take off. This turned out to be a wasted trip. I could've gone my entire life without learning that Iris's garden gnomes were put into sexual positions."

"Yeah, she was mad about that." Grandma laughed. "I thought it was kind of funny."

"Somehow, that doesn't surprise me." I waved and moved closer to the door.

Edmund had made a big show of pretending he didn't see me when he'd stepped inside. He eyed Dick in a way that made me uncomfortable, and I wanted to nip the potential problem in the bud before it got out of hand. Unfortunately for me, I was too late.

Edmund's ghost was sprier than his age would suggest, and he took a running leap before throwing himself at Rick. The senior center director was fixated on his phone screen, and the only visible reaction he gave was to stop blinking.

Dick didn't struggle or try to evict Edmund. I had no way of knowing if he even understood how to do that. When Edmund stretched inside Dick and forced the man's arms up, I knew that he'd accomplished what he'd set out to do.

I stormed up to him. "What do you think you're doing?" My frustration was big enough to need its own zip code.

"Whatever do you mean?" Dick asked innocently.

I'd only talked to him a few times, but nothing about his reaction suggested he was thinking for himself. No, it was all Edmund.

"Get out of him," I warned in a low voice.

"I'm minding my own business," Rick—or rather Edmund— replied. "Why can't you do the same?"

"Because that's not your body."

"Speaking of bodies, how about we rub yours against mine and see what happens, huh? I bet it would be magical."

I wanted to vomit all over him. "Get out of there." I had to force my voice to stay low and even. "You're not supposed to be in there. It's ... wrong and ... gross and ... wrong. Did I mention it's gross? You need to cross over and leave this place."

"Yeah, I don't think I'll do that." Apparently over talking to me, Edmund fixed his gaze on a spot beyond me. "Look at all the fine ladies playing today," he drawled.

"Yeah, I'm pretty sure one of those 'fine ladies' killed you," I shot back. "You might want to slow your roll."

"And you might want to bug off," he argued. "You don't even belong here. You're not a senior."

"And you're not alive."

"Death is a state of mind." He smoothed the front of his shirt, then shooed me to step aside. "Now, if you don't mind, I would prefer if you moved along."

I grabbed his wrist before he could step around me. "Don't," I warned when he tried to shake me off. "I won't just sit here and let you take over a life that's not yours. Leave him alone."

"No."

"Yes."

"No!" Edmund's eyes flashed. "Let me go!"

He jerked hard, but I had already gathered my magic. Before I realized what I was doing, I pulsed a burst of fire through him. I didn't intend to burn Rick but to chase Edmund out before he got too comfortable. It worked.

Edmund flew from Rick's body like a weak shadow and smacked into the wall. The ghost's eyes went wide when he realized I'd forced him out of the director. He took several seconds to collect himself, his eyes moving back to Rick, who bent over at the waist, seeming confused. I couldn't blame him.

Then, slowly, Edmund turned back to me. "Stop getting in my way!" he screeched.

I wanted to respond but couldn't with Dick in control of his faculties again. Explaining why I was talking to a blank wall wouldn't go over well. Whispers would start because the senior center regulars were gossips.

Instead, I focused on Rick. "Are you okay?"

Dick slowly lifted his eyes. "Yeah." He forced a smile that he likely didn't feel. "I felt woozy for a minute, but I'm fine now. I should probably eat something."

"Definitely." I did my best to look concerned but not freaked out. "Do you need me to help you to a table?"

He waved me off. "I'm fine. Don't worry about me. Thanks though."

I nodded, then flicked my eyes back to where Edmund's ghost had been floating seconds before. He was gone. I had no idea what was going on, but there was no way Hunter could chalk it up to a dream. Not that time. *Just what in the hell is going on here?*

Eight

I felt shaky when I got home. Even the sight of Hunter standing in front of the stove, cooking barefoot in his comfortable clothes didn't do much to shake the chill that had taken over during the long walk across town.

"Hello." He beamed at me and opened his arms for a hug. "How is my favorite roommate doing this evening?"

He was in a good mood. I didn't want to ruin it. I forced a smile and accepted the hug.

Tuned to my moods, though, Hunter realized almost immediately that something had happened. "What is it?" His smile had disappeared when he pulled back to take in my features.

"It happened again." I couldn't keep it from him, especially since Edmund had painted Hunter as a target.

"What happened again?"

"The thing with Edmund. He jumped into another body."

Disbelief blew over Hunter's face before he reined himself in. "Tell me what happened."

I caught him up, leaving nothing out. He listened, intent, and didn't remove his arms from around my waist. By the time I finished, I realized he was swaying back and forth—a motion to offer comfort without being obvious.

"Well, I guess you weren't dreaming." He tapped my chin to get me to look up, gave me a soft kiss, then released me. "You managed to shove him out again, though, so that's good, right?"

"Sure, but the only reason I knew what he'd done is because I happened to see it. He won't make that mistake again. He'll just take over somebody when I'm not watching."

"I hadn't considered that." He rubbed my shoulder and then turned back to the stove.

To my surprise—and delight—he was making the goulash he had mentioned earlier in the day.

"Well, what do we do?" He was a man who liked a plan. Give him a list he could check off, and he was perfectly content.

"If I knew what to do, I wouldn't be freaking out," I barked.

His eyebrows hopped, but he didn't yell back. "I'm just trying to help."

Sheepish, I nodded. "I know. I'm sorry. I just ... it's totally making me lose my mind. I don't know what to do."

"Well, what about the Winchesters? Can't you ask them?"

I wanted to slap myself in the face. *Why didn't I think of that?* "Yeah. I can. I totally should've done that as soon as my shift was over."

"How could you when you had my voice in your ear telling you that it was your imagination?" He offered a rueful smile. "I'm sorry I doubted you."

It was all I needed to hear. The bulk of my anxiety disappeared at the words. "It's not your fault. I probably sounded like a crazy person."

"It doesn't matter. I know you. If you say something, you mean it."

"Yeah, but it's like a movie. Why wouldn't you be dubious?"

"I hate to break it to you, Stormy, but our entire lives are like movies now." He laughed as he stirred the goulash before turning off the heat. "It needs to thicken for twenty minutes."

My stomach rumbled, and I cast a forlorn look toward the food as he led me to the couch. "I'm hungry."

"You'll be happy we waited in twenty minutes." He was firm. "Now, tell me what everybody said when you grilled them at the senior center. Did you settle on a particular suspect?"

"Oh, no way. They're all freaking nuts." I got comfortable next to him on the couch and rested my head against his shoulder. "They were all involved with Edmund, and yet no one seemed to care that he's dead."

"You've talked to him since his death—twice now—and you don't seem to like him," Hunter pointed out. "Maybe there's a reason."

"Did you know him?"

Hunter took my hand and flipped it over so he could trace the life-lines on my palm. "I never really thought about him, to be honest. Before he retired from the garage, I took my truck in from time to time. He always seemed fair with repair estimates and time frames. I guess I based my opinion of him on that. I never thought about him outside of work."

"Yeah. That makes sense. As I walked back from downtown, I kept trying to think of the times I crossed his path when I was a teenager. I never remember him being a gross pervert or anything."

"He wouldn't likely have risked that, given who your grandfather is. You treat him like a giant teddy bear and ignore his meltdowns, but other people in town are afraid of him. They think all his bluster is real."

"Oh, sometimes it's real." I smiled despite myself. "He warned me before I even opened the doors this morning that there would be hell to pay if anybody ordered poached eggs. I had to tell anybody who asked— Monica was the only one, in case you're wondering—that they'd been recalled. Good luck explaining that, by the way."

Hunter chuckled. "I didn't realize Monica still visited the restaurant."

"She doesn't have a lot of options for breakfast. Most people don't want to drive fifteen minutes one way for eggs and hash browns."

"Was she alone?"

"No. Phoebe and Celeste were with her."

"Well, that's interesting, isn't it?" His eyes lit with intrigue. "How is Phoebe handling turning herself in every weekend?"

"It's not as if she confided in me, but my guess would be not well. She didn't look like herself."

"Good. She deserves some consequences for the things she's done."

"I don't disagree. I kind of felt sorry for her this morning, though. She looked pretty sad and rundown."

"That's such a you thing to say." He tickled my ribs. "She spent years—decades really—trying to make your life difficult. Now you feel sorry for her, even though she got off easy. I mean ... she was blackmailing Lorenzo. She threatened to go public with his sexuality. If anybody deserves punishment, it's her."

I didn't disagree. "Speaking of Lorenzo, he was hanging around with Sebastian earlier. They seem pretty tight."

"Did you mind your own business?"

"Of course."

"Stormy." Hunter's voice was low and pointed.

"I did," I insisted. "I didn't say anything that might embarrass them."

"You thought it, though."

"I'm just curious." I refused to apologize for that. "If I ask any busybody-like questions, I'll direct them toward Sebastian when we're alone. I won't embarrass Lorenzo."

"Be good." He tapped the end of my nose and then prodded me to stand. "Come on. Let's get dinner."

I was more than happy to oblige. He handled dishing out the food while I lit the candles, and once we were seated across from each other at the cozy table, talk returned to Edmund.

"I'll call Bay tomorrow and tell her what's going on," I volunteered, referring to the Hemlock Cove necromancer. "If anybody has heard of anything like this, it's her. She'll know what to do."

"What if she doesn't?" Hunter forked goulash into his mouth and smiled. He didn't speak until he'd swallowed. "I'm glad you reminded me of this stuff. It's amazing."

"It's pretty good." My stomach was happy for sustenance, so that was what mattered most to me. "How did the rest of your day go? Did you find anything? I should've asked you that right away."

"I'm more than happy to have gotten through your stuff first," Hunter replied. "It sounds more dire."

"I think your stuff and my stuff overlap."

His eyes gleamed. "That's the plan for later."

I shot him a dirty look. "I'm serious."

"I am too." Hunter sobered. "I had another sit-down with Marty. He says he washed his hands of his father's activities, and I can't blame him. I couldn't deal with that either. The only other tidbit we got was from the medical examiner. Edmund died of the stab wound. It nicked his heart. It wasn't a knife, though. It was a letter opener."

The statement caught me off guard. "Seriously? Who stabs someone with a letter opener?"

"I'm honestly not certain. To me, that suggests it was a crime of passion."

"Like ... someone saw him outside and decided they just had to kill him, and they were opening mail at the time?"

Hunter chuckled. "Or the letter opener was on the counter or something. It was an expensive letter opener. I looked it up online. It retails for three hundred bucks."

"Um, who spends that much on a letter opener?" I was dumbfounded. "Especially in this town."

"I'm not certain, but it's a lead. I've placed a call to the manufacturer. They're looking into sales in the state. That might not go anywhere, though. I'm hopeful they can at least point me toward a store."

"Yeah." I rubbed my chin. "Well, it doesn't sound like either of us got as far as we would've liked today," I lamented.

"No, it doesn't, but tomorrow is a new day."

"Yeah."

"One other thing." He averted his gaze, telling me whatever he planned to bring up was difficult for him. "We want to be ready to get the McDonald house in the spring."

"Is that not going to happen?" I tried to tamp down the bitter ball of distress that appeared in the pit of my stomach.

"No, it'll happen. Matt Kenzie is the loan officer over at the bank. He dropped off some paperwork for me today. I spoke to him about it before. He asked me to file it for preapproval next month and wanted to give me time to fill out the paperwork."

"Okay." I had no idea where he was going.

"I'm not comfortable without you on the house deed, Stormy." He gripped his fork tightly. "That puts you at a disadvantage. I can put your name on the deed and my name on the mortgage, but it would be easier to do both together."

My stomach tightened. "This is the part where you ask about my finances, right?"

He forced himself to meet my gaze. "I know you don't want to talk about it."

"I really don't."

"We're melding our lives, Stormy, so I need to know what I'm dealing with. It's a lot of debt—you've already told me that—and I won't give you grief. I need to see the bills, though, so we can come up with a targeted attack to pay them down."

My eyes burned as I stared down at my plate. "Okay," I barely whispered.

"Okay?" He looked hopeful.

I nodded. I couldn't delay it forever. We wanted a life together. I'd dug myself into an unbelievable financial hole before returning home. Even though I was embarrassed, I understood we needed full transparency to move forward. "I'll show you after dinner."

He reached over and grabbed my hand. "Thank you. I swear I'll make this as painless as possible."

"I'm mortified by all of it. I'm sorry."

"Don't." He was firm. "This isn't going to turn into a thing. I just need to know."

"Yeah. I get it."

"Now, eat your dinner." He inclined his head toward my plate. "I should've waited to bring it up after you were finished. I want you to eat all of that, though."

Despite my trepidation for what was to come, I smiled. "I'm okay. I'll probably feel better when it's over with."

"You probably will. Just know, no matter what, we'll tackle it together. You have my word."

. . .

I SET HUNTER UP AT THE KITCHEN TABLE once the dishes were cleared and washed. I logged him into my credit card and bank accounts, then paced the small kitchen as he absorbed the numbers. I was a nervous wreck, which seemed ridiculous because I'd faced any number of monsters since I'd been home. That was different, though. My statements were a shining example of my failure, and I hated it.

"This isn't as bad as I'd imagined," Hunter said softly as I paced past him. "Stop that." He grabbed my hand to keep me from gnawing on my thumbnail. "It's not that bad."

"It's a lot."

"It is, but we can handle it." He sounded more upbeat than I felt. "Is this it, though? There's nothing else, right?"

I shook my head. "That's it. I didn't buy a house or car and go into debt that way. I just started living off my credit card. I should've run out of money two years before I did, but they just kept raising my limit."

"And you thought you could write your way out of the mess," he surmised.

"Yeah. I'm such an idiot."

"No. No, you're not." He tugged me onto his lap and held tight. "It's okay, baby," he whispered as he kissed my cheek. "We'll start paying down the debt next month."

I immediately shook my head. "That's my responsibility. You're not touching it."

"Um, I beg to differ."

"No." I would not allow him to take on my debt. "I'm paying it down."

"We'll argue about that later. For the mortgage documents, though, I think we'll have to do it the hard way. I need to put the mortgage in my name."

"Okay." *Really, what else can I say?*

"Your name will be on the deed though."

"If you're paying for it, then it should only be your name."

"It's our house. Shh." He pressed his finger to my lips before I could respond. "I don't want to argue about this. You're my future. We're getting married eventually. Don't bother arguing. That will be your house as much as mine. I don't care who pays for what. Since we're still single, though, I can leave your name off the mortgage application. That will be better for both of us."

"I'm sorry." I didn't know what else to say.

"Stop it."

He wrapped me tight, arranging me with my chin on his shoulder, and I could see through the sliding glass doors. Hunter had lowered the lights so the glare was minimal, and I could make out the ground by the storage shed. Krankle's tail lashed back and forth out there, and I figured he was hunting something.

"I don't want you making yourself sick over this," Hunter instructed. "That house has to be ours. You'll help pay off the mortgage. It will just be in my name."

"I'm still sorry. I don't know how I let things get so out of control."

"It's fine."

He rubbed my back, and I closed my eyes. It felt good to let myself lean. When I opened my eyes again, I realized Krankle was still next to the storage building. He wasn't hunting, however. He also wasn't alone. Slowly, I went stiff in Hunter's arms.

"I just told you not to get worked up about this," he chastised.

"I'm not worked up. I just ... a guy is down by the storage building."

"What?" Hunter kept me close as he got to his feet and turned to look out the window. "I ... where?"

"Right by the corner of the building." I pointed. "He's talking to the cat."

"You can't be serious." Hunter released me and moved closer to the glass, his expression impossible to read, but he didn't look happy. "Unbelievable," he muttered after a few seconds of watching. "He really does look as if he's talking to the cat."

"Can you tell who it is?" My anxiety reached a whole new level from what it had been before.

"No. It's too dark." Hunter glanced left and right. "Hold on." He unlocked the sliding glass door and stepped through it. Though barefoot on the balcony, in the cold, he didn't seem to care. "Here, kitty kitty," he called pointedly.

The figure Krankle had been talking to disappeared behind the shed.

For his part, the cat didn't move. He continued to lash his tail and stare in the opposite direction.

"Come on," Hunter called again. "It's time for bed."

The cat didn't respond. He also didn't follow Hunter's order. Instead, he remained rooted to his spot.

"Don't make me come out there," Hunter threatened.

Even from such a great distance, I could see the cat's smirk. He was amused that Hunter would say anything of the sort. We all knew that by the time Hunter got his shoes and coat on, Krankle would be long gone.

"Fine. Do whatever you want," Hunter said. "This conversation isn't over, though." He returned to the kitchen, shut the sliding glass door, and killed the light. The kitchen was completely dark when he slipped his arm around my waist and stared down at the storage shed.

The human shadow didn't reappear.

"It could've been someone just walking by," I said. "Maybe they were talking to him like a random cat."

"Maybe."

"But you don't trust him."

"Neither do you."

"Yeah." I blew out a sigh. "What do we do?"

"I don't know. We need to figure it out though. He's clearly up to something."

But what?

NINE

I slept as well as could be expected. Between Edmund running around, trying to hop into bodies and Krankle being Krankle, I had a lot on my mind. Still, my lack of sleep from the previous evening and the weight of my financial situation being out in the open meant I passed out despite my anxiety. When I woke the following morning, Hunter was already up and checking his emails.

"Anything good?" I murmured as I rolled to rest my head on his chest.

He adjusted to slip his arm around me and pressed a kiss to my forehead. "Not really. I hoped I would have some information on the letter opener, but nothing yet. How did you sleep?"

I knew what he was worried about. "I'm glad you know," I admitted. "I just ... it's embarrassing. I don't know how I let myself get into this mess. I'm usually way smarter than that."

"It's not about being smart. It's about the pressure you felt. You didn't want to come back."

"But did I really not want to come back, or was it more that the town expected me to succeed, and I didn't want them to see me as a failure?"

"I don't know. I think it was fear regardless. It's okay, though. We'll figure it out. In a few years, we'll have it taken care of, and we won't ever have to think about it again."

"I still feel as if it should be my responsibility. I'm the one who made the mess."

"Then write a book."

The fast, succinct statement came completely out of the blue. I balked. "What?"

He laughed. "The fastest way for us to get rid of the debt would be for you to write a book, wouldn't it?"

I'd thought about it—so many times—but I felt frozen in place when it came to writing. "And if I waste all my time writing a book that doesn't sell?"

"Then you can write another one. We already know you can write something that sells. The only one who currently doesn't believe that is you."

"And Phoebe."

"Screw Phoebe. She doesn't count. Why do you care what a black-mailer thinks?"

He had a point. "I don't even know what I would write." I sounded petulant, but I couldn't stop myself.

"Maybe you should write a book about a woman who comes home after years away, falls back in love with her high school boyfriend, finds out she's a witch, and hijinks ensue."

My mouth dropped open. "I can't write *that*."

"Why? It's not as if anybody would believe it."

"Because ... because..." No words came to bail me out of my predica-ment. The sad thing was it wasn't the worst idea I'd ever heard. "I think we should deal with other stuff first." I opted to be pragmatic. "Like, for example, perhaps we should track down that cat and see who he was talking to last night."

"I'm not opposed to that. You can multitask, though." He planted a loud, hard kiss against my forehead. "I promise not to push you too hard on the writing, but I see no reason you can't start thinking about it. If you're not ready for the witch book, why don't you try some-thing light? You used to talk about writing romantic comedies all the time."

I pressed my lips together. I did love a good romantic comedy. "Maybe." I didn't commit either way because I didn't know what to say.

"You could write about a woman who comes home after ten years and falls in love with her high school boyfriend all over again. She works in the family restaurant. Hijinks ensue."

I had to bite the inside of my cheek to keep from laughing. "You're kind of fixated on that potential story."

"I am. Make sure the hero is handsome."

"I'll think about it." I gave him a squeeze, then rolled out of bed. "Come on. I'll make the coffee. I really do want to track down that annoying cat."

Hunter needed little prodding. "Yeah. Let's beat the crap out of him."

I stilled next to the bedroom door, which we'd taken to closing upon finding out Krankle was a gnome shifter. "We can't beat up a cat." I was horrified by the thought.

"He's not a cat, as you've pointed out multiple times."

"Yeah, but he still looks like a cat."

"And he's lying to us."

"That's neither here nor there." I was firm. "We're not beating up a cat. We'll have to get our information another way."

"If you say so."

"I do."

Krankle sat in the middle of the kitchen. His luminous eyes fixed on us when we switched on the light, and his tail lashed back and forth. "You're late," he announced. "My breakfast was supposed to be here twenty minutes ago."

"We're not your slaves." Hunter glared at the cat and moved to the counter to turn on the coffee maker. "If you're so hungry, learn to feed yourself."

"Yes, I'll open the can of tuna with my claws." Krankle shot me an incredulous look. "Can you believe this guy?"

I couldn't believe a lot of things about the situation. I only wanted to talk about one thing, however. "So, what friend were you talking to last night?" I wasn't good at small talk, so I didn't bother to ease into the conversation. I went straight for his jugular.

"I have no idea what you're talking about." Krankle kept his unblinking eyes focused on me.

"Last night, you were talking to someone behind the storage shed," I pressed. "We saw you."

"It could've been when I ordered that skunk off my turf. I thought your grandfather's afternoon bathroom visits were the worst thing I would ever smell. I was wrong."

"It was a man." I was at the end of my rope. "We saw his shadow. Don't bother denying it."

All light, Krankle regarded me with faux innocence. "I think you're mistaken. I didn't see a man down there. Occasionally, someone will cut through the alley coming from the grocery store, but I don't remember seeing anybody last night."

"But you were talking to him," I snapped. "I saw you!"

"Yeah, I think you imagined things." He edged toward his bowl. "I'm hungry. Feed me, or I'll crap in this one's shoes." He lashed his tail toward Hunter.

I lifted my eyes to take in Hunter's dark expression. He merely shrugged at my unasked question.

"Fine, but we need to talk." I stomped to the pantry to grab a can of tuna. "You can't stay here if you're keeping secrets. We give you a wide berth to do your thing, but we expect some loyalty in return. For all we know, you're plotting against us."

Krankle gave a withering glare. "If I were plotting against you, you would know it."

"And yet here we are." I popped the tab on the can, ripped off the top, and upended it in his bowl. "You've been evasive for weeks. You're barely up here."

"Since you guys play naked games every night, I thought you would prefer it that way." Krankle pounced on his bowl. "I don't want to be part of those games, and you guys don't want me around either."

"You're the one who said you have to stick close to me," I challenged.

"Just because you haven't seen me doesn't mean I haven't been close." Krankle slid his eyes to me. "What do you want, Stormy?"

"I want to know who you were talking to last night."

"I wasn't talking to anybody. I think you're seeing things."

"Then we both are," Hunter snapped. "She's not the only one who saw that shadow."

"I don't know what to tell you." Krankle's tone was icy and even. "I wasn't talking to anybody."

Gaslighted by a cat, and I couldn't do a thing about it. "Whatever." I turned on my heel and huffed toward the bathroom. "We're not done with this conversation. You might try to come up with a better response for the next round."

"I'll work on it."

"You do that."

GRANDPA WAS IN A GOOD MOOD—FOR HIM—when I joined him downstairs. I immediately handled the coffee filters, then opened the restaurant's front door. As per usual, a handful of regulars waited in their vehicles, and they immediately popped out when they saw me. They were all coffee drinkers, so I let them find their spots and brought out mugs. Then I returned to check on Grandpa.

"Do you ever worry about Grandma's fixation on euchre?" I asked as he dropped a dollop of oil on the griddle.

"No. I think it's good for everybody to have a hobby. That's her hobby, and it keeps her out of my hair. Why?"

I shrugged. "She's just a little intense."

"She is, but that's her thing. Everybody has a thing."

"Hunter doesn't have a thing." I realized after the fact that my words could be taken in a different way. "Wait, that came out wrong."

Grandpa chuckled. "Let's not get bogged down with Hunter's thing. Seriously, though, you both need hobbies. You can't spend every moment of every day together. You'll wear on each other. You need outside interests."

"I have zero outside interests," I lamented.

"You have writing."

I had to bite back a sigh. I should've seen that coming. "Why are you so interested in me writing again? I was under the impression that you thought my leaving was a mistake."

"No. You leaving was what had to happen. You coming back was smart. Embracing this life while giving up your dreams is a mistake though. You need to find balance, kid."

"Ugh. You sound like Hunter."

"He's a smart boy. He always has been. You should listen to him."

I thought of how calm Hunter had been when looking at my credit card debt the night before. He could've flown off the handle, called me an idiot, and stomped around. He'd done nothing of the sort. Sure, he had learned I was in debt when we got involved. I hadn't provided him with the specifics, though. It had to have been jarring, and yet his expression hadn't changed. His biggest worry had been how I would react to things.

"Hunter is the best thing that ever happened to me," I agreed. "He's a good guy. I'm just not ready to write yet."

"Then when?"

"I don't know."

"Have you considered that perhaps you don't have to write the best novel ever written? Just get words on the page. They don't necessarily have to be good words. Just write something—anything will do, at this point—and go from there."

I hated that he was right. "I need to check on the customers."

"You're going to pout," Grandpa countered when I turned my back to him. "Do what you want to do. Just know, I'm not falling for your crap. You want to write. You just think that because you gave up everything else from that life, you can't have writing either. You're an idiot for thinking that."

"I love you too."

THE SHIFT WENT FAST. BY TEN O'CLOCK, I was coasting toward lunch and grateful that I would be finished in two hours. Then Pete Winkle, a guy I'd gone to school with, walked through the front door. I hadn't seen him since I'd been back, and he brightened considerably when he saw me.

"Hey, Stormy." He went in for a hug, which I didn't expect. "How's it hanging?"

I returned the hug haphazardly. When I pulled back to study Pete's face, I was awash in confusion. We'd always been friendly but never really friends. He had favored the cheerleaders, and once Hunter and I had gotten together, he wouldn't have dared spend too much time with me because he revered Hunter. Their relationship was the tighter one. I only knew him in passing.

"Um, things are going well." I offered a smile because I had no reason to dislike the guy. Perhaps I just remembered him wrong, or maybe he'd grown bolder since high school. That was known to happen. "You probably know Hunter and I are back together."

"I do. Everybody knows that. It was the talk of the town when you came home. They had a pool going to see when you would get back together."

"I heard about the pool." And I was still mad about it, but I didn't mention that. "I take it you didn't win."

"Nope." He smiled and then glanced over my shoulder to where several regulars drank coffee at a table.

"Do you want to join them?" I shifted so I wasn't directly in front of them. "I can bring you a coffee."

"Yeah, I think I do." Pete's smile widened. "I'll have two eggs over medium, hash browns, sausage, and white toast."

I wasn't prepared for his order, but I had a solid memory, so I just smiled. "Sure. Have a seat, and I'll bring you the coffee after I put that in."

"Awesome." To my utter surprise, he slapped his hand against my butt as he passed. Hard. "I'm glad you're back in town, Stormy."

My mouth dropped open, and I stood rooted to my spot. *Did he just slap my butt?* I was convinced something was off about Pete. Because I didn't know what else to do, I jotted down his order on my notepad and took it in to my grandfather, who was eating rather than working. He had egg yolk stuck to his cheek.

"What's wrong with you?" he asked midchew. His manners weren't always top of the line.

"Pete Winkle is out there," I replied.

"So?" Grandpa didn't look bothered by the news. "He comes in every once in a while. Not usually in the morning, but it's hardly shocking news."

"He smacked my butt." I hadn't meant to say it, but apparently, I couldn't hold it in.

Grandpa's forehead creased. "What do you mean?"

"I mean that he smacked my butt. Like ... bam!" I mimicked what had happened for Grandpa's benefit.

"That doesn't sound like him." He looked baffled. "Why would he do that?"

"I don't know. Maybe he's different from how I remember him or something. Did his inner pervert come out while I was gone?"

"That dude is more vanilla than frosting," Grandpa countered. "He doesn't go around smacking women's behinds. That's not who he is. Besides, even if it were, he's friends with Hunter. He wouldn't make a move on you because of that alone."

That was what I thought. Still, a niggling suspicion wormed its way into my head, and I moved to the swinging doors that looked out on the café section of the diner. I could see over the top, and Pete hadn't joined the locals as he'd suggested before I went into the kitchen. No, he'd switched to another table to sit with Celeste, Monica, and Phoebe.

"What are you thinking?" Grandpa asked, curious enough to join me at the swinging doors. He scowled when he realized who Pete was with. "Since when does he like her?"

I flicked my eyes to my grandfather. "He doesn't like Phoebe?"

"Nobody does, but he especially doesn't. She dated him like three years ago, then cheated on him with some traveling salesman. At least I think that's how the story goes. He openly hates on her."

I could see that, on both sides. Phoebe was always looking for something better, and Pete wasn't the type of guy to just put up with someone using and abusing him. "And yet, now he's over there hanging out with her."

Phoebe laughed at something Pete said and lightly slapped his arm. She looked to be having the time of her life.

"I didn't realize Pete was that funny," I said.

"I don't know anybody who finds that guy funny," Grandpa replied. "Dependable? Yes. Pleasant? Yes. Funny? That's a hard no."

"He's funny now." Worms squirmed in my stomach. "Was Edmund considered funny?"

"I never thought so, but the women found him hysterical. Why?" Grandpa's bright eyes focused on me.

"Just checking." I forced a smile I didn't feel. "I guess Pete is turning over a new leaf."

"No, it's more than that. What are you thinking?"

I couldn't share my belief that Edmund had taken over Pete's body. That was a bridge too far for Grandpa to accept. "It's nothing," I lied. "He just threw me with the butt slap."

"I can kick him out."

"That's not necessary." I meant it. "Let him stay. I'll just watch my butt."

"If he touches you again, I'll break his hands. Heck, when Hunter finds out what he did, I don't think he'll have anything left to break. Your boyfriend will grind him into glue."

That was a worry, but I had a far greater one. "Just cook his breakfast. I have a feeling he won't hang around long once he's eaten."

"I have a feeling you're right," Grandpa said. "Twenty bucks says he leaves with Phoebe."

The notion made me feel ill. "I'm not betting on that. Just make his breakfast. I kind of want to see what he does."

TEN

Pete didn't leave with Phoebe—apparently, she had to get to work—but he didn't hang around long after she left either. I watched from my spot in front of the swinging doors when he exited, and my every doubt was reinforced when he paused halfway through the door, glanced over his shoulder, and shot me a smug look.

It was definitely Edmund. That was the only explanation I could find. *What am I supposed to do about it, though?* I couldn't very well chase him into the parking lot and use my magic on him in broad daylight. Someone would see. That meant I had to wait.

I finished my shift, though my heart wasn't in it. I showered after and headed out through the restaurant's back door. I didn't have time to mess around, so I took my car to Sebastian's funeral home. He was alone when I let myself in, which was good because I had a lot to tell him.

"Pete Winkle smacked your butt?" Sebastian sounded understandably horrified by the story. "Is he trying to get himself killed? Nothing will be left of him once Hunter gets his hands on him."

"First off, Hunter is not a Neanderthal. He won't kill him or anything." Maybe I just hoped that was true. "Secondly, I don't think it's really Pete. Did you miss the rest of the story?"

"No, but I have trouble believing it." Sebastian cocked his head.

"What? That's next-level movie stuff there, Stormy. How am I supposed to believe that?"

"You were kidnapped by monsters three weeks ago," I reminded him. "They used magic to do it. I have a talking cat you've conversed with numerous times. Why is this a bridge too far?"

He held out his hands and shrugged. "I don't know. It just is."

"The point is that's not Pete. It's Edmund."

"Okay, let's say I believe you—I'm not saying I do, but let's say I do," he said. "What do we do about it?"

"We'll find Pete and isolate him, and I'll use my magic to force Edmund out."

Sebastian blinked twice. "Then what?"

"What do you mean?"

"Well, what do we do with the ghost when he's out? It sounds to me as if you don't have a way to stop him from jumping into another body."

"That doesn't mean we can let him stay in Pete."

"No, but ... at least we know where he is now. If we force him out, he could jump into somebody else's body, and we might not figure it out next time."

He had a point. Still, I couldn't stomach the idea of doing nothing. "I remember Pete as a nice guy."

"He is."

"Well, we can't just allow Edmund to screw up his life." I was firm on that. "What if Pete has a girlfriend?"

"He doesn't. He was at the bar two weeks ago complaining that all the women in town are either taken or evil."

Frustration had me by my innards. "What about his job? Edmund obviously isn't doing whatever Pete does for a living. He's off screwing around."

"Pete sells insurance," Sebastian replied. "Plus, he owns his own agency. I think he's okay if he doesn't show up for a day or two."

"Are you trying to kill me?"

Sebastian let loose a long, exasperated sigh. "No, but you obviously won't be dissuaded from this plan. My question is, how do we find him?

If he's not at work and he's not at home—which I assume is our first place to look—how will we find him?"

That was a fair question. I didn't have an answer. "We'll figure it out."

"Oh, we'll figure it out." Sebastian rolled his eyes but didn't move from the settee.

"Are you going to change your outfit?" I demanded after several seconds. "You can't wear that to spy. You'll complain the whole time."

"Oh, don't kid yourself, honey," he drawled. "I'll complain the entire time regardless."

"Sebastian," I growled.

"Fine." He was resigned when he stood. "I just want you to know, I'm doing this against my will. The only reason I'm even considering participating is because Hunter will beat me up if I don't go with you."

"What is it with you guys thinking Hunter will beat everybody up?" I demanded. "He's a pacifist."

"Oh, he's not his father—and we're all thankful for that—but he's hardly a pacifist," Sebastian shot back. "He gets all growly and testosterone-y when it comes to you. Denying it makes you look idiotic."

"Just change your clothes." I couldn't take much more. "If you're not ready in ten minutes, I'm leaving without you."

"Is that a threat? It doesn't sound like one to me."

"Do what I say."

"Yeah, yeah, yeah."

WE STARTED AT PETE'S HOUSE. HE WASN'T there, and I hadn't expected he would be. We checked the insurance agency afterward, but he wasn't there either. Shadow Hills wasn't very big, so it didn't take us long to drive end to end. Ultimately, it was a fluke that uncovered him, though I wanted to kick myself after I realized he was back at the senior center.

"Of course he's back here," I complained as we parked at Sebastian's funeral home. "This is where all his women hang out."

Sebastian was morose as we climbed out of my car. "What a waste of time that was."

"It's not as if I could've known," I argued.

"I'll never get that hour of my life back, Stormy. It's gone forever."

"You're on my last nerve."

We trudged across the road and entered through the main door. The group playing cards at the tables looked largely the same, except for one at the center. There, Pete sat with Iris, Florence, and Gwen. They looked to be playing euchre and having a good time with a lot of giggles and furtive arm touches.

"You still don't believe me?" I demanded of Sebastian, trying not to be smug.

"You want me to believe we're stuck in a very boring *Invasion of the Body Snatchers* remake simply because Pete is playing cards with three women?" Sebastian didn't look the least bit interested in the scene.

"Just wait." It wasn't about me being right—at least I told myself that as we cut through the room—but Sebastian's refusal to believe me simply because it was the right thing to do irritated me on several levels.

"Nice hand," Pete commented as Iris gathered the cards to shuffle. While paired with Florence, he seemed to pay all three women equal attention. "I love a pocket ace like you wouldn't believe."

Iris beamed at him. "I do too."

"You've always been good with the pocket aces," Pete crooned.

I would've thought Iris would react to Pete saying it, but she didn't.

"I'm good with everything," Iris purred.

"Oh, I bet you are."

I wanted to punch him. "Hello, all." I grabbed a chair from a nearby table and planted it directly between Pete and Gwen. "Is everybody having a good time?"

Iris arched an eyebrow as she regarded me. "Twice in as many days. Why do we merit so many visits in such a short amount of time?"

"Maybe I just like you," I replied.

"No, that's not it," Florence countered. "You're up to something."

While I only cared about Pete at that point, the statement rankled. "Why would you say that?"

"Because you have the same look on your face that your grandfather gets when he's up to something," Florence replied. "You're not very good at hiding your intentions."

That showed what she knew. I thought I hid my intentions extremely well. "I just like visiting my grandmother," I lied. "She's here most afternoons."

"Over there." Gwen waved toward the east side of the room. "She's not here with us."

"That doesn't mean I can't stop to visit with you guys."

"Uh-huh." Gwen looked unconvinced. "If you say so." She waited until she had all five of her cards before looking at them. "You play euchre, right, Stormy? Maybe you should go play against your grandmother. I'm sure she would like that."

"Yes, we don't need you over here," Florence agreed. "You'll be nothing but a nuisance."

"I'm actually here to talk to Pete." I couldn't let the conversation continue unchecked. The women would have me booted if I wasn't careful. That was their way. "Do you think we can head outside and have a conversation, *Pete*?"

"I'm good." Pete looked utterly relaxed. If he worried I might cause a scene, he didn't show it. Of course, from his perspective, I was the one who would look like a deranged idiot if I accused him of anything.

"Oh, come on," I wheedled, batting my lashes and offering up my best "come hither" look. Flirting wasn't my forte. "I just want to have a quick chat with you outside."

"No offense, but I would much rather spend time with these lovely ladies here." Pete smiled at each woman in turn. "You're not my type, Stormy."

"You're also spoken for, last time I checked," Florence pointed out. "How would Hunter feel about you trying to entice one of his good friends to join you outside?"

I narrowed my eyes. "I'm not trying to entice him. I just want to talk to him."

"Have a pressing insurance need, do you?" Iris challenged.

"I do. Hunter and I are looking at buying a house, so we'll need insurance."

Pete snorted. "Have Hunter stop by when he has a chance. I'll take care of him."

"I'm stopping by now."

"No offense, but I would prefer to deal with Hunter. He'll understand the numbers better than you."

I raised my chin and glanced at Sebastian, who looked much more interested in our mission after spending a few minutes near Pete.

"Did he just...?" I didn't finish the question.

"Yes, that was the male equivalent of a pat on the head and a 'you're a female, so you won't understand it,'" Sebastian confirmed.

"That's what I thought." I was more determined than ever to talk with Pete. "Let's go outside."

"I'm in the middle of a game," Pete argued. "Why are you being so aggressive?"

"Yes, why are you being so aggressive?" Gwen prodded. "I haven't spent much time with you since your return, but I don't remember you being this ... demanding."

"She gets it from her grandmother," Florence complained. "Stormy's just like her, right down to the way she orders men around. It's sickening really."

"Come on!" I grabbed Pete's arm and forcibly yanked him out of his chair.

Surprise registered on his features, and he put up a fight, but I had momentum on my side and managed to drag him away from the tables before he got his wits about him.

"What do you think you're doing?" Pete hissed when we were out of his harem's earshot. "I'm just trying to enjoy a game of cards. What's the matter with you?"

"Don't play games with me, *Edmund*." I kept my gaze on his face to gauge his reaction.

He didn't seem surprised that I used his real name. Amused was the better word.

"You're not even going to deny it, are you?"

"Why would I?" Pete—it was hard to call him Edmund when he was in the wrong body—smugly smoothed the front of his shirt. "If I didn't want you to know, I wouldn't have bothered hitting up the restaurant this morning."

"You need to stop doing this," I snapped. "You're dead. You don't get to keep living when you're dead."

"Who says?"

"Says ... everybody." I couldn't remember ever being so frustrated. "That's not your body."

"So what? He wasn't using it for anything good. I mean, everybody in town called him a loser. Technically, I'm making his life better."

"How do you figure that?" Sebastian seemed more intrigued than upset as he followed the conversation.

"Well, for starters, Pete can't catch a woman. I'm good at catching them."

"Yes, I'm sure Pete's new reputation as a romancer of women at the senior center will do great things for his reputation," I replied dryly. "He's not even thirty years old."

"Hey! Don't you be talking about my ladies that way. I don't like it!" Genuine irritation bubbled in Pete's eyes. "Why do you even care what I do? I'm not trying to get into your boyfriend. I get why you were upset about that—though I could've made things so much better for you than he ever has—but why do you care about this?"

"Because it's not right," I replied. "Also, don't be gross. Hunter is ten times the man you could ever be."

Pete snorted. "You don't know what you're missing."

"And I never will. You need to get it together." I felt like a nagging mother. Since that was the position he'd cast me in, I decided to channel my mother. "Don't you feel even a little guilty about stealing Pete's life?"

"No. He wasn't living it properly." He tapped the side of his head. "I know way more than he does. I have a chance to live life all over again and to do it right this time. I don't see a downside to this."

Of course he would think that. "Pete has a downside. You're stealing everything from him." Something occurred to me. "Is he still in there? Can you, like ... talk to him when you're sharing his body?"

"Pete is taking a nap. It's better for him if he doesn't know what's going on."

I couldn't decide if Pete's lack of awareness was a good or bad thing. Ultimately, I decided on optimism. The less he knew, the better. Though he would have a heckuva mess to clean up when he got his body back, and I would make that happen whether Edmund liked it or not.

"Listen—"

"No, you listen," Pete barked. "I've had enough of you. I don't know what your deal is. I don't know why you could see me as a ghost. And I don't care about any of that, but I think you do."

What does that mean?

"If you want to keep your secret, then you'll keep mine," he continued. "Unless you want people knowing you can shoot glittery stuff from your hands—and I'm sure it doesn't stop there—you'll back off."

Is he really threatening me? This is unbelievable. "Do you think people will believe you?"

"I don't know. People have always found you weird, though. A lot of strange things have happened since you came back to town. I guess we'll just have to see."

I didn't know how to respond.

After a few seconds, he backed away and graced me with another smile. "Now, if you'll excuse me, my ladies await."

With that, he sauntered back to the table he'd just vacated. His cadence told me he was flirting with his lady friends, but I didn't hear his words. It didn't matter.

"Well, that was bracing." Sebastian moved closer to me. "What will you do?"

"I don't know." I kept my voice low. "He can't keep Pete's body. We can't allow that."

"You also can't walk up to him in the middle of the senior center and conduct an exorcism."

"No. I certainly can't." I let loose a breath. "What a mess."

"Yeah. It's definitely a mess."

We moved to a spot near the door and watched Pete charm everybody in the room. The longer he talked and carried on, the more people surrounded him. My grandmother found us glowering between games.

"You look upset." Not commenting out of sympathy, Grandma was clearly curious. "Is something going on with Pete Winkle?"

"You could say that." I didn't know how much to tell her—*would she even believe me if I tried?*—so, ultimately, I forced a smile. "Just watch him. I get the feeling he'll be hanging out here and in your neighborhood on a regular basis."

"Why would Pete hang out in our neighborhood?"

"He's just not himself right now."

"Okay, but that wasn't really an answer."

"I don't have an answer at present. I just need you to be careful."

Grandma stayed silent a beat, then sighed. "This is some of that woo-woo crap you've gotten yourself involved in since you've been back, isn't it?"

"Yes."

"Then say no more." She held up her hand. "That's your business. I don't want to be dragged into it."

"As long as you stay away from Pete, you should get your wish."

"Then that's what I'll do."

ELEVEN

I watched for another two hours then headed home. Sebastian only stuck it out twenty minutes before getting bored. He made me promise to call him should something entertaining pop up, but it never did. Pete stayed close to the others, ensuring I didn't have a chance to get near him without someone seeing, and when he left, it was with multiple members of his harem in tow. He winked as he walked by, his smug smile making me want to shake the daylights out of him, then the building was empty.

Dejected and frustrated beyond belief, I stomped up the stairs to the apartment.

Hunter was there, dressed in comfortable jogging pants and a T-shirt, and his eyes went wide when he saw me. "I take it you didn't have a good day."

"Nope." I stripped out of my coat, kicked off my shoes, and threw myself onto the couch with the sort of dramatic ridiculousness that I associated with my grandfather. "I had the worst day ever."

Hunter calmly lifted my legs and settled beneath them. He immediately took one of my feet and began to rub. "Tell me what's wrong."

"Edmund is in Pete Winkle's body."

Hunter pressed his thumbs into my arch, causing me to moan, and cocked his head. "Are you sure?"

"He admitted it when I confronted him at the senior center."

"I think you'd better fill me in."

I did just that. When I got through everything, he looked flabbergasted.

"Well, that is just all kinds of crazy."

"Is that all you have to say?" I propped myself on my elbows and moaned again. "Man, don't stop doing that. Like ... ever."

He smiled, but his features held an edge. "Did he really slap your butt?"

"Yes, and now is not the time to worry about that. It wasn't really Pete."

"That doesn't mean I can't smack him around a bit."

"Um, yes, it does." I was firm on that. "If you punch Pete and Edmund leaves his body, then Pete would be left with a black eye he didn't earn."

"I'm still annoyed." He kept rubbing. "I guess I see your point, though. I guess it will be payback enough for everybody to tease him—probably for the rest of his life—about picking up senior citizens when he's twenty-nine years old."

"Yeah, that will be a thing." I closed my eyes and tried to get comfortable. Hunter was doing his best to lull me, but I couldn't quite relax. "Edmund said Peter is still in there but suggested he's asleep."

"Like ... he's trapped in his own mind?"

"Essentially."

"Hmm." He moved his hands down to my heel and kept rubbing. "Did you call Bay?"

"I did, and I left a message. She hasn't called back yet. I don't want to bug her when she has her own stuff to deal with."

"You help with her stuff."

"I do, and she's helped us more times than I can count. If I don't hear back from her tonight, I'll bug her again tomorrow."

"Okay." He switched feet. "What do you want to do about Pete?"

"I want to get Edmund out of his body."

"And you're certain you can do that if we get Pete alone?"

"I've done it twice before. I don't see why I can't do it a third time."

"Then we need to find him." Hunter's orderly mind was on full display as he mulled over our problem. "We need to think like Edmund, right? He might look like Pete, but he's really Edmund, so we need to figure out what he would do on a Wednesday night in Shadow Hills."

"And what would that be?" I was all ears. If Hunter could think of something, I was more than happy to go on an adventure.

"The bowling alley."

He said it with such conviction, all I could do was sit and blink.

"What now?" I asked when he didn't expound.

"It's senior night at the bowling alley. Edmund is part of the league."

"Huh." I ran it through my head. "Do you think we can separate him from people when we're there?"

"It can't hurt to try." He gave my feet a squeeze and then shifted them from his lap. "Come on. We can at least scope it out." He extended his hand to me.

"What about dinner?" I felt fairly pitiful. "I was hoping for goulash leftovers."

"We can eat when we get back, or we can save it for tomorrow."

"And do what tonight?" I couldn't help sounding surly.

"We can eat at the bowling alley. They've got burgers, fries, hot dogs ... that sort of stuff."

It wasn't the worst offer I'd had all day. "Do you really believe me?"

He was earnest when he shifted to meet my gaze. "Of course I do. If you say Edmund is inside Pete, then he's inside Pete. I think this is our only option to stop him tonight."

"Okay." I smiled as I sat up and opened my arms for a hug. "That's all I needed to hear."

He pulled me to him and rubbed his hands up and down my back. "I think maybe your ego isn't what it should be," he whispered. "Things went badly for you, and it's eating away at your self-esteem. I will always be on your side. Do you know why?"

"Because I'm awesome."

I was half joking, but when he pulled back, his earnest look told me he was serious.

"You are awesome. It's okay that you're still a little unsteady. I'm here to bolster you though. I know I gave you a hard time when you told me Edmund tried to get inside my body, but that wasn't fair. You wouldn't make that up. If you say it's true, then it's true."

"I think him threatening me today threw me. I don't want what I am to come back and hurt you."

"Nothing about you could ever hurt me." He gave me a soft kiss. "I promise." He squeezed me for another second, then let go. "Let me change into some jeans, then we'll head out."

"Now I'm kind of excited for bar food," I admitted.

"See. I knew you would come around."

THE BOWLING ALLEY WAS PACKED, CATCHING ME off guard when we walked through the door. Hunter nodded at various people who called out his name and waved with his free hand. All the while, he kept a firm grip on me with his other hand.

"Let's sit over there." He directed me toward a table raised on a platform above the lanes. It would allow us to watch the goings-on without being on top of the bowlers.

Catelynn Weaver, one of the local girls who had only been out of high school a year or two, arrived at the table within seconds of us sitting down. "Hi, Hunter," she cooed on a giggle.

"Hello, Catelynn." Hunter's smile was warm but not flirty. "You remember Stormy, right?"

Catelynn's smile faltered, but she nodded. "I remember her. She babysat me when she was a teenager."

"I remember that," I enthused. "You used to hoard bags of Twizzlers and eat them in one sitting. Your mom melted down all the time over the candy."

"Yeah, I remember that too," Catelynn said. "You used to spend all your time on the phone with Hunter, and the only real babysitting you did was to tell me not to turn on the stove."

Yup. That sounded about right. I was a crappy babysitter. "Good times, huh?" I smiled because I knew it would irritate her.

"I didn't know you bowled," Catelynn turned back to Hunter. "Are you part of the league?"

"Isn't tonight the senior league?" Hunter rested his hand on top of mine on the table. "I think I have a few years before I'll qualify for this league."

"Oh, you're so funny." Catelynn touched his shoulder and batted her eyelashes as if her life depended on it. "Do you want something to eat?"

"Um, yeah." Hunter grabbed the menu from the middle of the table. "I will have a chicken sandwich and fries—a Coke too please."

"Cool." Catelynn turned to leave, but Hunter stopped her by clearing his throat.

"I believe Stormy would like to order too," he said pointedly.

"Oh, of course." Catelynn smiled at me without warmth. "What do you want?"

Trying to order fancy in a bowling alley would be a waste of time, so I went basic. "I'll have a burger with ketchup, pickles, mustard, and onions. I'll have onion rings too."

Hunter cleared his throat. "No onions. How will I kiss you if you're loaded up on onions?"

"I'll make sure there are extra onions," Catelynn promised before taking off.

I had to fight to keep a straight face as I met Hunter's gaze. "How many members are in your fan club these days?"

He chuckled. "Only one I care about." He squeezed my hand, then started searching the lanes for our target individual.

It didn't take Hunter long. Pete was stationed one lane over from Florence, Iris, Gwen, and Blanche. He wasn't with any of them, but rather Maggie Baldwin, a different local, who happened to be several decades younger than Edmund.

"How old is Maggie now?" I tried to do the math in my head.

"She's eighteen," Hunter replied darkly. "I know because she got caught trying to buy vodka with a fake ID at the grocery store three weeks ago. I didn't charge her, but when I questioned her, that came up."

"Huh."

I cringed when Pete leaned in to whisper something to her. She giggled like a loon when he finished.

"Oh, I think I might be sick."

"You're not the only one." Hunter's expression was dark. "What are they even doing down there?"

"Are you talking about Pete?" a man asked from our left, causing me to jolt.

The bowling alley was so packed, it was virtually impossible to find a space where we couldn't be overheard. I made a mental note to be careful. I didn't want the wrong person to hear us.

"Hey, Rick." Hunter smiled at the man edging toward our table. I didn't recognize him, but Hunter clearly did. "You remember Stormy, right?" He gestured toward me. "Stormy, this is Rick Fields."

It took me a moment to remember the name. "Oh, right." I smiled. "You were ahead of us by about three years and quarterback of the football team."

"That's me." Rick's smile was friendly. "Now I own the Shadow Hills Bowling Alley."

"Ah." I nodded. "I haven't been in since I got back. It looks nice."

Technically, it looked the same. But I hadn't seen it in more than ten years, so that felt like a feat in and of itself.

"I'm surprised to see you guys here," Rick supplied. "I heard you were moving in together, above Two Broomsticks, right?"

Hunter nodded. "We plan to buy a house in the spring." He didn't mention which house, which was likely on purpose. "For now, we're saving money by selling my house and living above the restaurant."

"That sounds smart." Rick watched as Hunter returned his gaze to Pete. "You're wondering about the same thing I am."

"I'm just curious how Maggie and Pete hooked up," Hunter replied. "I didn't know they were a thing." He played it off casually, but the muscle working in his jaw told me it bothered him.

"I'm trying to figure that out myself." Rick lowered his voice. "Pete came in with the fearsome foursome over there." He inclined his head toward Edmund's harem, which watched him from one aisle over. "They were all having a good time, laughing up a storm. It felt weird, but I figured he was just being nice. That's Pete's way after all. Things changed when Maggie came in," he continued. "She stops by a few times a week because she likes Clark."

He pointed toward a twenty-something young man standing behind the shoe counter. His eyes were also trained on the couple, though he looked agitated.

"They flirt constantly but have yet to do anything. Still, I figured it was only a matter of time. Then Pete started cozying up to Maggie the second he saw her. It's very ... odd."

I cringed when Pete leaned closer to Maggie, their lips almost brushing. Some sort of weird mating ritual was clearly being played out.

"She's an adult," Rick noted. "Technically, there's no reason to question what's going on. It's just ... she's barely an adult."

"And Pete is definitely an adult," Hunter agreed.

"Do you think we should do something?" Rick looked uncomfortable at the prospect.

Hunter cocked his head, considering, then smiled. "You know what? I'll watch the situation while we're eating dinner. If I feel a discussion needs to be had, I'll pull Pete outside when we're done and ask him what's going on."

Rick let loose a relieved breath. "I think that sounds like a good idea. I don't want to cause a scene, but she's a girl. Sure, she has a wild streak, but she's still just a girl."

"And he's a man," Hunter agreed. "Don't worry about it. I'll try to be discreet when I draw him outside."

"Thanks a lot, man." Rick clapped Hunter's shoulder. "You guys have a good dinner. It's nice to see you two so happy again."

"It is nice." Hunter winked at me. "It's pretty much the best thing that's ever happened."

WE WATCHED PETE PLAY PERVERTED GAMES with Maggie throughout dinner. Neither of us had much of an appetite, but we plowed through our food. As interesting as I found Pete's attitude toward the teenager, his harem's reaction to the scene struck me as most fascinating.

"They're mad," I said as Hunter paid the bill and left a generous tip for Catelynn. "They're furious, and yet they're not doing anything to stop it."

"The problem is, I don't think they're mad on Maggie's behalf." Hunter shoved his wallet into his pocket. "They're mad because they feel they're missing out. It's not altruistic anger."

"No, definitely not."

Hunter pointed me toward the door. "How about you head out? I'll bring Pete to you. I think it will cause more of a stir if you're with me when I ask to talk to him. It will just look like two friends having a heart-to-heart if I'm alone."

"Okay." I started in that direction, frowning when I looked down at the spot where Pete had sat with Maggie only minutes before. "Where did they go?"

Hunter straightened, looking again. "Crap. They were just there."

"Let's not panic." The last thing I needed was him flying off the handle. "Let's check the parking lot."

We hurried in that direction. The parking lot appeared empty—everyone was inside playing games of some sort, after all—but then I noticed a set of foggy windows. "Oh, please don't tell me that's Maggie and Pete." I would hurl. I just knew it.

Hunter stormed in that direction and threw open the car door without hesitation. I scurried to keep up, and when I looked over his shoulder, I found Maggie was, indeed, inside. Pete wasn't with her though. Clark was.

"How...?" Honestly, it didn't matter how they'd gotten past us. What mattered was that a pervy senior citizen wearing Pete's body wasn't taking advantage of Maggie.

"What are you doing?" Maggie shrieked, her cheeks flushed. She looked a little sweaty and seemed to have someone else's hand up her shirt.

"This is private property," Clark barked.

"Yeah, yeah, yeah." Hunter waved his hand. "You guys can make out until the cows come home. I don't care about that. What I do care about is Pete Winkle. You were with him inside, Maggie. Where did he go?"

"I wasn't with him," Maggie hedged.

"Yes, you were. You two were this close to mounting each other in public." Hunter held his fingers about an inch apart for emphasis. "Don't bother denying it. We saw you."

"That was just for show," Maggie protested. "I was trying to make Clark jealous." She turned sheepish. "Obviously, it worked. I've been trying to get him to make a move for weeks. Pete was just gracious enough to offer his attention for an evening to help me achieve my goal."

"Uh-huh. And where did Pete go when you threw him over for Clark?" Hunter queried.

Maggie shrugged. "I have no idea. I saw him leave though. He didn't hang around once I told him that I thought it was best we just be friends."

"Great. Go back to your previously scheduled groping session." Hunter slammed the car door and slid his eyes to me. "He must've known we would come for him."

It made sense. As we walked away from the car, muted voices caught my attention near the front door. There, Iris, Gwen, Florence, and Blanche watched us with flat eyes.

"I thought they were enemies," I mused.

"Me too. Maybe something else is going on."

I'd just been wondering that exact thing. It wasn't the place to question them though. Even if it were, I had no idea what to say. "This just keeps getting weirder and weirder."

"Yup." Hunter moved his hand to my back. "Do you want to hang around in case Pete comes back or call it a night?"

"He won't come back." I was sure of that. "Let's go home. You can get some secondhand onion action."

He smirked. "Oddly, I think that sounds like a fantastic idea."

"You're a multifaceted kind of weird."

"I can live with that."

TWELVE

W e checked Pete's house on our way home. I knew it was likely fruitless, but we had to try. We drove past Edmund's house, too, but no lights were on.

"He could be anywhere," Hunter mused. "If he were smart, he would leave town."

"I don't get the feeling he's all that smart."

"No. I don't get why he's sticking so close to his lady friends. I mean, if the goal is to steal Pete's life, why not start fresh?"

It was an interesting question. "I think he's getting off on the attention. The way Marty talked, I got the feeling that those women fighting over Edmund turned into an ego thing."

"Sure, but from what your grandmother said, those women aren't really interested in him. They're interested in beating each other."

"Yeah. I don't understand any of it." I rubbed my forehead, trying to relieve the impending headache.

"I do think you should get Bay in on this tomorrow if at all possible," Hunter said. "She's the expert on ghosts. For all we know, she can nip this problem in the bud without having to go public. She can command ghosts, right? She could just order him to stay out of other people's bodies."

I hadn't considered that. "Actually, that's an interesting theory." I checked the clock on the dashboard. It was after ten.

"You need sleep," Hunter volunteered, seemingly reading my mind. "You can call Bay tomorrow."

"What if Edmund comes for you tonight?"

"That would put him in harm's way. He seems driven to taunt you, so you would definitely recognize it's not me. I don't think he'll risk that again."

I hoped that was true.

Hunter parked in what had become his designated spot in the lot. Instead of heading straight for the building, however, he turned toward the storage shed.

"What are you doing?" I scampered to keep up.

Hunter dug in his pocket until he came back with his cell phone. When he engaged the flashlight app and pointed it at the ground, I caught his intentions.

"You're looking for footprints," I surmised.

"I am." He dropped to his knees. His forehead creased in concentration. "I don't see anything though."

"The ground is hard," I reminded him. "The mornings and nights have been cold, so it's not as if any shadow feet can sink into a bunch of mud."

"No, I'm still bothered by the entire thing." Hunter glanced over his shoulder, toward the small group of trees making up the back acre of space behind the restaurant.

It couldn't be considered a forest by any stretch of the imagination, but it was thick enough to allow various critters a safe place to eat and sleep. The trees were also big enough to hide a human.

"Krankle's being squirrelly." I watched Hunter prowl the ground. "Something is going on, and he doesn't want to share it with the class."

"I think we should kick him out."

I couldn't be certain if Hunter meant to say that part out loud, but he'd clearly been giving it some thought. Truthfully, so had I. That scenario introduced a few problems, however.

"He's still a cat," I murmured. "I can't kick a cat out with winter bearing down."

Hunter lifted his eyes to me. "He's not really a cat, though, baby. He's something else, and he's obviously been manipulating us from the start. I'm not comfortable allowing him to continue. I think we need to issue an ultimatum. He provides answers, or we cut off the tuna train."

I turned my back to him so I could think. The only significant source of light in the area was the grocery store, which was closed. Inside, workers still prepared for the following day, but the parking lot showed no movement.

"It's your show, Stormy," Hunter added when I didn't speak. "I'll do what you want on this one."

"Why?" I asked in a low voice, keeping my gaze from his handsome face. "If you're so upset, why let me make the decision?"

"Because, ultimately, you're the one who has to deal with him."

"So do you. I mean ... you love me, right?" I turned a rueful smile in his direction.

"More than anything," he agreed.

"That means you get a say in what happens with our home."

"Yes, and when it comes time to battle it out over paint colors, I'll be more than happy to engage in that fight. This is different." He stood and dusted off the knees of his jeans. "You're the magical one. He's seemingly part of that. Even though he's annoying, you've been inclined to trust him on multiple occasions."

"I don't know if 'trust' is the correct word," I hedged. "He's helped us a few times."

"Yes, but we've had to back him into a corner to do it. I'm just afraid that if we keep ceding control to him, you won't feel safe."

That made me smile. "I feel safer here, with you, than I've felt in a very long time."

"And I'm glad, but we're living a temporary existence right now."

My shoulders jerked, but I didn't speak. I couldn't.

"Not how you're thinking." Hunter made a testy sound deep in his throat and glared at me. "We're not temporary, but our living arrangements are. We'll settle in here over the winter, and that will be fun. I've never lived over a restaurant before, and I can't wait to see what that's like. But we won't stay here forever.

"In the spring, we'll buy our house and probably stay in the apartment until at least June or so," he continued. "I've already talked to your grandfather about it. Once we buy the house, we have to wait for Nora MacDonald to move. Then painting and replacing carpet will be easier when nobody is living there. So, it will probably be early summer before we get our house. By then, I would really like to have the Krankle situation in hand."

"Because you don't want to take him with us," I surmised.

Hunter hesitated, then held out his hands. "I have no problem taking him with us if I'm certain he's a friend. I don't think we've determined that yet though."

"He's never actively worked against us," I protested.

"No?" Hunter arched an eyebrow. "What do you call hanging out behind the storage shed, talking to some shadowy figure?"

"We don't know that it's an enemy."

"We don't know it's a friend either."

He had a point. On a hefty exhale, I closed my eyes and considered his words. "Can I have a little time to think about it?" I asked when I'd found my voice.

"Sure." He smiled easily. "That's more than fair."

"I get that something needs to be done. I just don't know what that something is. He's barely been around the last two weeks."

"Yes, and that worries me even more than that he likes crapping in my shoes."

I couldn't contain my laughter. "I just need to think. The whole thing with Pete is throwing me. I want to get that situation settled. Then we'll deal with Krankle."

"Okay." He sidled over and slipped his arm around my waist. "Whatever you want is good with me."

He said it—he meant it—but that wouldn't be the end of it. Hunter wanted to protect me. He also liked things neat and orderly. As of yet, he hadn't managed to put Krankle in a box. *Friend or foe?* We honestly couldn't be certain. Hunter needed that stability. And truth be told, so did I.

"I'm ready to get some sleep," I said as we started toward the back door. "Tomorrow, no matter what, I will get a handle on this."

"I don't think it'll be as easy as you hope."

"No, but sometimes things in life are hard. I can't let Edmund keep living in Pete's body."

"Definitely not. As bland as Pete is, he's still a good guy, and he deserves to live his life. We can't let Edmund steal it from him."

"I think figuring things out will be easier when we're rested."

"Here's hoping."

SIX SOLID HOURS OF SLEEP HAD ME FEELING improved. Eight hours would've been nice, but the excursion to the bowling alley —and the subsequent search—had made that impossible. Six hours was better than nothing.

Hunter paused by the downstairs door before sending me to Grandpa for my morning shift. "You're going to call Bay, right?" He looked annoyed at himself for nagging, but I understood the worry.

"I am," I promised. "If I have to go over there after my shift, I will. I need help. I'm out of my league here."

"No, you're in the top league. You just don't understand the rules yet." He gave me a quick kiss and pushed open the door, stopping short when a white truck popped into view. "Who does that belong to?" He looked over my shoulder, into the restaurant. "Did your grandfather get a new truck?"

"That seems unlikely." I walked toward the front of the kitchen.

The apartment door led into the back, by the dishwasher rack, and thanks to the exhaust fans, I couldn't always hear what went on at the front of the kitchen from that location. When I turned the corner and the griddle came into view, I found Grandpa working like normal. He wasn't alone, though. A man stood with him, talking business.

I pulled up short, drawing Grandpa's attention when my shoes squeaked on the linoleum.

"You're late," he offered.

I scowled. "I am not. I came down right on time. I was just talking to Hunter." I gestured toward my boyfriend, as if his looming presence weren't obvious. My attention remained on the stranger, however.

He looked normal. Well, whatever "normal" was in the grand scheme of things. He had dark hair cut longer on top than on the bottom, and he wore khakis and a polo shirt with a name embroidered on it. Thanks to his coat, I couldn't make out the stitching.

"This is Kyle Morton," Grandpa volunteered, gesturing toward the man, who had one of those smiles that could eclipse the sun. Unfortunately, it looked forced. "He just took over as the distribution rep for Northridge Farms."

It took me a moment to place the name. Northridge Farms wasn't an actual farm in the area. It was a food distributor with a solid footprint in the Midwest. Things were starting to make sense.

"Hello." I smiled at Kyle, who looked out of his element.

It had to be his first day on the job, or at least his first meeting with my grandfather. He wasn't comfortable yet.

"Hello." Kyle's eyes flicked to Hunter dressed in his police jacket. "Is there a problem? I thought it was okay to park in the back alley. Your grandfather said no deliveries were due."

"It's fine." Grandpa waved off his concern. "He's not here on official business. His only business is doing filthy things with my granddaughter."

Kyle relaxed, if only marginally. "I see."

"We live upstairs," Hunter volunteered, shooting my grandfather a dark look. "Something I believe you were gung ho about just three days ago."

"I'm okay with this living arrangement because it means you'll have her out of here in six months," Grandpa countered. "You won't be interested in living upstairs over the long haul, so you'll be motivated to get out of there. And because you two are attached at the hip, you'll take her with you."

"If I didn't know I was your favorite, I would be hurt by your tone." I moved to one of the coolers. The racks affixed to the wall above it held stacks of aprons. I grabbed one and tied it around my waist. "Don't let my grandfather get to you," I said to Kyle. "His goal in life is to make people uncomfortable."

"I think it wise to stick with what you know." Grandpa's eyes flicked to Hunter. "Anything on Edmund?"

Hunter shook his head. "Not really. Except ... the murder weapon didn't turn out to be a knife at all. It was a very expensive letter opener.

No one in your neighborhood was bragging about buying a letter opener, were they?"

"No offense, kid, but that's not the sort of stuff we brag about in my neighborhood," Grandpa replied. "Got a new truck with four-wheel drive? That's something to crow about. A letter opener is just a letter opener."

"Yeah." Hunter rolled his neck. "It's not turning into the lead I hoped it would."

"Who is Edmund?" Kyle asked blankly.

"My neighbor," Grandpa replied. "He was stabbed the other day and left in the street. As you can imagine, that doesn't happen all that often in Shadow Hills. People are on edge. They want the killer caught."

"You don't think it's like a serial killer or anything, do you?" Kyle looked horrified.

"It's unlikely," Hunter replied in his "official" tone. "I believe it was a crime of passion. We still need to find who did it." He leaned in and pressed a kiss to my cheek. "Remember what I said earlier. Make that call. I'll text you later to let you know where I'm at on things. If I can make it in for lunch, I will."

"Okay." I waved him off, my heart pinging when he disappeared through the back door. When I turned back, I found Kyle watching me with curious eyes. "Sorry. We're a little schmaltzy."

"They're gross is what they are," Grandpa groused. "They were together as teenagers, and I thought that was the worst thing I would ever see. I was wrong. They're actually worse as adults."

"You love us, and you know it." I moved toward the coffee pot so I could start on the filters.

Kyle was in the way, and I accidentally brushed against him as I tried to maneuver around him.

"Sorry," I said as a weird chill ran through me. It wasn't exactly dread. It wasn't a happy emotion either though.

"Oh, it's fine." Kyle's demeanor didn't change as he moved. "I didn't realize I was in your way."

Did he not feel that chill? How is that possible? I ran my tongue over my lips as I grabbed several bags of coffee and the razor. "You're new to the route?" I asked, fighting overtime to keep my voice even.

"I am," Kyle confirmed.

"Myron Jefferson had the route before him," Grandpa volunteered. "You remember him. He's sick, though, and needs to retire."

"Oh, no. That's sad." It really was. I'd always found Myron funny. "What sort of sickness?" I expected to hear Myron had a heart condition or something.

Instead, Grandpa looked solemn. "He has gonorrhea."

I froze with the filters in my hands. "Um..."

Kyle, perhaps rightly reading the deer-in-the-headlights look on my face, chuckled. "It's not as bad as it sounds. Myron was having an affair with the office secretary, who also happened to be the boss's wife, and some gonorrhea got involved. The boss decided it was time for Myron to retire."

Well, that was better than I had pictured. "At least it's not cancer."

"Definitely." Kyle tapped his clipboard. "I've got your order for next week. Do you want to double-check it?"

"Do I need to?" Grandpa asked.

"I would feel better if you did." Kyle managed a smile. "I plan on being very good at my job. This is the first week, though, and I'm a little nervous. Your reputation isn't something I can ignore. I won't ask you to double-check it every week, but if you could this week... " He trailed off.

Grandpa took the clipboard with a raised eyebrow and scanned the list. "Looks good to me." He handed it back.

"Great." Kyle beamed. "I'll put this in today. It was great to meet you."

Grandpa had already lost interest in the conversation and faced the grill. "Tell me if you still feel that way in a month."

Kyle shifted his gaze to me. "It was nice to meet you too." He extended his hand.

I eyed it for a beat, debating, then took it. The same frigid wave overtook me when we made contact. I couldn't drop his hand fast enough. "It was nice to meet you too," I lied, a fake smile on my face.

Curiosity ignited in the depths of Kyle's eyes, but he didn't push me. "I'm sure I'll see you around."

"I'm sure you will too."

Thirteen

Once Kyle left, I decided to question Grandpa about him, trying to be sly. I couldn't pull that off with a man who knew me so well, though.

"So, what's his deal?" I asked.

Grandpa's forehead creased. "You're not looking to trade down, are you? Because that would be a mistake. Hunter is the one for you."

I glared at him. "I'm not looking to trade down. I'm just curious. I mean, the gonorrhea thing is horrible, but where did Kyle come from?"

Grandpa made a face. "How should I know? He just showed up. As for the gonorrhea, I'm not surprised. Myron was always a bit of a wild card."

"You have to be an idiot to sleep with the boss's wife."

"I agree. As for that Kyle guy, I don't know yet. Let's see if he manages to get the order right. I'll reserve judgment until then. Myron was a dirty dog, but he almost never screwed up my orders." In Grandpa's book, that was all that mattered.

I couldn't blame him. "I'll start the coffee, then open up the front. I expect a calm day today."

"Oh, you just jinxed us," Grandpa complained.

"How did I do that?"

"When you voice your wishes like that, everybody knows you get the opposite."

"I'm pretty sure that's an old wives' tale."

"And I'm pretty sure you'll regret saying that."

"Whatever." I set about my work. When I opened the front door five minutes later, the regulars were lined up. They greeted me with smiles and nods, but nobody seemed to be in a conversational mood. That was good for me.

The first hour was quiet. We didn't get hit with a rush, so I had no problem keeping up with both sides of the diner. By the time my cousin Annie arrived, I'd already waited on ten breakfast tables and three coffee tables. I wasn't close with Annie, but she wasn't irritating like her sister either. Thankfully, she had gossip, which kept us going another hour.

"I'm telling you, people say Phoebe is delusional or something," Annie insisted as we stood shoulder to shoulder waiting for Grandpa to get us plates shortly before nine. "She pretends she isn't reporting to the jail every weekend."

"I just saw her two days ago," I argued. "Well, actually I saw her yesterday too, but just two days ago, she acknowledged reporting to jail on the weekends."

"Well, apparently, she decided to change things up yesterday." Annie's eyes sparkled. "Nina Corbin said she asked Phoebe what jail was like, and Phoebe actually said, 'How would I know?' in response. I mean ... what's up with that? It's not like we can just forget she's reporting to jail."

That was weird. "Nina isn't usually wrong about her gossip."

"Definitely not," Annie agreed. "I think Phoebe might be losing her mind or something."

"Or she believes that if she denies it enough, people will believe her." I shook my head. "What a freak show."

"Right?"

I took the plates Grandpa handed me and swooped through the swinging doors. The breakfasts were for two of Grandma's friends, who had taken over one of the booths in the café section. In the time since I'd taken their orders, two more people had arrived, one of them my grandmother.

"This is a surprise." I retrieved my order pad after delivering the plates. "You don't usually come in for coffee and gossip so early in the week. I thought you preferred doing it at home."

"I come in once a week," Grandma countered. "On very special occasions, I come in twice a week. I like a change of location as much as the next person."

I knew better than that. She was up to something. That was her business though. If she wanted me to know, she would tell me. Since I had the opportunity to ask questions of my own, however, I used it. "So, what's the deal with Iris, Florence, Gwen, and Blanche?"

Grandma wrinkled her nose. "Do you really want me to answer that?"

"Yes. I was under the impression that they hate each other, yet they bowled together last night."

Grandma snorted. "Oh, that's just Harold Mulligan's idea of a joke. He runs the senior league. They're all part of the same league, but they started getting irritating about three years back because they refused to bowl together, which made it difficult for Harold to organize the lanes. He started purposely putting them together every time. He's mean when he wants to be. He said it stopped them from irritating other people, just each other."

Well, that was interesting and diabolical. "Is he trying to get them to quit?"

"Oh, everybody would prefer if they did. They won't, though. They're not eager to make others happy."

I could see that. "They were with Pete Winkle last night. Or rather, they came with Pete. Then he dropped them so he could flirt with Maggie Baldwin. They didn't seem happy about it."

"Maggie Baldwin?" Grandma sat straighter in her chair. "Isn't that girl a teenager?"

"She's eighteen," I confirmed.

"She's still too young for Pete. What was he thinking?"

I didn't tell her Pete's body had been commandeered. Not only did we have an audience, but it was too convoluted to explain. "He didn't get what he wanted anyway. Apparently, Maggie was just trying to make

Clark jealous. They ended up making out in her car together, and Pete took off."

"Well, that couldn't have made the harem happy," Grandma mused. "I got the feeling at the senior center yesterday that they'd decided to move the goalposts and compete over Pete now that Edmund is dead. If he threw them over, they're probably plotting his demise."

I hoped she was just being dramatic. "They wouldn't really plot his demise, would they? Like ... nobody has another letter opener sitting in a desk that they'll plunge into his heart, do they?"

"I have no idea." Grandma held out her hands. "Anything is possible with those harpies. I'm still trying to understand Pete's part in all of this, though. I can't figure out why he was hanging around the center yesterday. I don't think I've ever seen him there before."

I averted my eyes. "Maybe he was trying to drum up business."

Much like my grandfather, my grandmother could detect a lie like a fart in a car.

"Yeah, most insurance people don't try to sucker customers that close to death," Grandma noted. "They go for the younger ones because that's where they make money."

"Right." I rolled my neck, growing increasingly uncomfortable with my grandmother's stare.

"You know something." Grandma leaned close. "You can tell me what it is. I promise to keep it to myself."

"I don't know anything," I lied.

"You do so. Hunter is a good police officer, but he's weak where you're concerned. He tells you everything. Don't bother denying it."

"I wouldn't dare deny it, but Hunter doesn't have anything yet. He's frustrated. Well, he knows the murder weapon was a letter opener rather than a knife. I guess he has that."

"A letter opener?" Grandma wrinkled her nose. "Who walks around with a letter opener?"

"Who walks around with a knife?" I challenged.

"Fair point. A letter opener is weird, though."

"It is, and it was some fancy letter opener. He hoped to track it, but he's not having much luck, so keep your ear to the ground in case one of your frenemies starts talking about losing a letter opener."

"Oh, they're not my frenemies ... and that's a dumb word. Speaking of frenemies, though, here comes yours." Grandma inclined her head toward the front door.

Phoebe, Monica, and Celeste breezed through it, fashion scarves on full display.

My hackles immediately went up. "I'm not friends with any of them."

"I thought you were friendly with Monica," Grandma challenged. "You have to be nice to her, or people will call you a home-wrecker. That's what people say anyway."

Technically, she wasn't wrong. "Yes, well, being polite and building a friendship are two entirely different things. You have to have times of friendship to have frenemies, and none of those women fit the bill." Despite my words, I waved at the trio and pointed toward a booth in the corner. "That table is open."

Monica matched my bland smile. "Thanks."

They headed in that direction, leaving me to scowl behind their backs.

"You were saying?" Grandma challenged when I returned my attention to her.

"Yeah, yeah, yeah." I rolled my eyes. "What do you want for breakfast?"

"Two poached eggs and toast."

I froze. *Is she kidding me?* She knew darned well Grandpa wouldn't make her poached eggs. "I believe the poached eggs have been recalled."

"You tell your grandfather that those eggs are for me and to shut up," she said. "If he has a problem, he can take it up with me."

Yup, I wasn't looking forward to that conversation. "I'll just collect the other orders, then put yours in."

I smiled tightly as I grabbed coffee from the counter burners and took the pot to Monica's table. The last thing I needed was to spend time dealing with Phoebe, though I was curious enough about Annie's gossip to push the issue. "Hey, guys. How are things?"

"As well as can be expected," Monica replied. "How are things with you?"

"They're good." I managed a fake smile.

"I heard you and Hunter are buying a house," Celeste volunteered. "Isn't it a little soon for you guys to be living together?"

Her question shouldn't have surprised me, yet it did. "We're already living together."

I darted a quick look toward Monica to read her reaction. I didn't regret being with Hunter. We belonged together. But Monica had been hurt in our hurry to secure our forever, and I did feel bad about that.

"You moved into his house?" Celeste wrinkled her nose. "That's weird."

"Actually, he moved in upstairs with me." No point denying it. They would find out eventually. "He's putting his house on the market, and we hope to buy in the spring."

Phoebe's eyes narrowed as they landed on me. "What house?"

I shrugged. I refused to share that information. It might get out, but it also might not. If she found out the actual house we wanted—my dream house—she would do everything in her power to stop us from getting it.

"We're still figuring that out," I lied. "What do you guys want for breakfast?"

"Are poached eggs still recalled?" Monica asked.

Given my grandmother's order, that put me in a difficult position. "Um ... I'm not sure. How bad do you want them?"

"They're the healthiest egg."

"Yes, but if my grandfather decides to go on a murderous rampage, will they be worth it?"

"I'll have two eggs basted, hash browns, and whole wheat toast." Monica smiled. She didn't look upset. That was a good thing. At least I hoped it was a good thing.

"You?" I asked Celeste.

"I'll have two poached eggs and whole wheat toast," Celeste replied pointedly.

Fine. If she wanted to face my grandfather's wrath, that was on her. "And you?" I asked Phoebe.

"Well, I'm on a diet." Her forehead creased as she perused the menu. She'd been to the diner a hundred times. The menu had nothing new. She was just being difficult to be difficult. "I'll have the pancakes."

That didn't sound like diet food to me, but I saw no point in arguing. "Sure. I'm guessing you don't get a lot of good pancakes on the weekends." It was a test. Either she would fail, or I would.

"Whatever do you mean?" Phoebe was the picture of innocence and light as she met my even gaze.

"Huh." I didn't know what I expected. Maybe that she would play coy. She was basically outright denying it. What benefit she hoped to gain from the particular move was beyond me. I was amused despite myself. "I guess the rumors are true."

"And what rumors are those?" Phoebe demanded.

Though I knew it would irritate her, I opted to tell the truth. "People around town are debating whether you're deluded or playing a game when pretending you don't have to report to the county jail every weekend for the foreseeable future." I took her menu. "Most people think you're playing a game. I have to agree with them."

"Jail?" Phoebe puffed out her chest. "Why would I go to jail?"

"Yeah, don't bother with me. I'm not going to fall for that. I'll be back with more coffee in a bit."

When I returned to the kitchen, I found Annie fluttering on the other side of the swinging doors, waiting for gossip.

"So?" she prodded.

"So, she definitely denied reporting to the county jail." I handed the two tickets to my grandfather. "She's not fooling anybody, but that's the game she's playing."

"Interesting." Annie bobbed her head. "I wonder what her goal is. I bet it has something to do with Pete Winkle."

I almost tripped over my feet as I headed toward the counter to start a pot of coffee. "Why would it have something to do with him?" I hoped my voice didn't sound too strained.

"Because Nancy Sullivan says that his vehicle was parked outside Phoebe's house all night last night."

Well, that answered multiple questions. We'd wondered where Pete had taken off to. "Are they dating?"

"That's the rumor, though nobody knows when it started."

I knew exactly when it had started. Before I could respond, Grandpa banged his hand on the rack to get my attention.

"What?" I demanded, looking at him.

"You have two orders of poached eggs here." He glared darkly.

"I do," I confirmed.

"I told you poached eggs were off the menu."

"If that's your stance, then you need to go out there yourself and tell the customers you won't cook the eggs."

"No problem." Grandpa started out from behind the grill in a huff. "Who ordered them?"

"Celeste Holcomb."

"She can get the hell out and never come back." His hand aimed for the swinging doors.

"And your wife." I did my best to keep a straight face.

Grandpa did a huge loop and returned to the grill, immediately turning his back to me. "I guess I can do poached eggs today. They're off the menu starting tomorrow."

"Got it."

Annie and I shared amused smirks before I grabbed the coffee pot and started for the café.

"Just out of curiosity, has anybody else talked about Pete?" I asked my cousin.

"I've heard he's been busy," Annie replied. "Some people say he was hitting on old ladies at the senior center yesterday. Lonnie Blackstone said he was trying to slip his pickle to Maggie Baldwin at the bowling alley last night. Maybe he's having a midlife crisis."

"He's not even thirty yet."

"So, a quarter-life crisis?"

That was as good an explanation as any. I made the rounds with the coffee, stopping at Monica's table last for refills.

"Are you really dating Pete Winkle?" I blurted to Phoebe, unable to keep the question from escaping.

Surprise registered on her face. "Are people talking about us?" She looked pleased. "I think we'll make a great couple. He's stable, owns his own business, and will present well in front of the judge."

"Judge? Why are you going in front of a judge again? Oh, geez, you haven't blackmailed someone else, have you?"

If looks could kill, I would be dead. "No. It seems the previous decision might have been an error, however, and my attorney believes I'll do well on an appeal."

A blatant lie—but it was so like her to think she could get out of trouble by parading someone like Pete in front of the judge. That explained why she was hanging with him, though they'd already fizzled as a couple.

"I thought you weren't reporting to jail every weekend," I challenged. "Why would you have to appeal a verdict if you're not paying a price?"

Phoebe's smile disappeared in an instant. "Why don't you mind your own business?"

I wanted to leave her to her fate. She deserved it. Still, Edmund wearing Pete's body wasn't a worry I could dismiss. "You should be careful around Pete. He's ... not himself of late."

"Because he's dating me?"

"There's that. He's also been acting out of sorts in other ways. Did you know he was hitting on the women at the senior center yesterday afternoon?" If that didn't shame her into breaking up with him, nothing would.

"Oh, he was just being nice to those old women." Phoebe waved off my statement as if knocking away pesky gnats. "We're the real deal, and we're going to be happy. You should spread the news. That's the good gossip."

"Oh, don't worry. I have plenty of gossip to spread." I tried one more time to make her see reason. "This could backfire on you. What if the judge decides to throw you in jail on weekdays too?"

Phoebe scowled. "Nobody is going to jail! What did I say?"

She'd clearly lost it. I couldn't talk her out of the bad decision. "Well, do what you have to do. Don't whine to me when it blows up in your face though."

"I'll handle my life. You worry about yours."

"That sounds like a fabulous idea."

FOURTEEN

Finishing my shift was akin to torture, but once it was over, I raced upstairs. Bay had finally replied to my message, though her response was terse. *Help incoming.* That was it. She was usually more verbose. That told me she was busy with something herself.

Help did indeed come. I was on pins and needles by the time the knock finally landed on my door, but when I opened it, it was not what I expected.

"We're here to save the day." Tillie pushed past me into the apartment. "Where's the cat?"

She'd been obsessed with Krankle since she'd found out he could talk. The gnome shifter part didn't interest her anywhere near as much as the talking part. I'd politely declined her generous offers to take him off my hands—that had disaster written all over it—and had even refused her offer to throw in her pet pig, Peg, as compensation.

"He's been making himself scarce." I turned my attention to Tillie's sidekick.

Evan the day-walking vampire had become a regular fixture in my life. He'd frightened me at first, but the more I got to know him, the more I liked him. Seeing him dressed in a Vampires Suck shirt threw me, however.

"Don't ask," he snapped when I opened my mouth to query his sartorial choice. The jeans weren't new. The T-shirt, however, was something I'd never seen.

"I think he looks nice." Tillie beamed. "He's got attitude, though. Just ignore him."

"We had time to stop at my place so I could change clothes," Evan barked, his disdain obvious. "There was no need for me to wear this ... this ... monstrosity. This shirt is the equivalent of drinking box wine."

Tillie didn't look bothered in the least. "Some of that wine isn't too bad. It's nowhere near as good as my wine, but sometimes faster is better."

"I'll have to take your word for it," Evan said dryly. "She spilled coffee on me. On purpose. She just wanted to force me into this shirt."

"Oh, now you're making things up," Tillie complained. "I said you could go shirtless. You're the one who refused to go that route."

Obviously, they were having a tiff—not unusual for them. Ever since Evan's soul had been forcibly shoved back into his body and "healed" by his best friend, Scout Randall, his moods had been unpredictable. When he'd first taken up residence in his late uncle's home in Hemlock Cove, I'd worried he might off himself. He'd felt a tremendous amount of guilt following his soulless wandering. He'd bounced back, though, and Tillie was one of the reasons. She'd refused to let him pout, instead forcing him out on day adventures. They'd turned into quite the twosome.

"I was kind of hoping for Bay," I said when they finished lobbing insults at one another.

"Bay is busy with her stuff," Tillie replied. "She sends her apologies —and promises to come herself if we can't fix it—but she's otherwise engaged today."

Well, that was a bummer. I loved Tillie—no, really—but she was not my favorite cohort when the mission required stealth. "Okay, well, did she tell you what's going on?"

"No," Evan replied.

"Yes," Tillie said at the same time. "She said you have a ghost that needs busting."

"Um, that's kind of a lame explanation," I replied. "It's more that I have a dead guy whose soul decided to make a run for it, and instead of haunting people, he's trying to steal their bodies."

Evan's eyes, which had been boring holes into the side of Tillie's head, jerked toward me. "What now?"

I caught them up, leaving nothing out. When I got to the part about Maggie, making sure to mention her age, Evan looked annoyed.

"He sounds like a predator," he noted.

"He's acting like a predator," I acknowledged. "Apparently, according to my grandmother, he was sleeping with every woman of a certain age in the neighborhood."

"Do you think one of them killed him?"

"That would be my guess. None of them stand out as guilty, though. To be fair, it's entirely possible they're all sociopaths. The more time I spend with them, the more they freak me out."

"It sounds weird," Evan said to Tillie. "I didn't know ghosts could hop into occupied bodies."

"Technically, they can't." Tillie looked thoughtful. "I have heard of it happening before. It doesn't occur regularly, but there are stories."

"What do we do?" I asked.

"You said you managed to evict him twice before," Tillie noted. "You should be able to do it again, right?"

"In theory, unless he's somehow found a way to combat my magic."

"That seems unlikely. Do you know where he is now?"

"Well, Pete—he would be the host—owns an insurance agency."

"You think this Edmund guy decided to hijack a body so he could go to work?" Tillie looked amused.

"No, but won't he have to work eventually? It's not like Pete can get Social Security. Edmund has to fund his lifestyle somehow."

"True, but it's been, like, two days. I don't think he's worried yet."

"Right." I tapped my chin. "Well, our options are the senior center —where he's shown up twice—his house, Pete's house, or Phoebe's house."

"And Phoebe is the one you hate, right?" Tillie queried.

"Yes."

"Then we'll start there."

Surprise washed over me. "Why there?" I thought for sure she would want to go to the senior center. "He's infiltrated the euchre games twice."

"Yes, so he'll expect you to intercept him there," Tillie replied reasonably. "The houses are easy places to look. If he thinks he's flying under the radar—and he doesn't strike me as bright, so that would make sense—then he'll go to this Phoebe person's house. Besides, you told her to stay away from him. Just to spite you, she'll want to spend time with him."

Sadly, that made sense. "Okay, let's go to Phoebe's house."

"I'll take over when we get there," Tillie said.

I had no doubt her mystery plan would be a doozy. "Sure. What could possibly go wrong?"

PHOEBE'S HOUSE WAS LOCATED ON ONE of the prettier Shadow Hills streets. The woods spread out on the east and south sides, allowing coverage for her backyard. I knew from hanging out in the area as a kid that a five-minute hike through the woods would lead to a small pond. It had been a regular party spot during our high school years when we were avoiding our preferred location at the river.

"She's here." We kept close to the tree line on the east side so as not to be discovered. I could make out Phoebe's car in the driveway though. "That's Pete's truck too. It looks like they tried to hide it along the side of the house, but that's totally his truck."

"Okay." Tillie narrowed her eyes. "So, they're inside. What do you think they're doing?"

I didn't want to think about it too hard. "Let's just get him out of the house."

"We should try to entice him into the woods," Evan supplied. "That way we can wrestle him down, and it won't matter how loudly he screams. Nobody will come for him, and we can deal with him at our leisure."

That was an odd way to phrase it. "By 'deal with him,' you mean evict Edmund from Pete's body and let Pete go on his merry way, right?"

"Sure." Evan showed his fangs when he smiled. The light in his eyes hadn't been there when he'd been forced into his new reality. Things must have been looking up for him.

"I know how to do it," Tillie volunteered out of nowhere.

I waited for her to tell us her plan. When she didn't, I held out my palms in exasperation. "How?"

"I'll broadcast a message into his brain telling him there are naked chicks in the woods."

That was the dumbest thing I'd ever heard. "And you think he'll come barreling out of the house because a random message about naked women crosses his mind?"

Tillie pointed toward the sliding glass door at the back of the house. It opened, and Pete, indeed, headed toward the trees.

"This is unbelievable," I muttered.

Evan smirked as he drew us farther into the woods. "I'll grab him."

"Don't hurt him," I ordered.

"I've got it. I'll be fast. You guys try to keep up."

"Who do you think you're talking to?" Tillie demanded. "I always keep up."

"You can't bring your scooter in the woods."

"Someone should totally make a scooter for the woods," Tillie lamented. "I would be all over that."

"I think it's called an off-road vehicle," I offered helpfully as Evan used his super speed to buzz forward.

He took up position behind a large oak tree and waited for Pete to cross the line.

"Yeah, I have one of those. Winnie won't let me drive it, though. She says it's an accident waiting to happen." Tillie's lower lip came out to play. Her niece, Winnie, who also happened to be Bay's mother, was a real thorn in her side. "She's zero fun."

"I—" Whatever I was going to say—and it was nothing earth shattering—died on my lips when Pete screamed like an eight-year-old girl in the presence of a boy band member.

"Help! Help! Help!"

I broke into a run, and when I got to the back side of the tree, I found Evan pinning Pete to the ground. He'd covered the terrified man's mouth, who looked close to melting down.

"Get the ghost out of him," he ordered.

I wanted to laugh. The scene—Evan in his shirt on top of the wriggling Pete—was funny despite the circumstances.

"Show him your fangs," Tillie ordered. "That will shut him up."

"Why do you think he's screaming?" Evan snapped.

"Oh." Tillie gave me a blasé look. "I told you he was in a mood. You'd better evict the ghost."

I had no idea why she didn't do it herself, but I didn't care. I would finally be free of Pete. I had to follow through. Dropping to my knees, I pressed my hand to Pete's forehead and pulsed the familiar magic into him. It took no time for Edmund's soul to detach from the body, and he didn't look happy as he observed the scene.

"You are the absolute worst!" he barked when he saw me. "Why can't you just mind your own business?"

"You know why." I removed my hand from Pete's forehead and waited for him to blink back into consciousness.

It was only then that I realized I had no idea what to tell him when he awoke with a vampire sitting on him in the middle of the woods. Thankfully—*or is it unthankfully?*—Pete didn't stir.

"Is he asleep?" I asked.

"He's dead," Edmund replied. "You killed him. I hope you're happy."

Tillie jabbed a warning finger in the ghost's direction to silence him. "He's not dead. He's just sleeping."

"Why is he sleeping?" I was honestly worried. "Did Edmund do something to him?"

"Yeah, I made sure he had fun for the first time in his life," Edmund shot back. "I should obviously be flogged."

"Don't make me hurt you," Tillie warned.

"I'm already dead. How much could you possibly do?"

"You would be surprised." Tillie glared at him before turning her gaze to me. "His body probably just needs time to adjust. Don't freak out."

"Should we take him to the hospital?" I felt immensely guilty for not getting Edmund out of Pete sooner.

"And say what?" Evan challenged. "Are we supposed to tell a doctor that he's been possessed for two days? How exactly do you think that would play out?"

He had a point, loath as I was to admit it. "Well, we can't just leave him here. We have to at least take him home."

"How?" Evan's voice was even, but it held an edge. "He can't walk. You can't carry him."

"You can," Tillie argued.

Evan made a face. "Well, great. I'll carry him to his truck, shove him inside, and drive it to his house. What happens if someone catches me?"

I could see why he was wary. Tillie, on the other hand, would have none of it.

"Oh, suck it up," she complained. "Stormy is groping for the trout in the river of this town's top cop on a nightly basis. You don't have to worry about that."

"Whatever." Evan got to his feet and leaned over to collect Pete. "This is the last time I go on an adventure with you."

"You say that every day." Tillie gave an impish smile. "You always come back for more because you love me."

Evan grumbled something I couldn't quite make out.

"Seriously?" Edmund screeched at our backs as we started walking toward the road. Getting Pete's truck wouldn't be easy. "You stole my body, and now you're just leaving me here? You're the absolute worst!"

"Go someplace else," I shot back. "Cross to the other side. Do something other than what you're doing."

"No. I'm not giving up. I'll just find a new body. You know it. I know it. All you've done is force me to search yet again. Speaking of, where is your boyfriend?"

I whirled quickly, venting a burst of fire before I realized it was happening. It blew into him, but as a ghost, he suffered no damage.

"Temper, temper," Tillie warned in a low voice. "There's that hellcat I knew was hiding in there."

Hellcat. It was a term she'd used to describe me more than once. I didn't have a full understanding of what she meant, but it wasn't the time for that conversation.

"You listen here." I stalked back in Edmund's direction and wasn't sorry when he cowered in front of me. "You will stay out of bodies that don't belong to you. Do you understand? This isn't a game. You lived your life. Somewhere along the way, your decisions cost you your life. You don't get to steal somebody else's as a do-over."

"You're not the boss of me," Edmund groused petulantly.

"Actually, I am. You need to go to the other side. I don't care how you do it. Just go."

"I don't know how."

"Figure it out."

I wheeled back around and found Tillie watching me with amusement.

"What?" I demanded.

"You're fiery," she replied. "Actually, fiery in more than one way. It's nice."

"I didn't mean to do that blow-my-stack thing," I admitted as we emerged from the woods near the sidewalk. "It just sort of happened."

"It was cool," Tillie replied. "In fact, it was very cool. I wouldn't mind seeing another demonstration."

"That makes two of us," a man said from somewhere on our right.

When I jerked my head in his direction, I found a familiar figure leaning against a white truck, his arms crossed over his chest.

"Kyle," I breathed.

"Who is that?" Tillie demanded.

"You mean *what* is that," Evan countered in a low voice.

I jerked my eyes to the vampire. "What are you saying?"

Evan grappled with Pete's dead weight, readjusting him, then grimaced. "I don't know what he is, but he's not human."

Is that news? It didn't feel like it. I'd touched Kyle exactly twice in the restaurant, and both times, a sickening cold feeling had permeated my being. I'd recognized then that something was off about him. I'd tried to push the feeling aside, but it hadn't worked.

"What are you doing here?" I moved in front of Evan.

"Get behind me," the vampire ordered when he realized what I was doing.

I ignored him. No matter how we tried to explain away what we were doing, from Kyle's perspective, we were walking out of the woods with a body in our arms. *Could he see the ghost?* I had no idea. Edmund hadn't followed us out of the trees though. He was still in there, likely sulking.

"This seems like a strange place to drum up business for bulk food orders," I noted.

Kyle's lips twitched. "I was just taking a break and happened to see you and your friends heading into the woods. It was such an odd thing to bear witness to, I thought I should stick around a bit longer. I guess that worked to my advantage."

What did he mean by that? "Our friend passed out in the woods," I lied. "We're just making sure he gets home. Apparently, our hike was too taxing."

"Your friend didn't go into the woods with you," Kyle countered. "He joined you after. He was conscious, and now he's unconscious."

"He fell and hit his head. He'll be fine."

"Uh-huh." Kyle's smirk widened. "I guess I should've known when you reacted to me this morning that it would be an eventful day. Now I know more than I did. I'll take that as a win."

I had no idea what he meant. "What are you doing out here?"

"Don't worry about it." Kyle turned on his heel and opened the truck door. "I'll see you around, Stormy Morgan."

I opened my mouth, debating if I should call out to him. Ultimately, I had no idea what to say. Like an idiot, I stood rooted to my spot and watched Kyle drive away.

"Well, that's not normal," Tillie said when he was gone.

"What was your first clue?" Evan snapped. "You've got a lot of weird stuff going on in this town, Stormy. You need to get a handle on it."

That was a great suggestion, in theory. In reality, however, I had no idea what to do. "Let's get Pete home. After that, we'll figure it out."

"Oh, sure," Evan complained loudly. "We'll figure it out."

"You know, you're turning into a real kvetch," Tillie said as he stomped toward Pete's truck. "It's not attractive."

"Stop talking to me," Evan growled. "The whole day went to crap when you forced me to wear this shirt. This is all on you."

"Kvetch, kvetch, kvetch."

"You're on my last nerve."

Tillie was blasé. "You'll survive."

FIFTEEN

Tillie and I waited in my car while Evan parked Pete's truck in his driveway and carried the unconscious man into his house. Tillie had her phone out and took a snapshot of him in the offensive shirt as he exited. She looked beyond amused.

"He's going to stop hanging out with you if you keep doing this stuff to him," I warned, drumming my fingers on the steering wheel. Kyle's appearance—and reaction—had thrown me. I couldn't figure out his game.

"No, he won't." Tillie was all smiles when Evan climbed into the car's backseat. "Right?" she prodded him.

"Whatever you think, I believe the opposite," Evan groused. Despite his grumpy demeanor, the energy about him hadn't been there when I met him. He was surly—don't get me wrong—but he was clearly enamored with Tillie. Not in a romantic way or anything. In a family way, however, she was his jam.

"Does she remind you of Scout?" I asked out of nowhere. I was trying to understand their relationship. It wasn't always easy.

Evan slid his eyes to me. He didn't ask who I was referring to. Obviously, it was Tillie. "Maybe." He managed a smile. "I do think Scout will be a lot like Tillie when she reaches a certain age. I can't wait."

"Will you age?" I'd never asked before. It felt rude to blurt it out, but I couldn't stop myself.

He shrugged. "Maybe. I don't know. I'm not technically alive. I guess we'll see."

It would be hard for him, I realized. He might be having fun currently—he was basically a superhero because he had all the strengths of a vampire and none of the weaknesses—but that didn't mean he would always enjoy his reality. When he started losing people, when he lost Scout, his reality would be different.

"Well, it's kind of fun to watch you guys hang out." I reversed out of Pete's driveway and pointed us toward the restaurant. It was later in the afternoon, and Hunter would be off work in two hours. "Thanks for the assist."

"No problem," Evan replied. "It was kind of fun, though we didn't do anything to stop the ghost. You might need Bay over here no matter what."

I'd already considered that. "Yeah. I'll figure it out."

Tillie turned to study me when we stopped at the light. "What will you do about the weird monster in the white truck?"

Her phrasing threw me. "You think he's a monster?"

"He's clearly not normal."

"Definitely not," Evan agreed. "I couldn't get a firm read on him, which means he's different from anything I've crossed paths with."

"He's not human." Why that bothered me so much, I couldn't say. "I think I sensed something different about him this morning. When I accidentally ran into him, I felt this ... chill. That's the only word I can think to describe it. Then, when he shook my hand before leaving, I felt another chill."

"You couldn't get a read on him?" Evan queried.

"No, but that doesn't necessarily mean anything. I'm new to this."

"We can do some research," Tillie offered. "We don't have much to go on, though. Have you considered asking the cat?"

"The cat has been nothing but a pain for the past few weeks. We rarely see him." I recalled Krankle talking to the shadow as I pulled into the parking lot. "He was talking to somebody outside the storage shed the other night." I pointed toward the back corner of the structure in question as I parked.

"Did you ask him about it?"

"He denied talking to anybody." I shrugged as I killed the car's engine. "I mean, it could've been somebody wandering through the alley on their way back from the store."

"But in our lives, that seems unlikely," Evan surmised. "Let's check it out just in case."

I led him to the spot where the shadow had disappeared.

He lifted his nose, scenting the air—Scout had explained his heightened sense of smell was strong but not the same level as a shifter's—and after a few seconds, he shook his head. "I can't detect anything. I might've if I'd been here sooner, but nothing's left."

"I don't know what to do," I admitted. "Things feel off, and it's not just Edmund jumping into random bodies so he can romance half the town."

"He sounds like a pip," Tillie noted. "Too bad I didn't meet him before he died. He might've been a fun date."

"Except he was dating half the town. My grandfather said word on the street is that he was 'hung like an elephant.' That's a direct quote. For some reason, my grandfather found the rumor debatable."

"That's a man thing," Tillie replied. "Men feed their egos through their penises. It's so weird. Can you imagine if we spent all our time comparing the size of our vaginas? It's so stupid. Still, hearing he was well endowed makes me wonder if I really did miss out."

I shot her a curious look. "I thought you were dating Whistler."

Rumor had it that Tillie had been spending her nights with a certain bar owner in Hawthorne Hollow. Whistler was part of Scout's crew. He rode a motorcycle and dispensed worldly advice. His rumored interaction with Tillie had everybody gossiping.

"I'm not controlled by any single man," Tillie replied. "Besides, that's new. I wouldn't have minded a spin on the anaconda before taking a ride on Whistler's hog. And, yes, I mean both of them. I tend to like a good ride."

I needed to burn that picture out of my mind. I opted to change the subject. "What should we do about Edmund?"

Tillie shrugged. "See what he does, I guess. If he jumps into another body, I don't see how we're going to fix this without Bay. I'll talk to her. She's been busy with her own stuff."

"Which is?" I was mildly worried.

Bay wasn't the quiet type, yet I hadn't seen her in weeks.

"Honestly, I think she's up to something for Christmas," Tillie replied. "She's got her eye on something special for Landon. He's still upset about how stuff played out with that junior agent who died. I think he's a little shaken. She's been babying him."

Evan made a face. "Is she babying him or being a good wife?"

"It's the same thing in my book," Tillie replied. "Anyway, I'll talk to her. I can try digging up something on that Kyle guy too. If we can't figure out what he is, we might need to set a trap and force him to tell us."

"He had no reason to be over there," I pointed out. "He's a food distribution rep. That's a residential area."

"He followed us," Evan said, "without a doubt. The question is, why?"

We talked for another twenty minutes but found no answers. Once they left, I gathered a few ingredients from the restaurant pantry—a no-no when my grandfather was present, but since my Uncle Brad was in charge, it was fine—then started for the stairs. Brad caught me before I could disappear with my haul.

"Did you know that the Disney corporation created *Frozen* as a distraction?" He leaned against the doorjamb, arms crossed.

"The movie?" I was confused—a normal experience when spending time with my uncle.

"Yes. Walt Disney froze himself with the aim of coming back stronger and better, and the Disney corporation was sick of people asking about it, so they created the movie *Frozen* to hack the Google search."

Oh, geez. Even if that were true, why would someone care? "Well, you learn something new every day." I was desperate to get away from him.

"Also, the Nazis had a secret base in Antarctica, and it's recently been refurbished and put back into operation," he offered. "It houses advanced technology."

"Like UFOs?"

He nodded. "The aliens are in the Arctic."

"Well, awesome." *Really, what am I supposed to say to that?* "Anything else?"

"Just that we're all living in the matrix."

"Does that mean Keanu Reeves is coming to save the day? Because —and I have to be honest here—I think Keanu might be the only man who could give Hunter a run for his money for my heart."

Brad rolled his eyes. "Keanu isn't real."

"Okay, well, it's been nice talking to you." I practically ran up the stairs. Desperate to make sure he didn't follow me, I locked the door, then headed into the kitchen to make dinner.

I was a decent cook. One couldn't grow up in my family and be anything other than solid in the kitchen. It was illegal. Because I had things to discuss with Hunter—things he wouldn't like—I decided to go all out for dinner. That included stealing two steaks from the kitchen and making mashed potatoes from scratch.

By the time Hunter joined me shortly after six, the entire apartment smelled like a comfort food utopia.

"Oh, if I didn't already love you, this would seal the deal." Hunter kicked off his shoes and scurried into the kitchen. He immediately moved behind me, hugging himself to my back as I whisked gravy. "Have I mentioned you're my favorite person in the world?"

I went warm all over. "Not today."

"Well, it's true every day." He rubbed his cheek against mine. "What's the special occasion?"

"I can cook, and it doesn't need to be a special occasion," I said defensively.

"Oh, well, that's convincing." He pulled back and eyed me with trepidation. "What happened?"

I made a protesting sound with my tongue. "Why do you think something happened?"

"Because I know you."

He did. He knew me better than anybody. That bond we'd forged as teenagers, though it had been subjected to a hiatus, grew stronger with each passing day.

"Some stuff happened," I admitted. "Get us something to drink. I want to get it all out in one shot."

"Okay."

Hunter grabbed a bottle of wine from the counter—we weren't fancy, so it wasn't an expensive bottle—and filled the glasses on the table. He also poured glasses of water and carried the mashed potatoes, asparagus, and gravy over as I grabbed the steaks.

"Tell me," he prodded the second we sat down.

"So, Bay was busy today, but she did send Tillie and Evan as reinforcements."

Hunter made a face. "I guess I should be grateful Evan was part of the deal."

"He was very helpful," I agreed.

"Go on."

"For starters, we tracked down Pete at Phoebe's house. She mentioned over breakfast this morning that she was dating him. She also mentioned that his reputation would likely help her with the judge when her lawyer appealed her sentence, but that's a whole other thing."

"Yeah, don't worry about that," Hunter agreed. "It won't happen. She's deluding herself."

"We went into the woods by Phoebe's house, and Tillie used her magic to lure Pete outside. I thought she was nuts because she broadcast into his head that there were naked women in the woods, but he came running like an idiot."

Hunter's lips quirked. "Well, we have to remember that you weren't really dealing with Pete. It was Edmund."

"It was still ridiculous. Anyway, Evan wrestled him down once he was hidden in the trees. I used my magic to evict him. Pete did not regain consciousness, but we're hoping that's a temporary thing. Edmund whined like a baby and promised retribution. We kind of ignored him, though. Without Bay, I don't know what to do with a ghost. I bet he'll just find someone else to take over."

"Well, at least you got him out of Pete," Hunter said reasonably. "That's the most important thing."

"Yeah. Well, let's see if you still believe that in sixty seconds." I took a breath to center myself. "Evan had to carry Pete. When we left the woods, we found a truck parked on the side of the road, and the driver of that truck saw us."

Hunter only revealed he was worked up by gripping his steak knife so tightly his knuckles turned white.

"It was Kyle Morton," I volunteered.

Hunter's forehead creased. "I don't know who that is."

"You met him this morning." I caught him up on the rest of it, watching his face closely. When I was finished, he was flabbergasted.

"So, let me get this straight," he started. "Your grandfather's new Northridge Farms rep is some sort of monster, and he's stalking you. Do I have that right?"

"That seems a bit simplistic, but you're not altogether wrong."

Hunter viciously swore under his breath. Then he shot me an apologetic look. "Sorry. I just ... don't even know what to say to that."

"Join the club." I was rueful. "He just stood there like it was the most normal thing in the world. It was almost as if he was taunting me, and I froze like an idiot. I can't help thinking I should've done something, but even now, I don't know what that something would be."

Hunter reached over and rested his hand on top of mine. "It's better not to react than to react poorly. I don't blame you for being surprised. What did Evan and Tillie say?"

"Evan says Kyle's not human but doesn't know what he is."

"Well, great." Hunter pressed the heel of his hand to his forehead. "That is just ... great."

I sank into my chair a bit. "Sorry."

"No, don't." Hunter vehemently shook his head. "Don't be sorry. You didn't cause any of this. It sounds to me as if you handled things better than almost anybody else would've."

I wasn't certain that was true, but it was still nice to hear. "Thanks, but I don't know what to do going forward."

He silently shoveled food into his mouth, seeming to contemplate our predicament. When he did speak, he seemed to be processing vocally. "Let me ask you this. Do you think Kyle had something to do with Edmund's death?"

I had considered it, but no matter how I ran it through my head, the numbers didn't compute. "Kyle isn't human. That's what Evan said. Why would he hunt Edmund?"

"I don't know. Maybe it wasn't about Edmund at all. Maybe it was about you. We were in the garage when it happened. Is it possible that Kyle wanted to draw you out and gauge your reaction? He could've been watching us."

I hadn't considered that, but it was interesting to mull over. Ultimately, I shook my head. "That doesn't feel right."

"Fair enough."

"I could be wrong though."

"I think we're better off following your instincts," Hunter replied. "They haven't led us astray so far. That means we have to look at what's happening with Edmund separately from what's happening with Kyle."

"They're happening at the same time, though."

"They are, but you're right. I can't fathom why Kyle would care about Edmund. He followed you to Phoebe's house. He wasn't there because of Edmund. You said yourself that he showed no interest in Pete."

"He didn't even seem to care about Evan and Tillie," I acknowledged. "He was only interested in me."

"So, that means he has a different agenda." Hunter planted his feet outside of mine under the table. "Well, we have help if we need it. On both fronts. The Winchesters will swoop in and offer their expertise the second we make the request."

"We don't even know what we might need them for, though," I lamented.

"No, but we'll figure it out." He shot me a small, heartfelt smile. "I don't want you getting worked up about this. Don't panic. That's when you make mistakes. We'll just take it step by step."

"What's the first step?" I was honestly curious.

"We'll eat dinner. We'll snuggle on the couch. We'll go to bed."

"How does that help?"

"I have no idea, but we both need clear minds to attack a new day tomorrow."

Because I didn't disagree, I nodded. "Okay. That sounds like a plan."

"Good."

LATER, AS I DRIED THE DISHES HUNTER washed, I meandered to the sliding glass doors. We'd dimmed the lights, so it wasn't hard to see outside. That was a deliberate choice by Hunter, and I didn't question it. If Kyle showed up, or if his truck suddenly appeared in the parking lot, we both wanted to know about it.

Kyle didn't appear, though. Krankle did. He stood in the same spot where I'd seen him several nights before, and he wasn't alone. The same shadowy figure hung at the back corner of the storage building. No matter what the cat said, no matter how he denied it, I was convinced he and the shadow were talking.

I opened my mouth to tell Hunter but ultimately didn't speak. We had enough on our plates. If the cat was plotting with someone, it would have to wait until we'd dealt with Edmund and Kyle.

"What do you want to watch?" Hunter asked as he washed the last glass.

I forced my attention away from the sliding glass doors. "Something fun. How about a romcom?"

"Like *Sweet Home Alabama*? Where she comes back to her small hometown for the love of her life?"

I grinned. "I think that sounds like a fabulous idea."

"I hoped you might like that." He nipped in for a kiss. "Some women have to leave to realize that everything they ever wanted is waiting for them in the exact place they left it."

"Some women do need that," I agreed. "I'm glad I figured it out."

"You and me both."

Sixteen

I was awake before Hunter the next morning and watched him slowly stir. He seemed groggy, so I went with my natural instincts.

"What color underwear did I wear under my dress at senior prom?"

"Good morning to you too," he muttered, rubbing the sleep from his eyes.

I waited.

He sighed when it became obvious I wouldn't let it go. "They were white. You complained the whole time because you didn't like them. You thought they were boring. You had no bra to pair them with because your dress was backless. I remember absolutely loving that detail."

I exhaled heavily. "Okay." I leaned close and rested my head on his chest. "Just checking."

He lightly rubbed his fingers up and down my back. "Do you really think he'll come for me again?"

"I think it's possible."

"Yes, but you'll catch on quickly, and he'll be knocked out just as fast."

"I don't want to risk it."

He rested his cheek against my forehead. "I wish you weren't wrapped quite so tight right now. It makes relaxing with you hard."

I had news for him. I wouldn't calm down until Edmund crossed over, we found his killer, and the Kyle situation was figured out. Actually, after thinking about it, I wasn't the relaxing type. It would never happen.

"What time is it?" Hunter asked after a long silence.

"We have to get up in five minutes."

He took my hand resting on his chest and brought it to his cheek. "I won't let him take me over, Stormy," he said in a low voice. "I promise."

"I don't think Pete had a choice in the matter," I replied. "You didn't even wake up when he tried to do it the first time."

"I know, but ... I just won't let it happen. Take a breath."

That was easier said than done. "I'll take a breath when I'm certain Edmund is no longer a problem."

"Fine." He hugged me tight and exhaled heavily. "Come on. Let's hit the shower. We'll have breakfast downstairs this morning."

The statement caught me off guard. Not that he refused to have breakfast in the kitchen when we were preparing for the day, but it was rare. "Why?"

"Because I want to talk to your grandfather about his new North-ridge Farms rep."

Oh, well, that made sense. I should've seen it coming. "What do you think he'll tell you?"

"Not much, but I can't just let it go. At the very least, that guy was following you. I won't tolerate that. When you add to the mix that Evan says he's not human, I think it makes a bad combination."

He wasn't wrong. "Okay, but no funny business in the shower. If we're eating down there, we have to be fast."

"Man, and I'd planned to dress like a clown and juggle for you in there."

"Clowns are never funny."

"That's a good point."

. . .

GRANDPA HAD TURNED ON THE GRIDDLE by the time we made our way downstairs. He hadn't done much else. Since I was thirty minutes early for my shift, he was understandably surprised by our sudden appearance.

"Oh, this doesn't look good," he lamented. "Whatever it is, I didn't do it." He focused on Hunter. "In fact, whatever Florence said, I definitely didn't do it." That meant he'd done something to Florence, and within the last twelve hours or so.

"Do we even want to know?" I asked.

"Don't you already know?"

I shook my head.

Grandpa straightened. "Oh, well, never mind, then. How's it going, Hunter? Do you like living upstairs?"

Hunter's lips twitched. Even when my grandfather tried for annoying—which was often—he was inevitably amusing at the same time.

"I happen to like it a great deal." Hunter followed me to the coffee machine. "I think it might be the company, though." He playfully bumped hips with me.

"Oh, good, now I get to watch you guys flirt first thing in the morning," Grandpa drawled. "That's always my favorite thing to do."

I pinned him with a dirty look. "We're not flirting."

"Speak for yourself." Hunter gave me a friendly pat on the rear end, coupled with a challenging look toward my grandfather, then took the razor from me so he could tackle the coffee. "I'll handle this. You do whatever else needs to be done."

I left him to it. He'd first helped with the coffee filters when I worked there as a teenager, so he was familiar with the job. That allowed me to get the eggs and potatoes from the cooler. The evening shift was responsible for boiling and peeling the potatoes every night, but we grated them ourselves.

"This seems like a strategic move." Grandpa motioned between us. "It's as if you're outnumbering me for a specific reason. What's going on?"

"What makes you think anything is going on?" I demanded. "Maybe we just want to spend quality time with you."

"That's not it." He focused on Hunter. "Spill."

Hunter didn't miss a beat. "I want information on your new Northridge Farms distributor. What do you know about him?"

"Kevin?" Grandpa made a face.

"Kyle," I corrected. "Geez. You don't even remember his name?"

"I just met him yesterday."

Well, that brought up an interesting question. "When did you find out the Gonorrhea King was leaving his position?"

Startled as he opened a bag of coffee grounds, Hunter had to catch the silver packet before it exploded in the air. "Who is the Gonorrhea King?"

I laughed at his reaction as I started grating the potatoes. "That would be Myron Jefferson. He had Kyle's job first. Apparently, he was having sex with the boss's wife and was forced to take early retirement."

"Is that true?" Hunter addressed Grandpa. "Do you have confirmation of that?"

Quizzical disbelief flushed Grandpa's features. "How should I know? Kevin is the one who told me the story."

"Kyle," I corrected again. "His name is Kyle."

"Yeah, yeah, yeah." Grandpa waved his hand. "If my order arrives correctly, then I'll call him Kyle. Otherwise, he's Kevin."

"Have you called Northridge Farms to confirm they actually employed him?" Hunter asked.

Grandpa's face was blank. "Why would I do that?"

"Because I want to know if the Gonorrhea King really retired."

Grandpa hesitated, then switched his gaze to me. "What's going on? No pussyfooting around this time. I want to know what has him worked up."

I held back a sigh, just barely. "We have reason to believe that Kyle might not *just* be a food distributor."

Grandpa waited. When I didn't continue, he motioned with his hands to get me to talk. "I need more than that, kid."

"He..." I looked to Hunter for help.

Grandpa wasn't in on all the magical gossip. That was his choice. *Would he really want to know everything going on?* I had my doubts.

"Kyle followed Stormy yesterday," Hunter volunteered. "You don't want to know what Stormy was doing. It will make your head implode. He saw her doing some funky stuff, though, and wasn't surprised."

Grandpa took a moment to chew on that, turning his back to Hunter so he could drop oil on the grill. "Did he try to hurt you?"

"No." I moved closer to him and smiled in an effort to soothe his obviously fraying nerves. "He didn't even get near me. I wasn't alone anyway. I'm more concerned about the next time. I don't think he's done with me by any stretch of the imagination."

"Could he have known about the woo-woo stuff when he came here yesterday morning?"

"I wouldn't have thought so at the time, but now I'm not sure," I admitted. "It feels pointed."

"Well then, we'll deal with it." Calmly, Grandpa turned back to Hunter. "Once I'm through the morning rush, I'll make some calls. I know the big manager out at Northridge Farms. If something happened to Myron, he'll tell me. If Kyle doesn't really work for Northridge, he'll tell me. Kyle had the sheets though. How would he get them if he doesn't work for the company?"

I could only think of one way. "Let's make sure the Gonorrhea King is still alive, huh?" I suggested. "If he's dead, or missing... " I trailed off.

"Then we're dealing with a real problem," Hunter finished. "I think that's a good place to start."

"No one will be at the office until nine o'clock," Grandpa said. "We'll finish the breakfast rush by ten. Then I'll call and see what I can find out."

"Thanks." Hunter flashed a relieved smile. "If he shows up today, I would appreciate it if you didn't leave him alone with Stormy."

I balked. "Wait a second—"

"No." Hunter vehemently shook his head. "I know you're a badass, but I don't want you talking to him alone. I feel that might end poorly."

"I'll watch for him," Grandpa promised. "He would have to be an idiot to come back, though, given what happened yesterday, right?"

"Unless he's not worried," I replied. "He didn't seem worried when he was laughing at us."

"Well, we'll just see about that." Grandpa was firm. "Regardless, I can request a different rep. Even if Myron legitimately did retire, I don't have to deal with Kevin."

"Kyle," I growled.

"I'll call him Teeny Weenie if he's not careful," Grandpa warned. "Let's just see what they say when I call the main office. We should have answers then."

"I knew I could count on you." Hunter winked at him while steadfastly ignoring my glare. "I—"

Whatever he was about to say died on his lips when someone pounded on the back door. It wasn't some dainty knock but a heavy, insistent banging.

"You stay right there." Grandpa swaggered around the grill tower. "If that's him, I'll handle this."

"Not alone you won't." Hunter abandoned the coffee and scurried after him to offer backup.

I refused to be left behind, so I followed.

When Grandpa opened the door, however, it wasn't Kyle coming to kill us. It was a wild-eyed Phoebe, and she didn't look happy.

"Get out of my way," she barked to Grandpa.

For his part, my grandfather looked more annoyed than worried. "Oh, geez. I would rather have the rats in the dumpster form a union and go on the attack than deal with you. What is that smell, by the way?" He leaned forward and sniffed her. "Is that desperation? It smells like desperation to me."

Hunter smirked, but the expression fled quickly when Phoebe's gaze fell on me.

"*You,*" she growled.

"I guess we know who she's here to see," I said.

"What do you want?" Hunter positioned himself to shield me with his body.

The worst she could do was pull my hair, but I appreciated the unnecessary effort.

"I want to talk to your girlfriend."

"She's busy."

"Will you just move?" Phoebe gave Hunter a terrific shove, but he was big enough that he barely shifted. "Call off your dogs," she growled at me.

I could've refused and waited to see how things played out, but that seemed like a waste of time. The quicker we heard her out, the more apt she would be to leave. "Let her through."

"No," Hunter shot back. "You don't have to listen to whatever crap she's spewing today. That's not fair to you."

Fair or not, I knew Phoebe. She wouldn't go until she'd shared her feelings with the class. "It's fine, Hunter. She can't do anything to me."

"Nothing I can do?" Phoebe bordered on apoplectic. "Nothing I can do? How about if I kick your ass into next week?"

I had to bite back a laugh. Even ignoring my magic, Phoebe couldn't take me in a fight. I'd grown up with a buttload of cousins. Most of us were close to the same age. We used to beat each other up for sport. I wasn't afraid of Phoebe.

"If you touch her, I'll arrest you," Hunter warned in a low voice. "I'm pretty sure the judge in your extortion case won't look kindly on you getting violent when you're supposed to be serving time on weekends."

"That was a mistake," Phoebe snapped.

"The only mistake was not sending you to a real jail," Hunter fired back.

"Just tell me what you want, Phoebe," I commanded. "Some of us have jobs to do."

"Oh, like you don't know what I want." Phoebe's nose wrinkled in disgust. "You took him from me."

"Who?" I asked blankly.

"Pete. Don't bother denying it. The neighbors saw you parked on my street yesterday. They even claim you had some guy with you who was carrying Pete ... though I'm not sure how that works unless you've decided to dedicate yourself to human trafficking."

I swallowed hard. "I see."

"What did you do with him?" Phoebe didn't stop until she was directly in front of me.

I refused to back away from her, despite my discomfort with her proximity.

"I know you did something because he refused to accept my calls all night."

Something horrible occurred to me. "Maybe he was ... sleeping." I darted a worried look toward Hunter, who kept his face implacable.

"He wasn't asleep," Phoebe sneered. "He ignored my calls. He finally answered this morning and had the audacity to ask why I was stalking him. Me? Like I would ever stalk him."

I released a pent-up breath. "He answered the phone? That's good. Like ... that's really, really good."

"In what world, you bimbo?" Phoebe shrieked. "We were together yesterday afternoon. Then I went to the bathroom, and apparently, he decided to go for a walk in the woods. I didn't have a clue what had happened until Mrs. Wakefield across the street said she saw you hanging out with three other people. One of them was carrying what looked like a body. He's the one who took off in Pete's truck."

Uh-oh. Apparently, Mrs. Wakefield had seen more than I'd realized. That was the downside of having busybody neighbors. "I think Mrs. Wakefield should probably have her cataracts checked," I said blandly.

Phoebe turned haughty. "That shows what you know. She had cataract surgery two years ago."

"What's your point, Phoebe?" Hunter barked.

"My point is that yesterday, Pete couldn't get enough of me, and now he wants nothing to do with me. Your girlfriend is the reason."

"How do you figure that?" Hunter asked calmly.

"Because he only changed his mind after she—I don't know—did something to him in the woods. If you really want to know the truth, I think she lured him out there, seduced him, and promised him free food or something if he dumped me."

"Yes, that sounds exactly like something I would do," I drawled.

Hunter placed a steadying hand on my shoulder. "That's not what happened."

"Wait, you know she was in the woods with Pete yesterday?" Phoebe demanded. "How are you not angry? She cheated on you."

"Yeah, she was in the woods cheating on me with those other people you mentioned as witnesses." Hunter rolled his eyes. "That makes sense."

"If she wasn't out there to seduce Pete, then what was she doing?" Phoebe demanded.

"She was hiking with some friends." Ever calm, Hunter unleashed the lie without batting an eyelash. "They ran into Pete. He seemed panicked and desperate to get away from you. He was also confused— we're not sure what that's about, but I'll make sure Pete sees a doctor— and they helped him out of the woods and to his truck. The other guy drove Pete's truck because Pete was woozy."

"And why was Pete carried?" Phoebe snapped.

"Not carried," I volunteered smoothly. "My friend let Pete lean on him, but he couldn't carry him. Pete is too big. Mrs. Wakefield must've been confused."

Phoebe crossed her arms over her chest. "Do you really expect me to believe that? Pete was twenty minutes from the promised land when he took off. Why would he leave?"

"I have no idea. You'll have to take it up with him."

"I'm taking it up with you. You're the reason he left." She turned back to Hunter. "I've never understood what you see in her, but surely this must be a red flag. She took my boyfriend into the woods yesterday; then he broke up with me. What do you think happened?"

"I think they went hiking, and Pete got woozy," Hunter replied calmly. "Stormy wouldn't cheat on me. That's not who she is."

"Besides," I added. "I think calling Pete your boyfriend is a bit of an exaggeration. Two days ago, you guys weren't even talking. You might've wanted to use his reputation to your benefit, but that doesn't mean he was your boyfriend."

"Are you really going to stand there and deny it?" Phoebe barked.

"There's nothing to deny. We were just taking a walk in the woods."

"Oh, that is it!" Phoebe threw her hands into the air and stalked away from me. She didn't stop until she was in front of the back door. "You might think this is over." She cast a final look over her shoulder. "It's not, though. I'll make you pay. Mark my words."

It was hard to get worked up over a threat from Phoebe when I had so much else going on. "I look forward to seeing what you come up with."

"You won't say that when I make you cry."

"I guess I'll have to wait and see."

"You'll be sorry," Phoebe warned as she shoved through the door and entered the chilly morning darkness. "Oh, boy, will you be sorry."

I waited until the door shut to speak again. "Well, that was fun."

"She's a concern, but not for right now," Hunter said. "We'll deal with her when the other stuff is behind us."

"What will you do today?" I asked him.

"I don't know. When I figure it out, I'll text you. Until then, I have a lot to think about."

He wasn't the only one.

SEVENTEEN

Grandma came in with her coffee crew shortly before ten o'clock. She had seven women with her, and they all seemed ready for a good round of gossip. Grandpa was upstairs in my apartment, talking to the Northridge Farms manager, so that meant I was in charge of the restaurant. It wasn't nearly as exciting as I would've imagined. The power associated with running a restaurant was fairly benign.

"Twice in one week?" I sidled over to Grandma's table. "Is this some special occasion I don't know about?"

Grandma's gaze was withering. "This is my normal coffee date. I just stopped in on a lark the other day." That was as close as she would get to admitting that she'd only come in on a gossip hunt the first time.

"Grandpa is upstairs making a call, so poached eggs really are off the menu today. I can't make them."

"Who is he calling?"

I hesitated. While not opposed to telling her—and not telling her might spark an argument—I didn't need her caffeine cohorts digging into my business. "He's doing me a favor and asking about the new Northridge Farms rep."

Grandma's eyebrows drew together. "I don't understand. You're not looking for a date, are you?"

I shot her a dirty look. "Yes, I invited Hunter to move in with me and immediately started looking for dates with random guys. That sounds just like me, doesn't it?"

"Nobody needs the mouth," Grandma shot back. "It was just a question."

I couldn't help being testy, but she didn't deserve my bad attitude. "It's just that the new rep was a little weird with me yesterday." I chose my words carefully. "I don't particularly like him, and he told a weird story about how he got the job. Grandpa's checking to see if the story is true."

Grandma lightly tapped her fingers on the tabletop as she studied me. "Does this have something to do with the friends you were hanging out with yesterday?"

That caught me off guard. "How do you know about that?"

"Everybody knows everybody else's business in this town. Plus, well, Tillie Winchester has a certain reputation. When she crosses the town line, everyone pays attention." Grandma leaned closer. "Nobody throws a party for her arrival either. Just FYI."

I tried to picture my grandmother and Tillie being friendly and came up short. They were both forces in their own right, but their lives didn't mesh. Tillie liked gossip as much as the next person, but she wouldn't play euchre three hours a day, five days a week to get it. She had other ideas of fun.

"She was helping me with something," I said.

"Yes, I heard." Grandma's lips curved. "You were spying on Phoebe. She's told everybody in town."

"We weren't spying on her." That was kind of true. "We were ... hiking in the woods and happened to run into Pete. He had some sort of episode. We were close to Phoebe's house by coincidence."

"Right." Grandma looked unconvinced. "That story makes perfect sense."

I glowered at her. "Speaking of that area, though, I had a thought while I was there. As kids, my friends and I used to hang out at the pond behind her house when we weren't by the river. Do the kids still hang out down there?"

"They do," Grandma confirmed. "In fact, last I heard, that's the primary party spot. Since you guys refuse to cede the river—something that drives the current crop of teenagers nuts—they've been forced to look elsewhere. The pond is one of their places as is that big pile of sand behind the road commission building. Why?"

"It's not important right now," I assured her. "I was just curious. Since I've been back, I haven't seen the teens grouping anywhere. It's odd."

"They'll be taking over that coffee shop you love so much now that it's getting colder."

"I guess that makes sense."

"Speaking of hiking in the woods, though, I did learn something you might find interesting." Grandma's eyes sparkled as she looked left to right to make sure nobody was eavesdropping. Even her friends didn't seem interested in our conversation. "Do you remember Sonya Struthers?"

The question caught me off guard. "Um, I think so. She was the woman who planted all the blackberry bushes on her property line because she was convinced her neighbor's son was peeping through her window, right?"

"Yes. That's her. She was seventy when you were in high school and thought the thirteen-year-old next door wanted to see her naked. What an idiot."

Grandma's eye roll had me biting back a smile.

"Just because she's stupid doesn't mean she's bad at gossip, though."

A whisper of excitement ran across the back of my neck. If my grandmother was dragging it out, she had something good. I just knew it. "What did she say?"

"Well, she visited her son a few days ago—he lives out in his hunting cabin on the Jordan River after his wife kicked him out so she could bang the UPS guy—and Sonya said she saw four vehicles parked at the Dead Man's Hill overlook."

Not where I thought she was going. "Okay."

"The vehicles belonged to Florence, Iris, Blanche, and Gwen. She recognized them all."

The news landed like a brick on ceramic tile. "What would they be doing out at Dead Man's Hill?" I was familiar with the scenic overlook —the area was beautiful in the summer and especially the fall—but I'd only visited once or twice since I'd been back.

"Nobody knows," Grandma replied. "I mean, let's face it. Those women don't care about physical fitness. Iris might walk around the neighborhood constantly, but she doesn't do it for exercise. She just wants attention."

"Dead Man's Hill is a steep incline," I said. "They're a little old to be hiking there anyway."

Grandma shot me a dark look. "Are you saying women my age can't hike? Because we can. I don't want to, but if I were interested in hiking, I could totally do it."

I held up my hands to placate her. "I didn't mean offense. I just don't understand what they were doing out there. Besides, I thought they hated each other."

"They do. Or at least they pretend to."

The way she emphasized the word "pretend" said she was holding out on me. "What do you know?" I demanded.

She licked her lips, clearly enjoying her status as the gossiper in chief. "I've been giving it some thought since Sonya mentioned seeing their cars together. It's true that they make a big deal out of fighting with one another whenever they're out and about in the neighborhood, but what if that's all for show?"

I was baffled. "To what end?"

"Maybe they're doing something else. Maybe they all worked together to kill Edmund because they were fed up with his crap. Maybe they left him for dead in the street, and they all claim they didn't see anything."

The theory was interesting. "I did wonder how nobody saw anything when you're all up in each other's business."

"Don't lump me in with them," Grandma warned. "I'm not like them."

She wasn't all that different from them—except in one key area.

"You would always be considered an outsider because you're married. Is that one of the reasons they don't like you?"

"They're jealous." Grandma smoothed her blouse. "Your grandfather is a catch. They wish they'd caught him."

"Yes, I'm sure they wish they had husbands who purposely flashed the neighborhood on skinny-dipping mornings," I readily agreed.

Grandma narrowed her eyes. "Your grandfather is a total hottie."

Hearing those words come out of her mouth shook me. But I wasn't prepared to argue. "I believe you. Let's go back to talking about Edmund's harem. What could they possibly have done at Dead Man's Hill?"

"That's your problem to figure out. I was just sharing the news."

"Right." I tapped my foot on the floor as I considered the gossipy tidbit. "I guess I could go there and look after my shift." I wasn't keen on the idea, but I didn't see another option.

"Knock yourself out. Just remember, the incline is steep as you mentioned. I wouldn't hike alone. Now that all the leaves have fallen, rarely anybody goes there. You need to protect yourself. You could die if you fall and nobody goes looking for you."

She had a point. "I think I can manage a hiking buddy. Thanks for the tip."

"You're welcome. Now, get my coffee ... and eggs. I guess they can be scrambled today."

"I'll get right on that."

GRANDPA CAME DOWNSTAIRS thirty minutes later. He didn't look happy.

My heart dropped. "Is Myron dead?"

Grandpa shook his head. "He's not. The gonorrhea story is true."

I let loose a shaky breath. "That's good, right?"

"I guess that depends on who you ask. Since I had to listen to fifteen minutes of Jed Landry ranting and raving about his wife sleeping with Myron, I would say it's not good."

While I had sympathy for Jed and his marriage woes, I couldn't muster the energy to care. "Tell me."

"Okay, sassy-pants." Grandpa sounded annoyed, but the glint to his eyes suggested he was more amused than anything else. "Myron was forced to retire. The gonorrhea thing became public about a month ago. Everybody in the company knew, and Jed is downright ticked."

I had to bite back a snarky retort. "That's horrible. I hope his divorce goes smoothly."

"Oh, he's not getting divorced. He says it will cost him too much money. He's just punishing his wife in other ways."

Whatever that meant, I didn't want to know. "As fascinating as this all is, I don't care about the Gonorrhea King. If he's still alive, that means Kyle didn't kill him to take his spot."

"Sure, but I have more." Grandpa grabbed a rag and wiped down the counter in front of the grill. He seemed antsy, which wasn't like him. "Jed said that there was a two-week stretch between the time he found out Myron was sleeping with his wife and when the retirement became official. As much as he wanted to fire Myron, he couldn't."

I forced myself to be patient. My grandfather told a great humorous story to a crowd, but when relating an important story that could be put in a nutshell, he was less reliable.

"He had to let Myron retire, and he couldn't advertise an open position until everything was handled behind the scenes," he continued.

Okay, we were getting somewhere.

"Once Myron was officially off the payroll, the other reps filled in until Jed could hire somebody," Grandpa explained. "Jed thought they might fill the position from within, but nobody was interested. That's why they had to look outside the company.

"Kyle just showed up," he continued. "Like, they hadn't even advertised the position, and suddenly, he was there, résumé in hand. He had good references. Jed checked them. The guy interviewed well. Jed was dealing with other stuff, so he saw no reason not to hire Kyle."

I shifted from one foot to the other as I absorbed the news. "Has Kyle been working out?"

"Jed says he's good. None of the customers he's given Kyle have complained. He asked me if I wanted to complain, and I said I would wait until after I received my first order. It's not like I can complain that he showed up outside the woods where you were doing woo-woo and expect him to be fired."

I made a face. "I wish you wouldn't phrase it that way," I complained. "You make it sound like I was doing sexy stuff in the woods."

"Maybe you were. I don't want to hear about it. That's your thing. It's none of my business."

"I wasn't doing sexy stuff in the woods with Tillie and Evan."

Grandpa raised his hand to silence me. "Again, that is not my concern. I'm just telling you what Jed said."

"Keep going," I prodded, resigned.

"Kyle has done his job so far. He hasn't complained. He hasn't made any major mistakes. He hasn't been a pain in the office. Right now, I think Jed's biggest concern is ensuring his wife doesn't give gonorrhea to the new guy."

"I would really prefer not to hear about the gonorrhea stuff again," I muttered.

"Hey, if I have to know about it, so do you." Grandpa was matter of fact. "Jed did tell me one weird thing. Though, I'm not sure he realizes how weird it sounds."

I perked up.

"Kyle asked that the bulk of his clients be in three towns. Would you care to guess which three he asked for?"

Something sizzled in the back of my brain. I knew without hearing his answer. "Shadow Hills, Hawthorne Hollow, and Hemlock Cove."

"Give the girl a doughnut." Grandpa smirked. "Now, I don't like hearing about you and the woo-woo, but I know enough to recognize that Hawthorne Hollow and Hemlock Cove are buried in it."

"It was a specific choice," I mused. "He wants to be close to the magic."

"He handles The Overlook," Grandpa noted. "Jed mentioned that. He likes to talk about the women there, and I know your new buddy's mother is the one handling food supplies for that kitchen. He also mentioned that Kyle handles supplies for the Dragonfly, and if I'm not mistaken, your new buddy's father owns that inn, right?"

I nodded. That was true. Bay's father, Jack, owned the Dragonfly with her cousins' fathers. "So, he's positioned himself close to the action." That felt important, but we didn't have enough details. "What about Hawthorne Hollow? Who is he handling there?"

Grandpa held out his hands. "Jed didn't get into specifics. He said that Kyle was handling a couple of restaurants over there. He asked for a bar, but the bar doesn't serve food and Northridge Farms doesn't distribute liquor, so he's only allowed to pitch snack options."

I knew which bar without asking. "The Rusty Cauldron. That's where Scout and the others hang out."

"I don't want to hear about the woo-woo." Grandpa's tone brooked no argument. "The woo-woo makes me go hoo-boy, and it doesn't benefit anybody."

I laughed, shaking my head. "You should have that put on a shirt." I rolled my neck until it cracked. "So, Kyle is in the thick of it. He wants to be close to the woo-woo."

"That would be my guess."

"Who is the target, though?" I mused.

"I'm not an expert on this stuff, kid, but I have to think you're the target. You're the one he spied on."

"Tillie was with me too."

Grandpa opened his mouth, then shut it. "She's the crazy one, right?"

"I'm pretty sure you would wish for gonorrhea if you ever said that to her face. She'd curse you with something way worse."

Grandpa puffed out his chest. "I'm not afraid of her."

Bold words for a man I knew would curl into a ball and cry if he actually had to face her.

"I can't figure it out," I admitted after several seconds. "Why go through all the trouble to get a job if he's after something else?"

"Maybe he wanted you to trust him. He could've thought you would be more likely to let something slip if you two were friendly."

"Okay, but if that's the case, why be antagonistic yesterday afternoon? He could've spied on us from one street over, and we never would've known. Why hang out in the open like he did and openly taunt us?"

"That's a fair question." Grandpa angled his head. "None of it makes sense."

"It really doesn't." I blew out a sigh. "I don't know what to do."

"You need to call Hunter. He should hear the update. I think he's anticipating the worst."

"Not knowing is worse than knowing. We have no idea what Kyle is up to."

"Yeah, from Hunter's perspective, believing this Kyle guy killed Myron is probably worse."

"I'll tell Hunter," I promised. "What will you do about Kyle?"

"For now, I won't do anything. I haven't even gotten my first shipment. I only order from them every three weeks or so. If I try to switch reps now, Jed will be suspicious." Grandpa took a breath. "If you're uncomfortable, though, I can push the issue." He didn't look happy about it.

I shook my head. "I don't think that's necessary. I kind of want to see what he does."

"And what if he does something bad?"

"Then you'll probably get a new rep sooner rather than later."

Grandpa considered it a moment. "Just make sure the next one has a name that's easier to remember than Kyle. I mean, is that a stupid name, or is it just me?"

"I hadn't really thought about it, but I'll do my best to ensure you get a rep named Dave or Bill."

"That's all I ask."

EIGHTEEN

O nce my shift was over, I ran upstairs to change. Dead Man's
Hill was calling, though I had no idea what I would find
there. Krankle was in the kitchen when I stopped in the living
room to tug on my boots, and he leveled a perplexing look at me.

"What?" I demanded.

"Did I say anything?" he challenged.

"You're clearly thinking something."

"I think a lot of things."

"Whatever." My agitation with the cat was off the charts. Despite
that, I wanted company for my hike. "Come on." I stood determinedly.

Krankle didn't move. "Where are we going?"

"Dead Man's Hill."

"Why?" His lip curled into what looked like a sneer, an unusual
expression for a cat.

"Because rumor has it that the four harem members were sighted
there the other day, and since they're supposedly die-hard enemies, I'm
suspicious."

"Harem members?"

"Oh, right." I nodded. "You haven't been around to hear the gossip.
In a nutshell, a man was stabbed to death in the street by my grandpar-

ents' house, and now his ghost keeps jumping into people, trying to take over their bodies. He was sleeping with the single women of a certain age in the neighborhood. Those women supposedly hate one another, but now I'm not so sure."

Krankle blinked. "And why do I care?"

"Because I do." I was firm as I motioned for him to move toward the sliding glass doors. "Meet me downstairs."

"And what if I don't want to go?"

"You don't get a choice."

"I'm pretty sure that of the two individuals in this room, I'm the boss of me."

"I didn't get a say when you moved in," I pointed out. "You said you're here for me. I need you today. I think that means you're required by law—or at least common decency—to accompany me on my hike."

"I'm a cat. I don't hike."

"Fine. Do what you want." I stormed toward the door and paused with my hand on the knob. "Just know, if you don't start pulling your weight, Hunter will kick you out. I've been standing up for you, but I'm not sure how long I can keep doing it. You've been surly for weeks and have offered nothing to balance it out. I feed you. I try to talk to you. You do nothing for me, though."

"Looks can be deceiving," Krankle countered. "How do you know I'm not doing anything for you?"

"Why would I possibly think you are?"

He didn't respond, instead blinking multiple times.

After several seconds, I got fed up and exited the apartment. I cursed the cat's name as I made my way downstairs. Upon seeing that my uncle had my cousin Annie backed in a corner by the freezers, his mouth going a mile a minute, I used the nearest exit to avoid him.

Once outside, I sucked in several mouthfuls of oxygen. I was at my limit with the cat. In my heart, I believed he was there for a reason. If he wouldn't explain that reason, however, it was probably best to cut him loose. He made me antsy, and I was figuring everything out on my own. The Winchesters were way better guides than he had been. If I kicked him out, I figured he would go back to where he came from, taking my resulting anxiety with him.

Halfway across the alley, I noticed him sitting next to my car. His tail lashed back and forth, his gleaming green eyes full of annoyance, but he was there.

I pulled up short in front of him. "I thought you weren't coming."

"Perhaps you should consider asking next time," he suggested. "I respond better to requests than orders."

Caught off guard, I didn't respond immediately. "You have a point. It's hard for me to balance your external appearance with what I want to believe about you."

"I won't always look like a cat," he grumbled.

"You won't?" He'd mentioned something similar before, but he'd never gone into detail about it. "What will you look like?"

"You wouldn't believe me if I told you." He inclined his head toward the car. "Come on. Let's go hiking. It's obvious you won't let the idea go."

I laughed. "No, I definitely won't. I think something is out there. Why else would four women who supposedly hate each other make a trip together?"

"Because they're hiding something," Krankle replied without hesitation.

"Exactly."

"Well, let's figure out what that is."

IT TOOK ME TWENTY MINUTES TO REACH our destination. Once there, I was relieved to find the parking lot—which only loosely fit the definition—empty. We hopped out, looked around, then edged toward the trail that led down the steep expanse.

"I love that this is considered a mountain," Krankle drawled.

"It's not called Dead Man's Mountain," I reminded him. "It's called Dead Man's Hill."

"And how did it get that cheery name again?"

"It happened back in 1910. Some logger was supposed to marry his high school sweetheart, but he lost control of the huge timber cart he was supposed to be driving, and it killed him."

"That's sad, but it's still weird to name a place after one incident."

"Not a lot happens in this area." I shot him a smile and started down the incline. "Let's go. It gets dark a lot sooner these days. We only have two hours."

"Then we'd better get to it." Though he was a cat, Krankle took the lead. He seemed in better spirits than I'd seen him over the past few weeks, as if he liked being away from the restaurant.

"Who were you talking to the other night?" I asked out of the blue.

"I already told you. I wasn't talking to anybody."

I didn't believe him. "Krankle—"

"Why can't you just let it go?" he complained. "I told you I wasn't talking to anybody. You don't believe me, and it drives me insane."

He was right. I didn't believe him. For the first time since I'd seen him with the shadow, however, something occurred to me. "Is somebody threatening you?"

Krankle jerked his eyes toward me. "Why would you ask that?"

"That wasn't a denial."

"I'm fine. Don't worry about me. Worry about yourself. Obviously, you have more going on than I had realized."

"I do," I readily agreed. "I have a lot of stuff going on. It's not good stuff either. For example, I'm curious how a ghost is managing to jump into bodies and take them over. If that was a thing, wouldn't we have heard more about it before this?"

"It's not normal."

"How do you know?"

"I know things." Krankle sounded agitated. "Why don't you ask your witchy friends in Hemlock Cove? Bay is supposed to be a ghost expert, is she not?"

"She is," I confirmed. "I'm asking you, though. Have you ever heard of anything like this?"

"Not off the top of my head, although ... once I did hear about something similar I guess. The soul was cursed to never find rest. Perhaps this Edmund was cursed."

I hadn't considered that, but since he brought it up, I had questions. "Do you think the women who make up his harem are witches?"

"You don't have to be a witch to curse someone. Though, I guess anything is possible." He was quiet for a beat. "Have these women displayed magical abilities?"

I shook my head. "Not that I'm aware of, but you have to remember that before I came home, I thought magic was make-believe."

"Or did you just tell yourself that?"

I slowed my pace for the steep incline. "What do you mean?"

"I heard your friend Bay talking to you one day."

I wasn't expecting that tangent.

"She said that she was brought up with magic, but she never truly understood the consequences of it until she returned to Hemlock Cove after spending a few years down in the city. She called herself a dabbler," he continued. "She said she was aware of magic and understood that it could be used for any number of things, but she didn't truly understand until she embraced it. Perhaps you believed, but you weren't ready to embrace it."

It was an interesting take on my situation, and I didn't want to dissuade him from talking. Still, I had questions. "Let's say I believe that," I hedged. "Why was I suddenly ready to embrace it when I came back?"

"Because, in your head, you'd lost everything," he replied matter-of-factly. "You were empty and needed to be filled. At the time, you realized you were embarrassed by the things that had happened to you, but you didn't realize they were important to your development." He stopped walking and focused on me. "You had to lose everything to start over. You couldn't adjust your mindset until you thought you'd lost everything you were supposed to be."

"You mean the writing stuff," I surmised. "Did Hunter tell you to have this conversation with me?"

Krankle chuckled and turned back to our trek as we approached the thicker trees. "Hunter doesn't want to have regular conversations with me. He doesn't trust me."

"Do you blame him?"

"No." Krankle lifted his nose and sniffed.

I recognized the change in his demeanor. "What's wrong?"

"Don't you smell that?" Krankle made a face. "It smells like something was on fire down here recently. Nobody is allowed to burn things in this area, are they?"

"Not in the summer months at least," I replied. "Nobody lives out here, and we have burn ordinances when it's dry. They wouldn't be as much of a concern now, though, because fall is so wet."

"Well, something definitely caught fire out here." Krankle lashed his tail. "This way." He darted into the woods, leaving me to follow.

I trusted his instincts, at least on that, and didn't complain. "Are you going to pressure me about the writing stuff too?" I asked as I followed him. "Hunter and Grandpa have been hounding me. I was at my mother's house a few days ago for our mandated weekly tea, and she mentioned writing again too."

"My understanding is that you used to love writing." The cat fixated on picking a path we could both easily traverse. "It wasn't just a job to you. It was more than that. Losing it means you've lost a part of yourself."

"But I failed."

"You're the only one who thinks that. Have you ever considered that you simply picked the wrong way to go about embracing your dream?"

"Only every day of my life," I muttered.

"Perhaps you were always meant to write here."

"It's hard for me to consider that because it means I screwed up by leaving," I admitted. "I left Hunter, broke both our hearts, and it was unnecessary."

"I didn't say it was unnecessary," Krankle countered. "I merely stated that perhaps your beliefs on the topic were mistaken. There's a difference. I happen to believe that leaving when you did was smart."

"And why is that?"

"Because you weren't ready for the truth, and if you'd grown too complacent here, you might never have been ready. Things happened how they are supposed to happen. That doesn't mean everything you were before is lost."

It was a fairly profound thing to say. "I'm not sure I'm ready to write again."

"Then don't. You'll know when you're ready."

"I guess. I..."

I forgot my thought when Krankle led us to a small clearing among the trees. When I looked overhead, the branches stretched thickly in every direction to create a protective canopy above. The ground, though, was different. Someone had taken pieces of wood—most looked to have been part of fallen tree branches—and created a pentagram at the center of everything. At some point, someone had set it on fire.

"Well, this isn't naturally occurring," I muttered, nudging a piece of burned wood with my toe.

"Definitely not." Krankle leaned close to the wood and sniffed. "There's magic here, but it doesn't smell like the magic I'm used to. It doesn't smell like your magic."

"Meaning what?"

"Your magic is older and smells richer somehow despite being fresh to you. Whatever this is, it smells new. It's almost as if someone wielded it who wasn't supposed to wield it at all. Like it was a temporary thing."

I had no idea what to make of it. "It has to be the harem."

"Yes." Krankle shifted his chin. "Tell me about these women again. What do you know of them?"

"I don't know anything. I know they live in the same neighborhood with my grandmother and none of them like each other."

"Was it always that way?"

"No." I shook my head. "When I was younger, my grandmother and Florence were friends. They kind of messed with each other, but they at least pretended to be friends. She was friendly-ish with some of the others too. I distinctly remember her hanging around with Blanche for a time."

"But none of those friendships lasted," Krankle said. "What does your grandmother say about these women?"

"Nothing nice. She's mean, but that doesn't necessarily mean anything. I love my grandmother, but she's not always the easiest woman in the world to get along with. She and her friends are very cliquey."

"Maybe the harem, as you call them, decided they didn't like being kept from the clique."

"But why do this? Even if they were angry about being excluded from the group, what good would this do?" I gestured toward the pentagram. "What were they trying to accomplish here?"

"That I can't answer. They clearly cast a spell."

"We don't know it was the harem," I hedged.

"Oh, no?" Krankle shifted to look directly at me. "You came out here expecting to find something. Now that you've found that something, you're backing away from what you believed. Why? We have confirmation."

"I know, but ... this isn't what I expected to find."

"What did you expect?" He feigned patience, but his tone held a chilly edge.

"Fair point," I acknowledged after a beat. "I didn't know what I would find. This somehow feels worse than anything I could've imagined, though." I touched my tongue to my top lip. "Do you think they worked together to do something to Edmund? Are they the reason his soul is acting so strange?"

"I think that's as good a guess as any," Krankle acknowledged. "I'm curious where they got the magic. This does not smell like witch magic, and yet the pentagram suggests that was their exact aim."

"Like ... what?" I was genuinely curious. "Are you saying they know witches are real and tried to emulate what they thought a witch would do?"

"Why not? Hemlock Cove is one town over. It's full of witches."

"Fake witches."

"Tell the Winchesters that."

"Yes, but nobody is supposed to know about the Winchesters," I protested.

"And yet it's an open secret," Krankle shot back. "My guess is that whatever spell they cast, they got the idea—and maybe even the means —from Hemlock Cove."

I hadn't considered that. "Well, how do we find out if that's what happened?"

"I have no idea. I—" Krankle's words died on his lips as a twig cracked in the space behind me.

I swiveled quickly, my instincts telling me to prepare myself, and fire erupted from my fingertips as I finished the turn.

"Oh, yay!" Kyle clapped as he appeared in the clearing. He wasn't dressed for a hike—he wore largely the same outfit as the previous day—and his loony laugh made my blood run cold. "Isn't this a fun surprise? Who doesn't love a pentagram in the middle of the woods?"

I waved my hands to extinguish the fire and openly gaped at the interloper. "What are you doing out here?"

"I'm here to talk," Kyle replied. "I should think that's obvious."

"Did you follow me?" I darted a look toward Krankle and found the fur along his spine standing on end.

"Let's just say I've been looking for an opportunity to have a genuine conversation," Kyle replied. "I believe this is our chance."

"Don't do it," Krankle muttered. "Don't listen to him. He'll try to manipulate you."

That was rich coming from the gnome shifter. Still, I was leery. "Fine." I didn't see that I had much choice, given our location. "Let's talk."

"Lovely." Kyle smiled so wide it almost swallowed his face. "I'm glad you're not being difficult. That would've made this so much worse."

NINETEEN

My mouth was dry. "What would've made everything so much worse?"

"Your attitude," Kyle replied. "You're not exactly what I would call a glass-half-full person. In fact, you always look at things from the darkest possible side. Why is that? I have theories, but I would rather hear it from the witch's mouth."

A shiver ran down my spine. "How...? You...? I mean..." *How does he know I'm a witch?* The question refused to eke out correctly.

"Oh, look how cute you are. I just want to—" He reached toward my face, seemingly intent on grabbing my cheek and giving it a jiggle.

I yanked away before he could.

"Ah, well. If you really want to hide the fact that you're a witch, you'll need to do a much better job of it. Not only has the magic in this town exploded since your return, but you've also been seen throwing around fire in multiple instances." He made a tsking sound with his tongue as he wagged his finger. "That is not the way to fly under the radar."

I didn't know what to say. In hindsight, making the trip to Dead Man's Hill had been a colossal mistake. I couldn't turn back the clock, though. "What are you?" I demanded. The time for playing games was over.

"I'm a food distributor." He smiled.

"You're way more than that. I want to know what you are."

"And I want to know why you keep bothering with nonsense." Kyle slid his eyes to the pentagram. "You should not be wasting your time here. You have a destiny, Stormy, and it doesn't involve this."

I glanced at Krankle and found him puffed out and preparing for an attack. That seemed ludicrous, given the size difference between the cat and the man, and yet the cat showed no signs of backing down. As if sensing me watching him, Krankle spoke.

"You need to go, Stormy."

I was flabbergasted. "What?"

"Go," Krankle repeated. "I'll handle this."

I wanted to laugh. Under different circumstances, I would've.

Kyle did it for me. "You've been warned already about your affection for the girl," he growled. "Do you really think now is the time to risk being called in front of the tribunal?"

"You don't have any say over me," Krankle snapped. "You don't even have a say over this situation. She's not yours."

"Do you think she's yours?" Kyle arched a challenging eyebrow.

"I think she belongs to herself," Krankle shot back. "I've already told you that, but you don't believe me. None of you believe me. You can't control her." The cat flicked his eyes at me plaintively. "Go."

Is he suggesting I leave him? "Krankle." I didn't know what else to say. I certainly didn't know what to do. The entire situation had spiraled out of control, and I was at a loss.

"You have to go." Krankle was firm. "You can't stay here."

I made up my mind on the spot. "Then we'll go together." I raised my hand to draw the fire I wasn't yet comfortable with and pointed it at Kyle. "You will let us pass."

Kyle didn't look fearful, and yet, something I couldn't recognize glinted in his eyes. "You're not the boss here, girl."

"I think I am." I believed that somehow.

Hunter kept saying my ego had taken a beating, given my failures over the last few years, and he was right. This wasn't my writing career, though, and I had yet to fail when it came to magic. Maybe if I believed in myself enough, it would force him to back down.

"Go," I ordered.

"No." Kyle's smile was benign enough, but I didn't trust him. "I think I'm good here."

"If you don't get out of our way, I'll hurt you."

"Oh, such bravado." Kyle mock applauded. "You're so brave. You're an idiot, but your courage is to be commended. You'll need it for what's to come."

I worked my jaw, debating, then exhaled heavily. "I guess I have no choice but to put on a little display."

"No," Krankle hissed. He stepped forward with a purpose. "Don't. You're not ready, and he'll use it against you. You have to go."

I couldn't fathom why he kept saying that. "What about you?"

"I can take care of myself."

Part of me believed that. The other part wondered if it was wishful thinking. "Krankle—"

"Go."

"But—"

"Go!" he roared, taking me by surprise when a wave of energy blew outward from him and knocked Kyle back on his heels. "Get out of here, Stormy!"

I didn't have time to think. I had to make a choice. As far as I was concerned, I only had one. I ran. I didn't go up the hill. Kyle could overtake me if I went that route. His legs were longer. He was stronger. The climb would give him the advantage. That meant I had to level the playing field.

I ran into the woods, keeping the sun on my right shoulder. I hurried through the trees, cursing under my breath when whatever spell Krankle had thrown at Kyle dissipated and the man screamed at the cat.

Will Kyle kill him? That was a fear I couldn't shake. I shouldn't have left Krankle. That sentence played over and over in my head as I cut through the trees. *I shouldn't have left him. I shouldn't have left him.*

When Hunter and I were kids, we'd hiked the Dead Man's Hill loop several times a year. We were familiar with the area. Sure, a lot of the time, our hiking was just to find a small creek and make out by it, but we still knew the area. I used that to my advantage.

I counted my steps as I hit a small hill, my memory plugging holes for me. *One. Two. Three. Four.* I ducked to the right behind a large tree. It wasn't as healthy as it had been when I was younger, but it still stood strong. I moved around it and slid into another much thicker crop of trees that afforded a hiding spot one had to know about to discover, then waited.

I gasped raggedly but forced myself to regulate my breathing. *In and out.*

Footsteps crunched on the path from the direction I'd come.

In and out.

The footsteps drew closer.

In and out.

Kyle cursed close by, and my stomach constricted. But he didn't know to look where I stood. It wasn't his terrain. Though I hadn't been a big fan of the great outdoors as a kid, Hunter had. He'd loved coming to the woods in the summer and fall. It was a way to hide from his father. We'd spent hours here. Sometimes, I would bring a notebook with me and write. Other times I would bring a book. He would fish, hunt for morels, or take a nap in the sun. It was one of our favorite spots, and I refused to let Kyle take it from us.

"Where are you, Stormy?" Kyle called.

I held my breath and angled myself so I could see his profile. He'd moved beyond me. I needed him to commit to a path. It didn't matter if he went left or straight. He would pass me either way, and I would be free to circle back.

"Come on, Stormy," Kyle wheedled. "You misunderstood my intentions. I just want to talk."

I didn't respond. I wasn't an idiot.

He tried again. "I have the answers you're looking for."

I wouldn't fall for that.

"Fine." Kyle viciously swore. "You'd better hope I don't find you, though. I'll make you cry if I get my hands on you. You should be playing coy here." With that, he headed south.

I watched him from my spot, knowing better than to move. Sure enough, he made it a good twenty yards before stopping suddenly and wheeling to check the path behind him. He couldn't see me. With another string of curses, he turned and hurried down a slope.

He likely didn't know where he was going, but I did. If things were as I remembered, he would hit a steep slope leading to the water. Thanks to all the leaves that had fallen and the frost that regularly hit those days, if he stepped wrong, he would slip and lose control of his descent, ending up in the creek or maybe stuck in the mud. Either way, it would be a significant distraction. That meant I had more than enough time to get back up the hill and out of the parking lot.

I carefully slipped out of my hiding spot. He was gone from sight, but he could hurry back if he figured out my plan. As quietly as I could manage, I reached the footpath. It was rutted, the ground hard, thanks to the cold, but no tree roots rose to trip me.

When I made it back to the pentagram, I found no sign of Krankle. The cat was gone. Thankfully, no blood covered the ground. I kept my wits about me long enough to take photos of the pentagram with my phone, then I headed up to the parking lot.

The climb was arduous, and I looked over my shoulder for Kyle so many times I knew I was slowing myself down. I saw no sign of him, though. I didn't realize I had expected Krankle to be at the car until I made it to the parking lot to find him absent. My heart sank, and I whispered his name in an attempt to get him to emerge from the underbrush, where I hoped he was hiding. The cat was nowhere to be found.

Because I couldn't help myself, I moved back to the rim of the scenic overlook to gander at the hill. Kyle wasn't there. Neither was the cat. I went back to the car long enough to insert the key and make sure it worked—I wouldn't put it past Kyle to disable it, after all—then I went to his vehicle to check it out. It was the same white truck that had been in the alley. The same one he'd been leaning against when we'd come out of the woods near Phoebe's house.

I didn't know a lot about trucks, but I'd picked up a few things over the years. Kyle had left his truck unlocked, so I opened the driver's-side door, hit the lever to pop the hood, and took a look at what lay beneath. The truck wasn't very old, so it didn't have much grime. Rather than give it a lot of thought, I started pulling on things. I removed caps. I yanked out wires. I detached the battery. When I was certain the truck wouldn't go anywhere, I returned to the overlook to check for Krankle one more time. He wasn't there, but Kyle had figured out my ruse and was at the bottom of the hill, making his way up.

"Clever girl," he called. "You almost had me. Stay up there. I just want to talk."

Rather than call him a liar, I backed away. "Have a nice walk home, jackass."

Realization hit him, and he increased his pace. He couldn't catch me, though. Scampering to my still running car, I then floored it out of the lot. I buckled my seat belt as I drove, which wasn't exactly safe, but since nobody was on the road to the hill, I wasn't too worried.

The whole way back to town, I obsessed about Krankle. *Did I abandon the cat to death? Is something worse going to happen to him? How did he know Kyle? Did he even know Kyle?* They didn't act friendly.

By the time I hit Main Street, my heart no longer pounded, and the constant need to look over my shoulder had abated. I drove directly to the police station, which wasn't overly large. Hunter was talking to the secretary and one of the other officers in the main room when I entered —they were yukking it up and having a good time—and when his eyes moved to me, he was smiling. All traces of mirth left his features when he saw my dirty face and clothes.

"Stormy?" He stepped toward me.

I'd held it together for what felt like a really long time. I hadn't panicked in the face of adversity. I hadn't lamented my lot in life or asked, "Why me?" I'd been calm, cool, and collected. Now that I was truly safe, though, all that mental strength flew out the window as I threw myself into Hunter's arms.

"Baby." He gripped me tightly against him, his hand moving over the back of my head to stroke and soothe. "What happened? Are you okay?"

I couldn't find words, so I sobbed.

"Stormy, I'm about to freak out." Hunter pulled back far enough to look into my eyes. "Tell me what happened."

When I finally managed to speak, my voice was ragged. "I went to

Dead Man's Hill. I was just looking around. Krankle was with me. Then Kyle was there."

Hunter's grip tightened. "He followed you there?"

I nodded. "He kept saying he wanted to talk." I had to choose my words carefully in front of the other officer and the secretary. "He was freaking me out, though, so I ran. He chased me, but I knew the area better. I hid in that spot where we made out when we were together the summer before junior year."

Hunter nodded. "I know the spot. I used to dream about it. You let me stick my hand up your shirt for the first time there. Well, the first time that wasn't an accident. It was glorious."

I pinned him with a dark look.

"Sorry." He sobered immediately. "You obviously got away." He hesitated for a beat. "Did he put his hands on you?"

"No." I shook my head. "I hid in our spot, and he headed toward the creek. I knew he could overtake me if I ran up the hill straightaway, so I didn't do that. When I got to the top, just to be safe, I ripped out a bunch of wires and unscrewed a bunch of caps under his truck's hood."

"Oh." Realization dawned on Hunter's face. "That's where all your grime came from."

"I guess." I shrugged. "I lost the cat."

Hunter was quiet for a beat, then nodded. "We'll find him." He pressed a kiss to my forehead and hugged me tight before turning to the officer. "Jared, can you and Ben drive out there and look before the end of your shift? You just need to go to the overlook and check the road on the way out."

"No problem," Jared said. "Who am I looking for?"

"Kyle Morton," Hunter replied. "He's a food distributor for Northridge Farms. He's shown up where he shouldn't be twice now. Both times he was following Stormy."

"That doesn't sound good."

"It's not." Hunter seemed lost in thought. "I doubt you'll find him. If his truck is still out there, though, impound it."

"It sounds as if Stormy did a number on it," Jared said. "That was smart, by the way." He grinned at me. "Did you leave all the wires and stuff under the hood?"

I shook my head. "Everything I could take with me, I did. It's in my car."

"That's even smarter." Jared winked then turned to Hunter. "If you know who this guy is, can't we pick him up tonight?"

"In theory," Hunter replied. "The problem is, I ran him earlier. He doesn't technically exist. Or, well, none of the information he provided Northridge Farms is legitimate. The address he provided goes to an empty lot on the east side of town. He's not real."

"Well, that's a little freaky." Jared was grim. "Okay. I'll grab Ben, and we'll head out. I'll let you know what we find."

"Thank you." Hunter smiled, but it didn't touch his eyes. When he turned back to me, his gaze held worry and something else. "Let's go to my office, huh? I want to hear the whole story from the beginning."

What he didn't say—but I knew he meant—was that he wanted to hear the parts I'd purposely left out. The magical parts would bring the story into sharper focus. "Sure." I managed a smile. "Can I hit the bathroom first, though? I've had to pee for what feels like forever. I didn't want to take the time when I was on top of the hill."

"Sure. I'll make you some tea. Then we'll break everything down."

Though he wanted to dig deeper, I knew he wouldn't get what he was after. He wanted a motive. I didn't have one for him. Things were definitely spiraling out of control. We both wanted answers. Unfortunately, I had no idea what to do about it.

TWENTY

The truck was still at the scenic overlook, but Kyle was gone with no sign of where he'd disappeared to. They also found no sign of Krankle. Hunter had asked Jared to be on the lookout for a black cat—which I was certain struck Jared as funny—but they'd come up empty.

Hunter loaded me into his truck. "He wanted to know why my girl-friend was out hiking with her cat."

We'd decided that dinner in Hemlock Cove was a necessity, so my car would remain behind at the police station.

"I could hear them laughing between questions."

I frowned. "That's not very nice."

"It's weird when you think about it. It's not like you took a dog with you."

"He's still out there."

"And he knows the way home. He's not a real cat, Stormy."

"He protected me."

Hunter was silent a beat as he pulled onto the highway. "I know," he said finally. "I'm grateful. He'll find his way home, though."

I wasn't so sure. "What if Kyle killed him?"

"You said there was no blood."

"There wasn't, but that doesn't mean he's alive."

"Well, what do you suggest we do about it?" He sounded exasperated. "Do you want to camp out there and hope he shows up?"

That sounded like a nightmare. I wasn't a fan of camping under the best of circumstances, of which these were not. "No."

"Then tell me what you want to do."

I didn't have an answer. Instead, I stared out the window for the drive. It was dark already—Michigan winters were always that way—so there was nothing to look at. I needed to think, though. Since the initial shock had worn off, my mind raced a million miles a minute.

Hunter let me stew. He knew me well enough to recognize I needed time to decompress. I was calmer when we pulled into The Overlook's parking lot. Though I wasn't happy with the turn of events by any stretch of the imagination, I no longer mentally treaded water in my own tears.

The Overlook was quiet when we let ourselves in. Nobody manned the front desk, but we were familiar with the property and followed the sound of voices into the dining room. There, Bay and Landon sat drinking wine and arguing with Evan.

"I'm not saying she's a criminal mastermind," Evan huffed. "I'm just saying that she's a pain in the ass."

I didn't have to ask who he was talking about. Clearly, he was still agitated from Tillie dressing him the previous day.

"Oh, she's a criminal mastermind," Landon countered, smiling easily when he glanced in our direction. "She just doesn't care if she's caught."

"Hey." Bay got up when she saw us. "I'm so glad you guys decided to come for dinner." She hugged me, her gaze searching. She must not have liked what she saw because she frowned instantaneously. "What did you do?" She looked accusingly at Hunter.

"Oh, apparently, *I'm* the criminal mastermind." Hunter flopped into one of the chairs at the middle of the table.

"He didn't do anything," I assured her. "This is ... all my doing."

"Don't say that," Hunter groused. "You didn't do this. You were just minding your own business when a psycho chased you through the woods. Do I think going out there alone was a good idea? No. It's not like you asked for it, though."

"Yeah, I think we need more information." Landon grabbed the bottle of wine and poured Hunter a glass. "What's going on?"

I filled them in, leaving nothing out. Hunter tucked me in at his side when I finally sat and handed me his glass of wine. I sipped it, the warmth that suffused me making things better, but I remained out of sorts, thanks to losing Krankle.

"The cat is still out there?" Landon asked when I finished.

"I couldn't find him." I held out my hands and shrugged. "I looked, but I didn't think it was smart to hang around for more than a few minutes."

"You did what you could," Hunter insisted. "You did everything right out there. You thought on your feet. You couldn't outrun Kyle on a straight climb, so you led him into the woods before losing him. Then you disabled his truck before driving away. That was an amazing decision."

"It was," Landon agreed. "You made it so he couldn't follow you. I'm sorry about the cat, though."

Not nearly as sorry as I was.

"We don't know that anything happened to him," Bay argued. "He could've done the same thing she did and hid once he was certain she got away. It's not as if he actually thinks like a cat. He's a gnome shifter, right? He can find his own way home."

I wished I felt as certain as she sounded.

"I can go out and look after dinner." Evan gave a quick, friendly smile. "I can cover a lot of ground out there, and the cat knows me. I might be able to sniff him out."

"If a predator hasn't found him," Landon said. "All sorts of things out there will eat cats."

Bay pinned her husband with a death glare. "Is this you trying to help?"

"Sorry." Landon raised his hands in supplication. "I don't mean to be a downer. I just don't want Stormy holding onto false hope. I mean

... it was a man against a cat. How often will the cat win in those circumstances?"

"More often than you might think," Evan replied. "Cats are amazing killing machines in tiny packages. We might have domesticated them, but they have ways to protect themselves. Again, though, we're not dealing with an actual cat. I think it's entirely likely Krankle headed home when he realized Stormy had gotten away. How many miles are we talking?"

"Getting home would be a decent hike for him," Hunter said. "He's also not used to hunting. All his food comes from a can."

"I'll go look," Evan promised. "For all we know, this Kyle guy is still out there anyway. I mean, how else did he get home? Do we think he walked?"

"It's unlikely," Hunter replied. "But we don't know if he's working with anybody. He doesn't exist apparently."

"Then how did he get the job?" Bay asked.

"I don't know. I'll chase that information tomorrow." Hunter rubbed my back. "Your grandfather called to check on him, right? You didn't give me a full update on what was said."

"Just that the Gonorrhea King wasn't killed," I replied. "The guy who owns the company confirmed that Myron was forced to retire. Kyle conveniently came in at a time when they were looking for someone. Apparently, they didn't vet him properly. His only request was that all his assignments be in Shadow Hills, Hemlock Cove, and Hawthorne Hollow."

Bay straightened, her eyes dark. "Well, that's interesting, isn't it?"

"It gets more interesting," I replied. "My grandfather managed to secure at least a partial list of the businesses he's serving. The Overlook is on it, as is the Rusty Cauldron."

Bay shifted her eyes to the swinging door that separated the kitchen from the dining room as her mother, Winnie, swung into view with a huge platter of pot roast. I hadn't realized how hungry I was until the scent hit me like a brick and my stomach growled.

"Do you have a new Northridge Farms rep?" Bay asked her mother.

Tillie, trailing behind her niece, had a breadbasket in hand. The question clearly caught her off guard. "Who cares?"

"I do." Bay shot her great-aunt a dirty look. "You should, too, since apparently the new Northridge Farms rep tried to kill Stormy today."

"Well, that's taking service to a new extreme," Tillie drawled. "What's up with that?"

I told the story again, this time in a nutshell.

When I finished, Tillie had a hunk of buttered bread in her hand and a perplexed look on her face. "Wait, the guy we saw by the truck is the new Northridge Farms rep?"

I nodded. "Yeah. My grandfather placed a call today. Supposedly, he's your rep too."

"Kyle." Winnie sat. "I've met him. He seems nice enough."

I glanced around the table at the many empty chairs. "Where's everybody else?"

"They're down at the town square," Winnie replied. "We're hosting a booth at a festival tomorrow. Terry has to check security, and Marnie and Twila are setting things up."

"Oh." I couldn't help deflating a bit. I loved little more than a raucous Winchester dinner. "That's kind of a bummer."

"They'll be here soon." Winnie patted my hand, looking concerned. "I don't understand why a food distributor would want to kill you."

"He's not a food distributor," Landon countered. "That's the problem. He took a job as a food distributor to get close to certain people."

"Witches," Hunter supplied. "He wants to be close to witches."

"Does that mean Stormy is the true target, or is he interested in all of us?" Winnie handed a set of tongs to Landon.

For his part, he dug into the pot roast with gusto. Even attempted assault couldn't kill his appetite.

"I think, likely, he has an interest in everybody," I replied. "He seems especially fixated on me, though. He followed us to Phoebe's house. He saw Evan carrying Pete out of the woods and didn't care."

"I didn't recognize him," Tillie mused. "I saw him here during your food order, but I didn't put it together."

"Well, we need a new rep," Winnie said.

"Obviously," Bay agreed. "I bet he doesn't come back, though. He wouldn't try to keep his job, given what's happened. He has to know that Stormy went straight to Hunter."

"And we have his truck now," Hunter said. "We impounded it. He can't just mosey back to work and pretend nothing happened."

"Unless he tries to play it off with me as the aggressor," I argued.

Hunter doled food onto my plate. "Nobody will believe that."

"We don't know that. Technically, it's just my word against his. Even what happened at Phoebe's house can't be used because we can't trot Evan out as a witness."

Hunter rubbed his cheek. "I didn't think about that."

"You can use me as a witness," Tillie argued.

"Yeah, unfortunately, your reputation won't stand up to that sort of scrutiny," Landon countered. "Stormy is right. If this guy is deranged, he might be bold enough to concoct a story about Stormy to cover himself."

"Except one of my fellow officers was present when Stormy came to the department," Hunter argued. "He saw how upset she was. She couldn't fake that."

"We know that," Landon replied reasonably. "Unfortunately, other people might not believe that."

My appetite was quickly fading.

"Eat, baby," Hunter prodded. "You need to keep up your strength."

"He won't keep his job regardless," Winnie said firmly as she sat. "There's no way. We'll drop him first thing tomorrow. Obviously, Stormy's grandfather will too. All we have to do is place a call to Whistler at the Rusty Cauldron over in Hawthorne Hollow, and he'll join with us. Northridge Farms doesn't want to lose our business. They'll at least transfer Kyle away from us."

"But if he works for other businesses in the area, he still might be around," I noted.

"I guess." Winnie leaned back in her chair. "He's not human, right? What are we dealing with here? Can we smite him?"

I practically choked on the bread in my mouth. I would've expected the statement from Tillie. Hearing it from Winnie shocked me.

"We don't know what he is," Evan replied. "I was directly in front of him and felt ... well, I'm not sure what I felt. He has magic, but it's not like any I've come into contact with before."

"It has to be tied to the cat." Tillie stuffed a napkin in the front of her shirt and went to town on her dinner. "It's the only thing that makes sense. You said you saw the cat talking to someone behind the shed. Then this guy shows up. From what you described, at the very least, they recognized each other for what they were. I don't think that's a coincidence."

"But is Edmund Hawthorne's ghost a coincidence?" Hunter queried. "I mean, is all of this tied together?"

"I don't think so." Bay shook her head. "From what Stormy described—and I want to see your photo of that pentagram—I think the Edmund stuff is separate. I've never technically witnessed a ghost take over someone else's body, but I have to think some spells out there can make it possible."

"Dark spells," Tillie confirmed.

"I think your four girlfriends—calling them a harem is hard for me —managed to get their hands on a spell book," Bay continued. "I have no idea where the magic came from, but if the cat said it smelled like borrowed magic, then I'm guessing that's what we're dealing with."

I dug for my phone, found the photo, and handed it to her.

Bay's forehead creased as she studied the photo, then she handed it to Tillie. "I want to see it up close and personal tomorrow. We might be able to detect something you couldn't see, Stormy."

"I'm game for that." I forced a smile I didn't feel. The last thing I wanted was to return to Dead Man's Hill. I didn't see a choice, though. "I have a shift tomorrow morning. We will have to go after noon."

"That's fine," Bay assured me. "We'll put together some potions just in case we can reverse the spell on site. It's unlikely but would solve one of our problems straightaway. As for Kyle, I don't know what to say, Stormy. We need more information on the guy. The only way we can get it is if he shows up again."

"That's not the only way," I countered. "Krankle knows what he is."

"Yes, but we don't know where Krankle is."

"Can't we cast a locator spell? You're good at them, right? I've tried before and managed to do it." I wanted to kick myself. "That's what I should've done before leaving him out there."

"You did what you had to do to survive," Bay argued. "That's the most important thing, and I'm willing to bet the cat would agree. He's the one who told you to run. As for a locator spell, we can certainly try. If he's walking home, though, we might be in for a long search."

"It's better than not knowing." I blinked back tears. "I have this sick feeling. I don't know how to explain it, but I'm afraid."

Hunter's hand landed on my back. "We'll find the cat."

He sounded a lot more certain than I felt.

"I hope so."

"We will," Bay agreed. "If he's out there, we'll find him. I would like to knock out this Edmund problem right away if we can. It's interesting, and annoying for the people he's taking over, but it doesn't feel as serious as the Kyle problem. Once Edmund and his unhappy harem are in the rearview mirror, we can focus the proper attention on Kyle."

"I just wish we knew his plan," Winnie said. "I had no idea he was such a creep. He seemed perfectly nice when he was here."

"Did he ask questions?" Landon asked. "Like, did he ask about Bay or anything?"

Winnie cocked her head as she considered the question. "You know, now that you mention it, I think he was here one of the days Bay and Stormy were practicing with Aunt Tillie in the backyard. It was one of the last nice days we had. He saw them and assumed they were doing yoga."

"I think we can surmise that he didn't really believe it was yoga," Bay countered. "He was obviously watching us."

"And for a lot longer than we realized," Tillie agreed. "I definitely don't like this guy. I don't know how to find him, though. Do we have anything of his?"

"Just his truck," Hunter replied. "Will that work?"

Tillie wrinkled her nose. "Maybe. Can I get inside the truck?"

Hunter looked caught off guard. "I guess I can get you into the impound lot. What do you think you'll find there, though?"

"I'm not sure. It doesn't hurt to look, though. If I can find some of his hair, I could fashion a locator spell."

"Then what?" Hunter asked.

"Then we'll track him down and smite him."

That time, I smiled. Being around the Winchesters always made me feel better. My appetite returned with gusto. "That sounds like a plan.

You can search the truck while I'm at work tomorrow. Then we'll go to Dead Man's Hill and hopefully deal with the Edmund situation."

"One catastrophe at a time," Bay agreed. "That's the way we like to do it in this house. We will deal with it, Stormy. You have my word."

I hoped she was right, but a small, niggling portion of my heart was terrified she was wrong.

Twenty-One

The rest of the Winchesters showed up before we finished eating. They happily insulted one another and made booth plans for the following day, making me smile and laugh at appropriate intervals. Inside, though, I was a mess.

Bay was good at reading people, and she caught me in the lobby while I waited for Hunter to use the bathroom on our way out the door. I was exhausted and ready for bed. Bay, apparently, had other ideas.

"You can't beat yourself up over what happened," she said.

I'd been staring out the front window, and she caught me off guard. When I turned, she was leaning against the front desk.

"Who should I blame?" I asked.

"Well, off the top of my head, I would say Kyle."

"I'm the one who went to the woods by myself."

"Yes, but you couldn't have known what would happen."

"I should've guessed. He followed me the day before."

"You'll find that there are a lot of 'should haves' in the witch business." Bay managed a wan smile. "Do you want to know how many things I should have done? Unlike you, some of my 'should haves' resulted in people dying."

"Krankle could be dead."

"And he could be perfectly fine. In fact, my money is on the cat. You need to stop beating yourself up over things you can't change. Krankle is out there somewhere. I'm willing to bet he finds you."

"I guess." I pressed the heel of my hand to my forehead. "It just feels like too much this time. I don't understand how you do it month after month."

She smiled genuinely that time. "You'll get used to it. Trust me. As for being too much, I know it feels that way now, but it will be okay. This is your first time dealing with two bad guys at once. It's a pain, but thankfully, it doesn't happen very often."

"You think Kyle is the bigger threat, don't you?"

"Oh, most definitely. That's why we need to handle this stupid Edmund problem as quickly as possible."

"Can you control him? I know he's different from other ghosts, but it would be great if you could stop him from jumping into other people's bodies."

"I'll do my best," Bay promised. "If I can't control him, then we'll take on the harem." She made a face after the term escaped. "I really hate using that word."

"And yet it's the most accurate one." I managed a smile as Hunter joined us in the lobby. "Thanks for coming to help. I know you're busy."

"We're all busy, and helping is what we do." Bay turned her attention to Hunter. "Get her to bed. She needs rest."

"That's the plan." Hunter slipped his arm around my shoulders. "We'll see you tomorrow, right?"

Bay nodded without hesitation. "Definitely."

THE SECOND WE GOT HOME, I RACED into the kitchen, looking for Krankle. If he'd managed to make his way back to the restaurant, he would likely be waiting there, disgruntled and starving. The kitchen was empty, though, with no sign of him. His bowl sat empty, and his usual spot on the couch was vacant.

"He'll show up, Stormy," Hunter said in a low voice, appearing behind me.

"What if he doesn't?"

"He will."

"You can say that all you want," I groused. "That doesn't make it true, though. We may never see him again."

"I don't believe that." Hunter wrapped his arms around me from behind and nudged me toward the sliding glass door so I could look out on the storage building and trees. "Do you know what's funny?"

"Romantic comedies?" I was going for levity, but my voice sounded flat.

He chuckled anyway as he gripped me tighter. "If you had asked me if I was okay with the cat dying twenty-four hours ago, I would've said yes."

I battled tears.

"Now, though, knowing he willingly risked himself for you, I can't help feeling this sense of loss."

I jerked my chin to look into his eyes. "That's exactly how I feel."

"I know, baby." His lips curved up, but he wasn't amused. His fingers gently brushed my hair away from my face. "It's okay to be conflicted. The cat has been a menace since he revealed the truth about himself. He's mouthy, opinionated, and secretive."

"And yet he saved me," I whispered.

"And yet he saved you." Hunter rested his cheek against my temple. "I'll give him eight cans of tuna when he gets back. I might even turn on the heater thing he loves so much and point it at him when he's sleeping."

Unexpected laughter bubbled up, unbidden. "I miss him, and I didn't think I would."

"I miss him too. At least I think I do."

"Can I ask you something?"

He nodded without hesitation. "Always."

"Do you ever worry that you'll come to hate this life? I mean ... this is not what you signed on for. When we met, none of this was part of your life."

"When we got together again as adults, I knew all of it. I don't regret one single moment of our time together. I won't regret it going forward either. I need you to have a little faith. Things are hard for you right now. Your ego took a bruising before you came home. If you can't have faith in yourself, though, have faith in me."

I swallowed hard. "I've always had faith in you."

"I'm not sure that's true. You did take off and leave me after high school."

My mouth dropped open. "I thought you let that go."

My outrage was apparently funny because he broke into a wide grin. "There she is." He leaned in and pressed a kiss to the corner of my mouth. When he pulled back, his eyes twinkled. "I did let it go. I believe things worked out how they were supposed to. Yes, we had some hard times, but I'm grateful for every moment I'm with you because this is how things are supposed to be."

I went warm all over at his earnestness. "Yeah."

"That means this was supposed to happen with Krankle too." Hunter was firm. "He'll show up when you least expect it. He's going to be fine."

"I hope so."

"And when he does show up, he'll give us the information he's been holding out on." Hunter's tone was icy. "Enough is enough. I feel he's been trying to protect you in some respects. I also feel he's done a poor job. We need to start working together."

I exhaled heavily and let my gaze slide back to the dark expanse behind the restaurant. "I really hope we get the chance to grill him."

"We will. Have a little faith."

"I have faith in you. My faith in myself and others is a work in progress."

"Then lean on me, Stormy. That's why I'm here. If you have bad dreams tonight, wake me. I want to be there for you."

It was a sweet offer. "I might take you up on that." I squeezed his hand. "I need to watch something mindless before bed, though. Like, I need a palette cleanser."

"That can be arranged." He nudged me toward the couch. "Which bad sitcom would you like to watch this evening?"

I considered it for longer than I expected. "Let's go with the *Big Bang Theory*," I said finally. "If Sheldon can't clear out my dreams, then nobody can."

"I think that is a great idea. The *Big Bang Theory* it is."

I DIDN'T THINK I WOULD BE ABLE TO fall asleep. I was too keyed up. Apparently, pot roast and cuddles were enough to kick me into a virtual coma, however. Somehow, I fell asleep without realizing it, and I didn't stir when Hunter carried me to the bedroom. I was down for the count—until Kyle found me in my dreams.

"What are you doing here?" I demanded when I arrived at the dreamscape Dead Man's Hill overlook and found him studying the landscape. Just like in reality, it was stark and cold because all the leaves had fallen for the season.

"I wondered if you would come back here." Kyle was all smiles as he turned to face me. "You are a predictable little thing, aren't you?"

I glowered at him. "What do you want?"

"I want to go back in time and reclaim my truck. Do you know what a pain it will be to get that thing back?"

I snorted. "Good luck with that."

"Oh, look at you." Kyle swung his hips and did a little dance. "You feel pretty good about yourself, don't you?"

"I *do* feel pretty good about myself." My smile didn't diminish. "I outsmarted you."

"Only because that mongrel sacrificed himself to give you an out."

A lump formed in my throat, and I had to fight off tears. "Did you kill him?"

A slow smile spread across Kyle's features. "Wouldn't you like to know?"

"Where is he?" Frustration grabbed me by the throat. "What did you do with him?"

"What makes you think I did anything?" Kyle's smile disappeared. "I don't suppose you've considered the possibility that he's the real danger to you, have you?"

Is he joking? "No. I haven't—and will never—consider that. He's not the one who followed me into the woods. That was you. He's not the one who threatened me. That was you."

"He is the one who entered your life under the guise of being a helpless animal," Kyle shot back. "He's pretty far from being that, isn't he?"

Kyle was trying to manipulate me. I refused to let it happen. "I don't care what you say about him. I trust him a heckuva lot more than I trust you. By the way, the Winchesters know about you. By tomorrow, Scout will too. You won't be welcome in any of the places you were so keen to infiltrate."

Kyle's eyes narrowed. "Is that how you plan to win? You'll alienate people from me, so they don't buy chicken strips? What a delightful plan." He gave a pronounced eye roll.

"Is winning what this is about?" I demanded. "I would like to know what I'm supposed to win before playing the game."

"You're not ready for that yet." Kyle looked smug. "You're growing in leaps and bounds—nobody expected you to progress this fast—but some things are still beyond your level of comprehension."

"Is that an insult?" I demanded.

"No. It's merely fact. You might have been born into this world, but you're coming up woefully short in the witch department. On one hand, your powers are progressing very quickly. Unfortunately for us, your mental game is lagging."

"If that's your way of calling me stupid, I really don't care. I'm a big proponent of that sticks-and-stones thing."

Kyle snorted. "I do like your mouth. Goddess help me, you're quick and witty. That will be the end of you if you're not careful."

"Yeah, that message might hold more stock if I hadn't met the Winchesters first. They're all mouthy and thriving."

"You are not a Winchester."

The simple statement landed like a punch to the gut, but I didn't respond.

"They are a different breed," he continued. "Do I wish you'd never met them? Yes. They will make your development difficult. You cannot compare yourself to them, however. Your path will be different."

"How so?"

"Do you want to know?" Kyle's enigmatic smile reappeared. "I'm more than willing to tell you if you join my cause. No more working against me."

"So, basically you want me to pledge myself to you."

"Not in a gross way or anything," Kyle replied. "Like, I don't expect sexual favors. Well, unless you want to bestow them upon me."

I glared at him. "You're disgusting. For the record, I will never join your cause."

"Never is a mighty long time. You shouldn't issue promises you have no ability to keep. You will join our faction, whether you like it or not."

"I won't."

"You will."

"No, I won't." I knew that beyond a shadow of a doubt. "I've already chosen my side. It's Hunter and Bay and Tillie and Scout."

Kyle grimaced at the mention of Scout. "You'll want to steer clear of the pixie witch. She's gearing up for trouble."

"And I'll be right there with her if she needs me. The only person who won't be there is you."

Kyle scowled. "You're making a big mistake."

"Maybe from your point of view. From mine, this was the only option I had. I won't take your side."

"I guess we'll have to wait and see if that's true."

"I guess we will."

I WOKE BEFORE HUNTER. HE SNORED LIGHTLY from his spot next to me, but I didn't wake him. I stepped lightly when I climbed out of the bed and hurried to the kitchen.

I didn't expect to find Krankle there. No, really. He would've woken me the second he got home and demanded tuna. Still, a small part of me had hoped he'd been so exhausted he'd curled up on the couch to take a nap. I planned to shower him with as much tuna as he could eat, but he was nowhere to be found.

"He'll turn up, Stormy," Hunter said from behind me when I moved to look out the sliding glass doors. "He might have thought it was a bad idea to travel after dark. That's when the bigger predators come out."

I made a face. "I don't want to hear about predators."

"I know you don't." Hunter's hands landed on my shoulders. "It's possible he's still out there. I've been thinking about it, and from his perspective, it might make more sense to hunker down."

"So, he was out there freezing to death all night?" I was horrified. "That doesn't make me feel better."

Despite the serious nature of our conversation, Hunter let loose a chuckle. "You're too much sometimes. Have I mentioned that?"

"Maybe a few times."

"Well, it's true." He kissed my cheek. "He won't have frozen, Stormy. He's got fur. Cats survive much colder temperatures than we saw last night. He's got magic too. If he's out there, he's fine."

"Why would he stay out, though?" That's what I couldn't wrap my head around. "Why didn't he go up the hill and wait for me at the car?"

"He might not have known your plan. He also might've panicked. He knows you'll come looking for him, though. He's been around you long enough to gauge how you react. If I were him, I would lie low and wait for you to come back with reinforcements."

"What if he expected me last night?"

"I don't think he did. He would consider trying to find him after dark a mistake. He'll have found a spot to sleep, a place that's warm enough and safe enough, and he'll be waiting for you today."

I wanted to believe that. "What if he's not out there? Honestly, the not knowing is worse than knowing."

"I get that, but we can't give up hope yet. We'll find him when we go out there."

It was the "we'll" that threw me. "You're coming with me?" I glanced over my shoulder, unable to hide my surprise.

"Absolutely, and for multiple reasons."

A smile tugged at my lips. "Oh yeah? Tell me these reasons."

"Well, for starters, having an official presence with you if Kyle shows up and decides to make noise about his truck is a good idea. Also, I'm armed. I can shoot him if he decides to rush us."

"I very much doubt he's still out there." I thought of the dream. "I'm sure he either hiked out or someone came for him."

"Yeah, I've wondered about that too." Hunter was grim. "I think it's unlikely he's working alone."

"I agree."

"You need me with you out there," Hunter insisted. "You and Bay will be working a spell. I'll watch your backs when you do it. The smartest move is for me to be with you."

Since I'd screwed up the previous day and had gone out with only Krankle's support, I didn't offer up a fight. "I think that's probably a smart move."

"Good."

"Getting through a shift with my grandfather first will be torturous."

"Yes, well, we all have our crosses to bear."

I smirked. "Is it wrong that I hope someone orders poached eggs? It will be a relief for somebody else to have a meltdown."

"Who knows? Maybe you'll get your wish."

"Yeah. I could use a mental break."

"Soon, baby. We'll get the cat back, deal with Edmund, and smite Kyle like Tillie wants. Then you can get your break."

That sounded like a lot of stuff to fit in before I got my reward. "I'm going to hit the shower."

"I'll go with you. I want to do as much as possible at the office this morning before we head out to Dead Man's Hill."

"No funny business in the shower," I warned.

"I can refrain. Well, maybe."

I smiled genuinely. "There's a first time for everything, right?"

"That's the spirit."

TWENTY-TWO

I tried to hide how down I felt when I joined Grandpa in the kitchen, going immediately to the coffee filters to stack them. He worked quietly in front of the grill, for a change, but I felt his eyes on me.

"You're not fighting with Hunter or anything, are you?" he asked finally.

I glanced at him and shook my head. "No. Hunter and I are good."

"Your car isn't here."

It was only then that I remembered we'd left my vehicle at the police station. "I met him at the station last night. We drove together to Hemlock Cove for dinner. I forgot all about it. I'll have to pick it up later."

"You went to Hemlock Cove?" Grandpa's expression was inscrutable. "That's not a good thing, right?"

He knew about the witch stuff. He didn't understand it, but on a basic level, he knew I was getting dragged deeper and deeper into a separate world from the one where he resided. I debated how much I should tell him and ultimately decided that cutting him out of the information entirely was a bad idea.

"I went over to Dead Man's Hill yesterday," I started. "I got a tip that Edmund's harem had been sighted out there a few days ago and wanted to check it out."

"If this is going to get weird, I don't want to hear it."

I ignored his grumpy face. "You don't need to know what I found there. Suffice it to say, it wasn't good. Those women are definitely up to something."

"I could've told you that."

"What's important for you to know is that Kyle followed me."

Grandpa froze in front of the grill, a spatula gripped tightly in his hand. "Did he hurt you?"

"No, but I think he wanted to. Unfortunately for him, I know that area better. I made a run for it and hid in a spot I remembered from when I was a kid. When he went looking for me down by the creek, I ran up the hill."

"Obviously you made it."

"I did."

"Where is he?"

"We don't know. Hunter sent some of his fellow officers out to take a look. His truck was still there, thanks to me, but he was nowhere to be found."

"Thanks to you?" Grandpa's eyes gleamed with curiosity. "What did you do to the truck?"

"I'm not entirely sure." I let loose a baffled laugh. "He left it unlocked, so I popped the hood and did as much damage as I could in two minutes. He was heading up the hill when I stopped to check, so I just left him there."

"That was smart." Grandpa nodded knowingly. "I might have waited for him to get to the top of the hill and run him over, though."

"I didn't want to risk that. I just wanted to get away."

"Well, good." Grandpa was grim. "I'll call Northridge Farms and make sure they understand he will not be my rep going forward. Of course, he'll probably be in jail by the end of the day, if I know Hunter."

"He has to find Kyle first. We don't know where he is. If Kyle's smart, he won't show up for work. Hunter couldn't find a real person to go with his name, so I'm guessing Kyle is in the wind. The Winchesters know about him, though. They're cutting him loose too."

"Well, that's just ... unbelievable." Grandpa slammed the spatula against the counter, catching me by surprise. "What the hell was he thinking? What did he want?"

"I'm not sure. It happened very fast. I decided not to hang around and ask questions, though I really wanted the answers. It was a fluid situation, and I went with my gut."

"You should always go with your gut, kid." Grandpa shook his head. His temper was a thing to behold. "That guy better hope I don't see him again. I'll be the one running him over."

My grandfather wasn't known for his driving prowess, so I could see that happening. "Once my shift is over, we're heading down there again. Hunter will be with us."

"I'm guessing the Winchesters are part of the 'us' you're referring to."

"They are."

"Well then, kick his ass." Grandpa's smile was feral. "I hope he cries when you're done with him."

I didn't have the heart to tell him we weren't actually looking for Kyle. Edmund was our first order of business. I returned his smile anyway. "That's the plan."

AN HOUR LATER, THE CAFÉ SECTION bustled with activity. That wasn't out of the ordinary—but Blanche, Gwen, Florence, and Iris deciding to join the party was, and none of them sat at the same table.

Annie joined me at the swinging doors to survey the people taking over the restaurant. "I see the old biddies are here. That's weird, huh? They almost never come in."

I had a feeling I was the reason they'd decided to change their routine. I didn't share that with Annie, though. "Yeah. I've interacted with them a few times since Edmund died. They're ... a lot of work."

"Do you want me to wait on them? You can take the diner section today. I'll handle the café."

"Are you sure?" Annie looked surprised. "You usually like when you have the diner section because the café doesn't get many tips."

She wasn't wrong, but I had other things on my mind than money for a change. "It's fine. As a trade-off, though, I need to get out of here as close to eleven o'clock as possible. My car is at the police station, and I'm meeting some friends for a hike."

Annie's eyebrows pushed together. "Since when do you hike?"

"It's a new thing I'm trying out," I lied. "I'm hoping to get in better shape."

"Okay, but why would you start hiking so close to the first snow? You won't be able to keep it up. It makes more sense to pick it up in the spring. You should try CrossFit or something."

"I'll take that into consideration." I grabbed a pot of coffee from the warmer. "I'll handle the old biddies, as you so eloquently called them. I just need to get out of here on time today."

"That shouldn't be a problem."

"Good."

I was all smiles as I approached Florence first. She sat at a table with two other women I recognized from the senior center. She didn't greet me as I approached, but I could feel her interest from a mile away.

"Good morning, ladies," I trilled. "Does everybody know what they want? Is it just coffee or breakfast?"

Jackie Dombrowski, who sat across from Florence, looked up from her menu. "Are the poached eggs still recalled?"

I could've said no. Grandpa was spoiling for a fight. I didn't want to set off an explosion, though. "Unfortunately, yes. It's the darndest thing."

Florence made a face. "How are poached eggs recalled? If something's wrong with the eggs, they would all be recalled."

I shot her a pointed look. "You'll have to talk to the chef if you want the answer. I'm just the messenger."

"Whatever." Florence rolled her eyes. "I'll have a fried egg sandwich and coffee."

I nodded. "And you, Jackie?"

"I need a minute."

I focused on the last person at the table, Minnie Carruthers. I barely knew her, but I'd never considered her difficult. "How about you?"

"I'm just having coffee this morning," she replied. "I ate before I left the house."

"Okay." I flashed a smile I didn't feel and waited for Jackie. To fill the silence, I flicked my eyes to Florence. "How are you feeling after Edmund's death? Are you still shaken?"

"Why would I care about him?" she shot back. "I barely knew him."

I considered playing the game according to her rules, but I wasn't in the mood to kowtow to her crabby whims. "That's not what everybody else in the neighborhood says."

"Oh, really?" Florence turned haughty. "And what does everybody else say?"

"That you were sleeping with him." Even I didn't expect I would blurt it out that way.

Florence's eyes went wide, and her jaw swung in the breeze with surprise at my fortitude. "Who said that?" she managed finally.

"Everybody," I replied. "I don't think anybody in town is unaware of your relationship with Edmund."

"Well, they're lying."

"Uh-huh. I'm sure they're lying about Iris, Blanche, and Gwen too."

Florence's eyes narrowed to slits of hate. "Did your grandmother tell you that nonsense? I'll sue her! She's such a gossip."

"My grandmother hasn't gossiped about you." That was a lie. My grandmother loved little more than gossiping about Florence, but it didn't matter. "The rest of the town, though, they're another story."

If Florence hadn't hated me before—which she had—she downright loathed me after that. "On second thought, I think I'll have the poached eggs and toast," she said pointedly.

"Okay. Expect a visit from my grandfather shortly."

I offered a sweet smile and took Jackie's order, then moved on to Iris's table. She was with a woman I didn't recognize.

"Are you guys having breakfast or just coffee?" I asked.

"Just coffee." Iris's expression lit with intrigue as she studied my face. "I saw you over there with Flo. Was she being difficult? She always is. You should just ignore her."

"Oh, she was just being Flo." I kept my face impassive. "She was upset because, apparently, everybody in town is talking about you guys fighting over Edmund. I don't know why she's so surprised about the gossip. You guys didn't exactly fly under the radar with your antics."

Iris might've been trying a different tack with me, but her fury was palpable when her smile disappeared. "And exactly who is talking about us?"

"Everybody in town. It was one of those open secrets." I let loose an empty laugh. "What I'm most curious about is how he managed to keep up with you all. That must have required a lot of Viagra. When you combine it with the Replens everybody's talked about, I bet the pharmacy loved you guys." Trying to be pleasant hadn't gotten me anywhere, so I went for purposely obnoxious to push her buttons.

"You shut your mouth," Iris hissed. "You don't even know what you're talking about."

"Okay then."

"I want poached eggs and whole wheat toast," Iris said out of nowhere.

The triumphant gleam in her eyes said she thought she was winning. Well, I had news for her. When Grandpa got the orders, he wouldn't care in the least that she wore an invisible tiara and puffed herself out like a haughty cat.

"Sure." I nodded. "Expect a visit from my grandfather."

I hit up Gwen next, who sat with five other women. For some reason, she seemed to enjoy her status as the harem member with the most friends. "Are those old goats giving you a hard time?" she trilled when I arrived with my order pad. "They're unpleasant. They can't help themselves. They've never been what I would call people persons."

"I can see that." I flashed an engaging smile. "You've been hanging around with them, though. I mean, you guys pretend you're not friends, and yet people have seen you out at Dead Man's Hill together. It seems strange that mortal enemies would be out there hiking as a group."

Whatever Gwen expected, that wasn't it. Her face drained of color, and she gripped the edge of the table hard enough that her knuckles turned white. "Who told you that?"

"I can't recall," I lied. "Were you guys trying to make nice with each other? I know the whole Edmund thing threw you. Losing him had to be hard. With him gone, though, you have no reason to keep competing with one another, right?"

Gwen worked her jaw. "I don't know what you've heard..."

"Oh, everybody in town is talking about the arrangement you guys had with Edmund." Even Edmund was still talking about it, but I couldn't bring that up, given the café's mixed company. "It sounds like it was a lot of work. You guys must be relieved now that he's gone."

Gwen made a protesting sound with her tongue. "You don't know what you're talking about, girl. If your grandmother is filling your head with lies, she needs to stop. A man died. Sure, he wasn't a good man, but he deserves some respect."

"Okay. Just out of curiosity, though, will you guys fight over who gets to dramatically throw themselves on top of the casket?"

"Shut your mouth!" Gwen barked, clearly at the end of her rope. "I'm here for breakfast, not a bunch of nonsense gossip."

"That seems fair." I kept my voice level. "What do you want for breakfast?"

"Poached eggs." Her upper lip curled into a sneer.

Obviously, my grandfather's aversion to cooking poached eggs had made the rounds, but if they thought they were torturing me with their orders, they had another thing coming.

"Do you want toast with that?"

"What do you think?"

I took the rest of the table's orders—thankfully, none of the other women were stupid enough to order poached eggs—then I hit up the final harem member. Blanche occupied a table by herself, but the coy looks she kept tossing the men drinking coffee one table over told me it was a strategic move.

"Are you going to order poached eggs too?" I asked her.

"I don't know." Blanche tapped her fingers on the tabletop and glanced between Gwen, Iris, and Florence. "Did they order poached eggs?"

It occurred to me that she was only asking as part of their competition. "They did."

"They sounded angry."

"They're mad because I asked them about the gossip."

"What gossip?" Blanche leaned forward, her flirty intentions with the men forgotten. "What have you heard?"

"Just that the four of you regularly played tickle games with Edmund. It was some competition or something. Oh, and that you were all seen together down at Dead Man's Hill the other day. The townsfolk are suggesting it's a sign of the apocalypse, but I'm guessing it's something else."

"Oh, yeah?" Blanche was clearly thrown. "And what do you think it is?"

"I don't know yet. I plan to find out, though. Do you want toast with your poached eggs?"

"I do. And coffee."

"Great." I jotted down her order, offered up a saccharine smile, then headed toward the kitchen.

Grandpa was waiting in front of the grill when I arrived with the order tickets. "I'm about to hate you, aren't I?"

"I think it's more likely that you're going to hate Blanche, Florence, Iris, and Gwen."

"Poached eggs?"

"Yup, and it was on purpose. They all did it as some form of a game."

"Well, I'll show them." Grandpa stormed out from behind the metal counter. "I don't know who they think they are, but this is my restaurant. I'll die before I cook them poached eggs."

I smiled as he disappeared through the swinging doors and cringed when he exploded, his voice echoing through all three sections of the restaurant. I couldn't make out everything he said through his anger. Annie's eyes were wide when she scurried into the kitchen from the dining room side. She looked terrified.

"Why didn't you tell them the poached eggs were recalled?"

I shrugged. "I kind of wanted to see what would happen."

"If Grandpa has a heart attack because of all the yelling, will you be as amused?"

"Probably not, but I'm sure he's fine. Yelling is his cardio." I slid over to the swinging doors to get a look. The harem members didn't look nearly as smug as they had when they'd sent me to the kitchen with the orders. "What do you know about their relationships with Edmund?" I asked when Annie joined me.

"Only that everybody in town made jokes about it," Annie replied. "Why? Do you think one of them killed him?"

"That's my guess. I just don't know which one. They were all capable."

"If they were sleeping with him, why would they kill him? Shouldn't they have wanted to appease him?"

"Maybe, but it was never about love. It was about winning. Someone decided the only way to win was to take him away from the others."

"If you had to choose right now, which one would you go for?"

"I honestly have no idea. They're all equally terrible." I moved back from the doors as Grandpa stomped in.

"They've wisely changed their orders to scrambled eggs," he announced.

I wasn't surprised. "I guess you won today."

"I win every day."

I grinned. "How much do you want to bet they're already plotting revenge?"

"Like I care." Grandpa grabbed a bowl to whisk the eggs. "All I care about is that I won."

I could see that. "I'll take the coffee around. Let me know when their orders are up. I expect a different sort of explosion when I hit up their tables again."

Grandpa's eyes narrowed. "You riled them up on purpose."

"I am your granddaughter."

That earned a chuckle. "I don't know what the goal is here, but I hope you're the next one who wins."

"If I win, we all win."

"Then I definitely want you to win."

TWENTY-THREE

Hunter arranged to have my car dropped off at the restaurant. He was ready and eager when Bay, Tillie, and Evan showed up for our foray into the woods.

"That's a lot of magic stuff," Hunter noted when he saw the bags Evan carried. "You won't set the woods on fire, will you?"

Tillie made a face. "I'm a professional. Do you think I set things on fire?"

Bay shot her a dubious look.

"When I do, it's on purpose," Tillie snapped at her great-niece. "I have no reason to set anything on fire today."

"If you say so."

We took Hunter's truck. Evan sat in the front with him, leaving the three females to look through Tillie's bags of tricks during the drive. When we arrived at the scenic overlook, Bay was alert. The way she scanned the area told me she was looking for Kyle. To nobody's surprise, he wasn't there.

"I talked to the manager at Northridge Farms today," Hunter volunteered. "He said that Kyle is no longer employed by them and acted shocked that none of the application's information was correct. The manager swore he planned to look into it, but I'm pretty sure they didn't bother checking the references."

"Does it matter now?" I asked. "He's gone."

"I very much doubt he's given up," Evan argued. "He didn't follow you all the way out here, chase you, and try to get you on his side simply to throw in the towel after one loss."

"But how would he get close?"

"One thing I've learned about evil monsters is that they're willing to think outside the box." Bay grunted as she hefted one of Tillie's bags out of the truck. "Seriously? What's in here?"

"Anything I thought I might need," Tillie replied as Hunter helped her out of the truck. "Don't give me grief. You'll be glad I have that stuff before it's all said and done."

Bay looked unconvinced, but she didn't argue either. Hunter took the bag from her and slung it over his shoulder. Evan took the second bag. Then we started for the incline.

"Why don't you hold onto me?" Evan suggested to Tillie when he saw the steep hill.

The look she shot him promised mayhem if he persisted. "Are you suggesting I can't walk down a hill myself?"

Evan didn't hesitate. "This hill? Yes."

"Well, I've got it." With a great deal of determination, Tillie started to descend.

On a sigh, Evan followed. He matched his pace to hers, and when her legs started to go out from under her—it was inevitable as far as I was concerned—he wrapped his left arm around her waist and anchored her at his side.

"I'm not a bag of potatoes!" Tillie groused as he carried her down the hill. "Just what do you think you're doing? I can walk myself."

When I glanced at Bay, I found her grinning.

"It'll be even worse when we have to go back up," I said.

Bay merely shrugged. "She'll survive."

At the bottom of the hill, Evan put Tillie back on her feet. He lifted his nose, scenting the air, and when he glanced back at me, he looked intrigued. "I smell a cat."

I started forward immediately and yelled Krankle's name. I held my breath, waiting for him. *Please be here. Please be here.* But he didn't emerge from the underbrush.

"We'll look for him," Hunter promised as he shifted closer. "Take us to where the pentagram is. While Bay and Tillie are determining what we're dealing with, I'll help you search for Krankle."

"I will too," Evan offered. "I don't think he's far away. His scent is strong."

"Could that be because he died?" I asked around a lump in my throat.

"I don't smell death, Stormy," Evan assured me. "Let's just tackle this one step at a time. Pentagram first."

I nodded. That made sense. I motioned for them to follow me. "This way."

It only took a few minutes to reach the pentagram, and as soon as Tillie saw it, she hissed and arranged her hand as if preparing for claws to spring forth.

"That's her Wolverine stance," Bay explained. "She's about to say something weird."

"It's dark magic," Tillie announced. "The type that will take your innards and twist them into a bow before they explode, causing you to die a painful death. Also, I never say anything weird."

"Right." Bay shook her head and circled the pentagram. She didn't move close enough to touch it, but she looked intent. "What's that smell?"

"Fire," I said. "I noticed that when I was out here earlier."

"No, something's underneath it." She leaned over and sniffed. "What is that?"

"It's several things," Tillie replied.

"You can barely smell yourself when you've gone three days without a shower," Bay argued.

"Hey!" Tillie's eyes flashed hot. "I have an excellent sniffer. I could be a professional police search dog, I'm so good."

"Yeah, yeah, yeah." Bay turned to Evan. "What do you smell?"

The vampire closed his eyes and lifted his nose. "Basil."

"That's used in protection spells," Tillie volunteered. "It can also be in love spells. People use it when they want to bring someone back."

I filed that away to think about later.

"Bay leaves," Evan added.

"They're a symbol of power and life," Bay explained. "They're also used for love spells."

It figured she would know that.

"Clove," Evan supplied.

"Clove can bring back lost love," Tillie mused. "Rosemary too. Do you smell that?"

Evan sniffed again, then nodded. "I smell hints of rosemary—and something else." He opened his eyes and nudged one of the branches with his foot. Then he bent to retrieve an object. When he straightened, he had what looked like a scorched flower herb.

"That's vervain." Tillie shifted closer. "It's used in protection spells. Like ... if someone wanted to protect their house or heart, they would use vervain."

"There's one more thing." Evan darted forward and grabbed another burned weed. "Lady's mantle?" he asked Tillie as he held it up.

"Very good." Tillie beamed. "You're coming along nicely."

"I actually learned that one from Scout," Evan replied. "People believe lady's mantle can prolong life."

"So, what exactly were they doing out here?" Hunter asked. "If all of them were together, what did they hope to do?"

"I have a few theories," Bay replied. "One involves protecting Edmund's soul so it wouldn't pass on."

"Is that possible?" I asked.

"Almost anything is possible if you're determined enough," Bay replied. "Why the pentagram, though?"

"The pentagram has had many meanings throughout history," Evan replied. "The Christians, for example, used it at one time to signify the five wounds of Christ. It was also the symbol of Jerusalem for a century and a half. For our purposes, however, I think the answer is much simpler. The pentagram is tied to the occult in this day and age. It has five points, and if you include your victim, your unholy harem relationship has five participants."

I jolted. "I would not have figured that out myself."

"We don't know if that's the reason. They could've opted for the pentagram because they didn't know any better. It's just a possibility."

"Well, it makes sense."

Tillie studied the pentagram for a few more seconds, then stalked toward the bag Hunter had placed on the ground. "It's amateurs," she insisted. "They aren't real witches."

"These fake witches somehow managed to enact a real spell," Bay countered. "How? One of them has to have access to real magic."

"Not necessarily," Tillie fired back. "Margaret managed to cast a spell, and she doesn't have a magical bone in her body."

"She got hoodwinked with a cursed coin. That's different."

"What if one of these women has a cursed object and doesn't realize it?" Tillie countered. "Isn't that just as possible as anything else?"

Bay opened her mouth, likely to argue, then snapped it shut. "That makes sense, I guess. I don't know if I'm ready to jump on that train, but I'll grant you that it's possible."

Tillie beamed. "Good girl."

"Oh, whatever."

Bay crossed her arms over her chest and watched as Tillie removed things from her bag. The potions I expected. The handcuffs I did not.

"Don't bother asking," Evan interjected when I prepared to voice my question. "You don't want to know."

That was fair. At least I thought so.

"Okay." Tillie came back with a potion. "Let's see what this does, huh?" Before anyone could respond, she threw the potion on the pentagram and watched with overt curiosity as purple flames erupted. They didn't consume the wood like a normal fire would. Instead, images appeared in the flames.

"What is that?" I dropped to my knees to get a better look.

"It's a truth spell." Bay joined me, almost looking impressed as she glanced at Tillie. "What made you think to throw a truth spell on a bunch of wood?"

"I'm wily," Tillie replied, not missing a beat. "Just because the wood isn't sentient doesn't mean it can't access certain memories."

"I would think that's exactly what it means," Evan argued.

"Not necessarily," Bay replied. "It's not the wood that has the memory, but the magic."

"What do you see?" Hunter's hand landed on my back. "I'm not sure I see anything."

"It's images," I replied. "It's ... fragments. I think it's whatever happened out here. Like, right there." I jabbed my finger toward a face. "That's Blanche. I recognize her."

"What about the others?" Bay queried. "Do you recognize them?"

I concentrated hard, then nodded. "That's Iris and Florence."

"They look to be arguing," Evan noted.

"That's all they do," Hunter replied.

"Except that's not all they do," I interjected. "They obviously did something else together."

"What, though?" Bay rocked back on her haunches, thoughtful. "Whatever spell they cast has to do with Edmund. He's not a normal ghost."

"Could you call him here?" I asked. "You've done that before."

"It's worth a shot." She smiled.

Before she could engage her magic, however, Evan turned his back to us, facing the bushes. He extended his hands, as if preparing for an enemy, and I braced myself for Kyle to appear. Instead, the creature that burst from the bushes was small—cat sized, to be exact.

Krankle's eyes were wide. Weird burrs clung to his fur, and he seemed to be running for his life. Though cats were supposed to be graceful, Krankle couldn't stop his forward momentum, and he skidded into the flaming truth spell.

"No!" I reached for him, but Bay shot out a hand to stop me.

"Wait," she commanded.

The cat went rigid the second he hit the spell. He didn't catch fire. He didn't burn. He did change, though.

Slowly, as if from a horror movie scene, the cat began to elongate. He grew. First doubling, then tripling, then he was human sized. He was no longer a cat, though. His fur disappeared, as did his claws as a man took his place—a very hot, very naked man. The former cat sputtered as he pitched forward, hands and feet replacing paws. Whiskers transformed to stubble. The same wild look that had been in the cat's eyes belonged to the man.

"What in the hell?" he demanded. That was Krankle's voice. It was a man, but he sounded like my cat.

"That was going to be my reaction." Evan cast the man a dubious look.

"Holy crap!" Tillie clapped her hands, seemingly delighted. "Somebody see if they can find a raccoon. I've always wanted a human raccoon." She cocked her head and looked at Krankle's penis. "I wonder if he would be as well endowed."

Bay nudged her great-aunt and focused on the man. "Hello," she said calmly. "Do you know your name?"

Krankle gave her a dark look. "Yes, and I know yours, too, Bay. What just happened?"

"We should be asking you that." Evan looked more intrigued than worried. "Is this what you look like when you're in gnome form? Because not to embrace stereotypes or anything, but I thought gnomes were supposed to be shorter."

"And have bad butts," Tillie agreed. "If you're the exception to the rule, I have to say, good job." She shot him a thumbs-up as she eyed his well-muscled rear and licked her lips. "Does anybody have a quarter? I want to see if I can bounce it off that behind."

"Knock it off!" Krankle roared. "I need to know what happened." He turned quickly and studied the still-roaring flames. "What is that?"

"A truth spell." The way Bay looked Krankle up and down told me that she was figuring things out. "You ran through a truth spell and came out looking ... like that."

"That means he's truly that gifted in the penis department." Tillie gleefully rubbed her hands together. "This is the best thing ever. Somebody find me that raccoon."

"Knock it off." Bay didn't look at her great-aunt. She was too fixated on Krankle. "Is this your human form?"

Krankle glanced down at his body, then shrugged. "I guess so."

"You guess so?" Bay challenged. "Shouldn't you know?"

"My form varies given the plane I'm on. Eventually, I was supposed to shift to a human. It wasn't supposed to happen yet, though."

"When was it supposed to happen?" I asked, genuinely curious.

"When your magic matured but not yet. Just ... not yet." He slapped his hand to his forehead. "Could this day get any worse?"

"I don't know," Tillie replied. "How opposed are you to me squeezing your butt?"

"No!" Krankle wagged a finger in her face.

He looked frustrated. I couldn't blame him. Nobody had expected that outcome.

"Have you been out here all night?" I asked.

"I knew you would come back," Krankle said mournfully. "I could've walked back, but that would've been a haul. I didn't want to risk being hit by a car or picked up by some seven-year-old kid who wanted to name me Whiskers and make me drink from a bottle. I figured it was best to wait."

"Well, yeah." I averted my gaze because it kept going to his crotch. "What are we supposed to do here?"

"I think we take him back to your place," Bay replied.

"Oh, sure." I threw up my hands. "That sounds like a great idea. How am I supposed to explain a naked guy living in my apartment?"

"I think you can get him some clothes," Bay replied. "I mean ... no rule stipulates that you have to be naked, right?" she asked Krankle.

"That would be a great rule," Tillie enthused.

"Clothes would be wonderful," Krankle replied.

"Ooh. I have something." Tillie darted to the second bag and came back with what looked to be a superhero cape and a scarf. "You can wear the scarf like a diaper, and the cape will keep you warm until we get back to the restaurant."

Krankle eyed the items with obvious distaste.

"It's that or climb the hill naked." Hunter didn't look remotely happy about the turn of events. "Unless ... can you change back into a cat?" He seemed hopeful.

"I have no idea." Krankle sounded morose. "This wasn't supposed to happen. Not for months. I—this is not good. Do you have any idea how not good this is?"

"You could tell us," Bay suggested. "I mean, if your plan is shot to hell anyway, you have no reason to be shifty now. I think we need to put all our cards on the table, don't you?"

Krankle was clearly exasperated. "You know what, I've had the worst twenty-four hours of my life, and that's saying something because I was a grunt in the Gnome Wars for eight years. I need to get out of here. I need something to eat. I need to not be hunted by a coyote. That's what I need."

He was so screechy, I almost didn't recognize his voice. Upon thinking about it, however, I realized he must be in shock. The best thing for him was to take him back and feed him.

"Then let's head home," I said. "We'll get you upstairs without anybody noticing." How we would do that was beyond me. "We'll get you fed. Then you need to start talking." I was firm on that.

"I just want to get out of here." Krankle grudgingly took the scarf and cape. "Stop looking at my butt," he ordered Tillie as he tried to make sense of the scarf. "It's undignified."

"Then you should have a worse butt," Tillie replied.

"I'm not a piece of meat!"

"No, but you have an interesting piece of meat hanging—" Tillie scowled when Bay lightly cuffed the back of her head to shut her up. "You're on my list," Tillie warned.

"Somehow, I think that's preferable to you finishing that sentence," Bay snapped. "Now, come on. Let's help Krankle maintain some modesty and get up that hill. After that, we'll figure it out."

I hoped she was right because all I had were questions, and the answers felt increasingly out of reach.

TWENTY-FOUR

The ride home was tense. We put Krankle in the front seat next to Hunter because he was still mostly naked, and the rest of us crammed into the backseat. Hunter kept casting sidelong looks toward the former cat, but he didn't say anything. When we arrived at the restaurant, Bay grabbed Tillie before she could follow us inside.

"I think we should let Stormy and Hunter deal with this for tonight," she said pointedly.

Tillie's mouth dropped open. "Are you kidding me? I just made a human being out of thin air. That means I get to be involved."

"That's not what you did," Bay said firmly. "We're going home." She switched her gaze to me. "Call me tomorrow when you know more, and we'll figure things out."

I nodded, secretly relieved. I loved Tillie—*who couldn't love her?*—but our situation was delicate. Her mouth would add a layer of instability to the conversation, and nobody needed that.

"Thanks." I glanced at Evan, who seemed completely focused on Krankle. "Thank you too."

"Don't worry about it." Evan managed a smile. "I can patrol the area around the restaurant overnight if you want. You know, just to make sure Kyle doesn't come calling."

I considered taking him up on the interesting offer for a full thirty seconds. Ultimately, I shook my head. "We should be fine. Hunter put in a security system. We're good."

"Okay. I'm only a phone call away if you need me."

With that, Bay and Evan each grabbed one of Tillie's arms and dragged her toward their vehicle. That left us to get inside the restaurant without anybody noticing Krankle's outfit.

"I'll take him up the outside steps," Hunter volunteered. "They're in rough shape—your grandfather should really get them replaced—but we can make it. Meet us in the apartment."

I wanted to argue that I should be the one to take Krankle up, but there was no point. Hunter's mind was made up. "Okay." I attempted a smile, but it came out as more of a grimace. "I'll see you in two minutes. Time me." With that, I bolted toward the door.

My plan was to cut behind the dishwashers and head up immediately. No muss. No fuss. No distractions. Instead, I ran into Uncle Brad, who held court by the meat slicer.

"There you are." He looked happy to see me—never a good sign. "These guys don't believe me." He gestured to several night workers, a few of whom I was related to. "Tell them the *Titanic* didn't sink."

Oh, well, good. He's chosen a realistic topic this evening. Not. "Why do you believe the *Titanic* didn't sink?" I demanded.

"Because they want us to believe it did," Brad replied. "It's just a story they tell. It was the *Olympic* that crashed into an iceberg and sank. All the people on the *Titanic* had to go into witness protection after the fact because the mobsters were out to get them."

"Oh, well, sure." I tried to edge around him to reach the stairs to my apartment.

"Also, and I was just reading up on this so I'm still getting all the facts, but Apollo 17 wasn't the last moon landing," Brad continued. "There was actually an Apollo 18, but aliens killed all the astronauts on the moon. The government had to hide it. We ceded the moon to the aliens."

I frowned. "How did we hide the space shuttle's takeoff for this moon landing gone awry?"

"It was the Illuminati."

"Okay then." I forcefully pushed him aside. Then something occurred to me. "I need to order some food." I turned to my cousin Alice. We were tight, but since Hunter and I had gotten back together, I hadn't spent as much time with her as I likely should have. "Can you send up three orders of fish and chips?"

Alice's forehead creased. "How hungry are you?" Wait ... are you pregnant?" She looked excited at the prospect.

"It's not all for me." I made a face and jutted out my index finger. "And don't spread the pregnancy rumor. I don't like it. Hunter is already upstairs." That was mostly true. "And we're hanging out with a friend."

"What friend?"

"You don't know him."

"Him?" Alice perked up, always on the hunt. "Is he hot?"

Krankle was most definitely hot, but I didn't want Alice sniffing around right then. "Totally," I agreed without hesitation. "Do you remember Jordan Stuckey from high school? He looks a lot like him."

Jordan Stuckey wasn't a bad-looking kid by any stretch of the imagination. He did, however, boast one detail that drove Alice up the wall.

"Ugh. Does he have that lower-lip-hair thing going on like Jordan?"

"Yeah." I kept my face blank. "Why? You like that, right?"

"No, I do not." Alice vehemently shook her head. "That's so gross. I'll get the food and bring it up, but I'll leave it on the top step, knock, then run like a maniac. I do not want to meet another lip-hair guy."

That was exactly what I'd hoped for. "Thanks. You're my favorite cousin for a reason."

I didn't wait for Brad to start in on another conspiracy theory. Instead, I bolted up the stairs, locking the door behind me when I made it inside.

Hunter and Krankle were in the kitchen when I peered around the corner. They weren't talking, but the way Hunter kept eyeing Krankle told me we were in for a doozy of an evening.

"Stop spying," Hunter ordered without looking up. He'd obviously felt my eyes on him. "What took you so long? You should've beaten us here by a full minute."

"Uncle Brad," I replied simply.

"Ugh."

"I also ordered food. Alice will leave it on the other side of the door. I went with fish and chips." I gripped my hands in front of me and studied Krankle's face. "Is that okay, or do you want a can of tuna?"

Krankle somehow managed to look imperious despite his superhero cape and a makeshift diaper. "Somehow, I think I'll survive." He glanced down at his outfit. "I really need different clothes, though."

"You can wear something of Hunter's," I volunteered.

Hunter shot me a dark look. "Excuse me?"

"He can't fit into anything of mine," I replied reasonably. "He's too tall and built."

"Oh, good grief," Hunter muttered.

"I'm sorry." I held out my hands. "I'll go to the store and buy him something tomorrow." I thought about the meager savings account I'd managed to accrue since returning home. "I can get him some jeans and sweatshirts. Hopefully."

Hunter looked pained. "It's fine. Don't go spending a bunch of money. I'll handle the clothes tomorrow."

"It's not your responsibility."

"Oh, don't start that again." Hunter stalked toward the bedroom. "We're in this together. That means your money problems are my money problems. No need to be a martyr." He slammed the bedroom door behind him.

"He just needs a minute to cool down," I explained to Krankle. "He'll be okay."

When Krankle looked up, for the first time since he'd turned into a human, I saw a hint of the amusement the cat used to show me when talking.

"Yeah, I don't think he's going to just get over this," he said.

"Probably not," I agreed. "It will be okay, though." I edged closer, for the first time picking up on the fact that he was covered in bruises. "How did this happen?" I leaned over to get a better look at his shoulder. "Why are you injured?"

"Injured isn't the correct word," he replied. "I had to hide a lot last night. In the bushes. Don't worry about it."

That was easier said than done. "Krankle." Only after his name escaped did I realize how odd it sounded to call a grown man the same name that had seemed so normal for a cat. "I can't call you Krankle now." I made a face. "It feels wrong."

"You didn't have a problem calling me Krankle before." His lower lip jutted out. "Why is it such a big deal now?"

"Because you're no longer a cat. Do you have a name other than Krankle?"

"Maybe."

"I would like something else to call you." I was firm as I regarded him. "It will make things easier."

"Maybe I don't want to make things easier. Have you ever considered that?"

"Only every single day that I've known you."

That nudged a smile out of him, though when he dropped his head into his hands and started rubbing, my sympathy reared up.

"Do you have a headache?"

"Everything hurts," he replied. "It's like I was tossed into a stretcher and pulled in a million different directions."

I hadn't even considered that, but it made sense. "It's probably like intense growing pains," I mused. "The food will help. I'll get you some ibuprofen. Once you're clothed, hydrated, and fed, we can start figuring things out."

Krankle's lips twitched. "You can call me Easton."

Relief I didn't know I so desperately needed washed over me. "Easton."

"It's my given name. Easton Krankle."

"Oh." A smile took over my lips, unbidden. "You have a full name like a..." I trailed off.

"You were about to say, 'Like a human,' weren't you?"

"Yes, but that's rude."

"It's also apt. Easton is fine."

"Easton." I repeated the name and cocked my head. "You kind of look like an Easton."

"Am I supposed to say you look like a Stormy?"

"No. I'm curious why gnomes have last names, though."

"Why do humans have last names?"

"I ... don't know." I pursed my lips. "Am I insulting you? I don't mean to."

He let loose a long sigh. "No. You have questions. I knew you would. That's why my reveal was supposed to be months from now." He lifted his hands and studied them. "It's nice to have opposable thumbs again, I guess."

That struck me as funny. "Why would you come to this plane as a cat?"

The door to the bedroom opened, signaling Hunter's return. I kept my gaze on Krankle. *Er, Easton.* That was definitely a better name. It would take some getting used to, though.

"It's a very long story."

"We have time."

"I need to wrap my head around things." Easton took the clothes Hunter handed him. "Thank you. I'm going to change." He started for the second bedroom. "I can still stay in there, right?" He almost looked afraid to hear the answer.

"Of course." I bobbed my head. "Get changed. Dinner should be here in a few minutes."

"Thanks."

I clenched and unclenched my hands as I watched him walk into the room and shut the door. "What do you think?" I asked Hunter in a low voice when I was certain he was out of earshot.

"I don't know what to think. This entire thing is unbelievable. I mean ... it's just freaking unbelievable. He's a man. How do we explain what happened to the cat?"

I hadn't gotten that far yet. "I think that's the least of our worries. We can say the cat ran away, though that makes me sound like an irresponsible pet owner."

"Yes, that's what we should worry about."

I had to press my lips together to keep from laughing. "Sorry. My mind goes weird places sometimes."

"Come here." Hunter pulled me into a hug. "What are you thinking? What do you want to do?"

I wished I had an answer for him. "I don't know. I think, for now, we should have dinner and not push him too hard. Kyle is the immediate concern. The other stuff can wait."

"Can it?" Hunter didn't look convinced.

"I think it has to. We need to deal with Edmund, our witchy harem, and Kyle. The cat who is now a man falls fourth in the lineup... That's a statement I never thought I would make."

Hunter caught me by surprise when he chuckled, and his grip tightened. "We'll figure it out," he promised as he squeezed tight and kissed me between my eyebrows. "Let's just get through dinner. We'll take it one step at a time."

ALICE, TRUE TO HER WORD, WAS already halfway down the stairs when I opened the apartment door after her knock. She had no interest in meeting another human with a hairy lip. It was her line in the sand when it came to picking dates.

I carried the food to the table, smiled encouragingly when Easton joined us, and poured wine because alcohol could only make things better at that point.

"Can you have this?" I held the bottle close to Easton's glass. "I mean, how old are you?"

Easton made a face. "I'm more than a hundred years old in human years. I think I'm fine. That being said, I don't need wine. I already have a headache."

I clucked my tongue sympathetically. "Is the ibuprofen I gave you helping?"

"Not yet." Easton attempted a smile, but it didn't touch his eyes. "I feel ... disjointed. That's not how a transformation is supposed to work."

"How is it supposed to work?" Hunter asked.

He'd positioned us on the same side of the table, across from Easton, so the gnome would have to go through Hunter if he wanted to get to me. I didn't anticipate that happening, but clearly Hunter had ruled nothing out.

"It's difficult to explain." Easton was finicky when cutting his fish, opting for small bites over the hunks Hunter forked into his mouth. "My development is supposed to be tied to Stormy's development as a witch. As she grows, so do I. It's supposed to happen in increments."

"Who decides when this development happens?" I asked. "I mean, who says you're supposed to do anything?"

"History? Destiny? Your magic is different from that of the other witches you surround yourself with."

"If you weren't supposed to change just yet, why did you?" Hunter asked.

"It was the spell," I replied. "Tillie's spell revealed the truth. Easton said himself that he would only be a cat for a short time—that it wasn't his real form. The spell forced him into his real form before he was ready."

"Yes," Easton agreed.

Hunter blinked twice. "Who is Easton?"

I pointed toward our guest. "His real name is Easton Krankle. I found that out when you were getting clothes in the bedroom."

"Ah." Hunter seemed to take the name change in stride. "That's better than calling an adult man Krankle, I guess. How are we supposed to explain who he is, though? Won't your grandfather ask questions about why we have someone living with us?"

I hadn't gotten that far yet. "Um ... huh. I don't know."

"You can say I'm a friend you met while away from Shadow Hills, Stormy," Easton volunteered. "Tell people I dropped in for a visit. They won't ask too many questions."

"Until two weeks from now, when you're still here," Hunter groused.

"You're just mad because it was easier to do the humpty dance under the same roof when I was a cat," Easton drawled. "You might not have to say anything, so hold off on that. I should be able to transform back into the cat if everything goes as planned."

"Oh." Realization washed over me. "You can shift at will."

"That's usually how it works," Easton agreed. "I don't have the energy to try right now though. I was already exhausted from being awake all night before I stepped into the spell, and the forced shift drained me."

"What can we do to fix that?" I asked.

"The food will help. The water. I need to sleep."

"For how long?"

"I'm guessing at least ten hours." Easton smiled ruefully. "Maybe twelve. We'll know more when I've finished my restorative sleep."

Well, that was something at least. It didn't feel like enough, though. "I have questions about the man who followed us to Dead Man's Hill. You seemed to know him."

"I don't know what I can tell you about him. Not yet anyway. Things are ... not as they were supposed to be." He appeared genuinely baffled. "I need time to wrap my head around things."

"And we need answers," Hunter pressed. "How long will you keep us in the dark?"

"Not much longer. My transformation will force things to come to a head early. I'm sorry about that, but it is what it is."

I didn't debate long before telling Easton what he wanted to hear. "Get some sleep. I'm off tomorrow. We can spend the whole day talking about things if we need to."

"I think we should force him to answer tonight," Hunter countered.

"Tomorrow is soon enough." I wanted answers, but Easton appeared miserable. "I look forward to hearing what you have to say."

"Yes, won't that be fun?" Easton said dryly.

Fun wasn't the word I would have used, but his reckoning day had finally arrived.

TWENTY-FIVE

Having Easton sleep in our apartment was uncomfortable for both Hunter and me. Thankfully, the second bedroom was at the opposite end of the residence, which meant we weren't on top of one another.

I went through my normal evening routine, washed my face, and changed into comfortable pajamas, then crawled into bed next to a shirtless Hunter, who was checking sports scores on his phone.

"What a day, huh?"

"You could say that."

"You haven't said much," I pointed out. "Are you mad?"

"What would I be mad about?"

"You know."

"Not really." He didn't look at me.

Irritation grabbed my innards and twisted. "Fine. Good night." I turned onto my side, putting my back to him.

When the bed dipped, I knew he was wrapping himself around me. Sure enough, his warmth enveloped me within seconds.

"I'm sorry," he whispered, his lips near my ear. "I just... I don't know what I'm supposed to do with this, Stormy. The cat is now a man, and he's sleeping in our office."

"We always knew he was more than a cat," I pointed out.

"Yeah, but I didn't expect this, or maybe I just wasn't ready for it. If he'd prepared us, it might not have come as such a shock."

"Yeah." I'd been thinking about that too. "He clearly has an agenda. The thing is, he put himself on the line to save me when Kyle followed us. I can't just forget that."

"I don't expect you to."

"This might not be what we anticipated, but it's our reality now. Easton is our responsibility, and I don't think that will change quickly."

"No, I don't either." He reached over and turned off my nightstand lamp before settling in. "It would be better if he can shift back into cat form. That way we don't have to explain who he is. People are used to the cat coming and going from the apartment."

"There's that. I don't want to look like a bad cat owner."

His lips curved against my cheek. "Not my Girl Scout."

"I just can't help feeling that he's keeping something big from me. I don't want it to go the same way as Scout's story."

"What do you mean?"

"She's been quiet. You've obviously noticed that."

"I have."

"It's because she learned about this big prophecy that says she's supposed to fight some huge battle. Other people have been making decisions about her life since before she even knew who she was. I don't want that to happen to me."

He linked his fingers with mine. "I don't think it's the same thing. It sounds to me like you're something special, but I don't think there's a prophecy or anything concerning you. I think ... well, I think it has something to do with your particular brand of magic."

I was all ears as he laid it out.

"Tillie says that the fire magic you have is special and that it died out over the years," he continued. "What if you being so strong in this particular magic means it will have a comeback or something? Maybe Easton and the Kyle guy are trying to gain your allegiance and get in on the ground floor of that movement."

His phrasing was interesting. I didn't disagree, though. "What will that mean for us?"

"Nothing. We'll be together regardless. It doesn't matter if people keep coming for you. I'll always be with you for those fights. The Winchesters will too. Have you considered that the Winchesters' presence in your life has thrown everybody for big loops?"

"Why do you think that's important?" Hunter had an orderly mind, and I really did want to hear what he had to say.

"Because I think Krankle—that's what I'm calling the cat even when we're referring to the man as Easton—was sent here to prepare you to use your magic. They clearly thought this would go a specific way. They couldn't have foreseen the Winchesters, though. They've truly been the ones guiding you. I don't think the people who are invested in however this goes wanted that."

"It's a good thing though, right?"

"I think it's a very good thing. Tillie can be a bit out there, but she's smart. Actually, she's wily. That works to our advantage. And as hard as it was to come to grips with a day-walking vampire with attitude problems, Evan seems like a good guy to have on our side."

"Yeah." I was in total agreement. "Did you see the way he looked at Easton? I think he'll be poring through the research books all night. Maybe he'll come up with something."

"That would be nice, huh?"

"It really would be."

Hunter rubbed his fingers over my arms in an attempt to lull me. "Go to sleep, baby. We'll force answers out of our guest tomorrow, whether he wants to provide them or not. We can sleep in—I already messaged the office that I will be taking the morning off—then we can have a leisurely breakfast before we get the answers you deserve."

"It feels weird to think I might finally know something."

"Oh, there's no *might* about it. Come hell or high water, tomorrow, that gnome will answer our questions."

EASTON'S BED WAS EMPTY WHEN I WENT to check on him while Hunter made coffee the next morning. He left no note—*could he even write?*—or any indication he would come back.

"So much for our answers," I grumped when Hunter arrived at my side with a steaming mug.

"I would like to say I'm surprised, but I'm not," Hunter groused. He checked the door that led to the stairwell, and the chain was still secured from the inside. "Does this mean he managed to shift into a cat again?"

"He could've gone down the balcony stairs as a human," I replied. "He could've gone down as a cat too. I'm not sure."

Hunter grumbled as we returned to the kitchen. "Have I mentioned that I hate him?"

"We don't know why he left," I argued. "Maybe something came up."

"And he couldn't leave a note?"

"Maybe he doesn't know how to write. He's just getting used to opposable thumbs again. He brought that up himself last night."

"I don't trust him." Morose, Hunter added sugar to his coffee. "He's a putz. I knew it the second he became human in that clearing and all anybody could talk about was his butt. That's a sure sign that he's evil if you ask me."

I had to hide my smile behind my mug. Our situation wasn't funny. Hunter's reaction to it was, however. "I didn't realize you were so upset about the butt talk," I said after swallowing a mouthful of caffeinated goodness.

"Why wouldn't I be? My butt is ten times better than his."

"Oh, so modest." I gave his rear end a playful pinch through his boxers. "That is a pretty nice butt."

"I'm serious. Why was he naked?"

"Probably because he wasn't wearing clothes when he shifted. That's my guess, anyway. He can control his body for the shift but not clothes. They're an entity all their own."

"Then where are his clothes now, smart girl?"

He begged an interesting question. I took my mug to the second bedroom to look around again. "They're not in here."

"And they're not on the balcony. I just looked."

"So, maybe he left in human form." Something occurred to me, and

I went to where we kept our shoes by the front door. "Are any of your shoes missing?"

Hunter joined me to look, his lips curving down after a few seconds. "He took my Nikes. I haven't even had them that long."

"Well, that answers that question," I mused. "He obviously left in human form."

"Because we told him we had questions. He left because he didn't want to answer them."

I saw no point in arguing. He was right. "Obviously, he's not ready to share the truth with us." I darted my eyes to the cat door. "Can you rig that so he can't get inside?"

"I thought we agreed he was in human form. He can't fit through that hole as a human."

"No, but eventually, he'll be able to shift, if he can't already. I don't want him to have access to the apartment when he won't share what's going on with the class."

"I can rig it so he can't get inside. It will take some work to close it permanently, if that's what you want, but I can do it."

I considered it but not for long. "Let's close it temporarily for now. After that, let's get cleaned up. I'll buy you breakfast downstairs, and we'll make plans for the day."

"Do those plans include a cute-butt search?"

I choked on a laugh. "Why would I search for what I already have?" I asked when I was reasonably sure I could speak without laughing.

"Fine. I want a big breakfast, though. I've earned it."

"I think that can be arranged."

THE RESTAURANT WAS BUSTLING WITH activity when we made our way downstairs. We settled in the café section because it gave us a better view of the door, which meant that nobody could go in or out without us seeing.

"Did you see your new friends are here?" Hunter settled across from me.

My attention had immediately gone to the corner booth, where Celeste, Monica, and Phoebe sat and glared. A quick scan of the café told me who he was talking about. Iris, Blanche, Gwen, and Florence were all present and accounted for, at separate tables again.

"This is turning into a pattern," I noted. "I don't ever remember them coming in like this. At best, I saw one or two of them a handful of times between when I came home in the spring and now."

"It does feel pointed, doesn't it?" Hunter pursed his lips. "I don't know what to make of it. I—"

His words died as Celeste slid into his side of the booth without invitation.

Though there was plenty of room, she plastered herself to his side. "It's so good to see you," she enthused as she threw her arms around him. "How are you?"

Hunter's face was priceless. It took everything I had not to laugh.

"I'm fine." Hunter forcefully eased Celeste's grip from him and nudged her to stay on her side of the booth. "How are you?"

If Celeste registered Hunter's less-than-happy greeting, she didn't show it. "I'm just peachy," she enthused. "I haven't seen you around much. I guess Stormy is happier hiding you from the rest of the world. Do you know she's telling people you moved in together?"

"I would guess she's telling people that because it's true. Do you need something, Celeste?" Hunter clearly wasn't in the mood.

Celeste blinked. "I just want to spend time with you."

"Well, now you have. If you don't mind, though, Stormy and I would like a quiet breakfast, just the two of us. We rarely get morning meals together because she usually has to work."

"Oh." Celeste didn't move.

"In other words, get off him," Phoebe barked from the booth Celeste had vacated to invade our morning meal. "He doesn't want you there, and you're not supposed to be sitting with the enemy anyway, Celeste. Get with the program."

Celeste, never the sharpest knife in the block, looked genuinely baffled as she glanced between Hunter and me. "Who is the enemy?"

"That would be me." I raised my hand. "I'm the enemy. Phoebe doesn't want you to sit with me."

"Oh, right." Celeste nodded knowingly. "You stole Pete from her.

That's such a shame." She turned to look at Hunter. "You heard about that, right? Stormy has been sleeping with Pete."

Oh, well, good. I was hoping Phoebe would spread *that* rumor.

"Stormy was helping Pete after he had a moment of lightheaded confusion in the woods," Hunter countered. "That's a little different."

"What were they doing together alone in the woods?" Celeste challenged.

"They weren't alone. Two other people were with them."

"Oh." Bewilderment rode roughshod over Celeste's face. "I didn't hear that part of the story." She shot an accusing look toward Phoebe. "It seems I'm only being fed certain things. Again."

"Perhaps you should stop believing the source who keeps feeding you those half facts," I offered. "Just a suggestion."

"Right. Are you guys going to the river party tonight?"

Celeste addressed the question to Hunter, so I let him answer it.

"I think it's unlikely this evening," Hunter replied, not missing a beat. "Stormy and I want to spend some time alone. You know, celebrate moving in together and everything." The statement was pointed.

Per usual, Celeste missed his meaning. "That's a bummer. Maybe we could all hang out together."

"No." Hunter shot a glare toward Phoebe's table. "Do you want to collect your breakfast companion?"

Monica got sheepishly to her feet. "Sorry. She doesn't always listen to reason." She smiled as she grabbed Celeste's arm. "You need to go back to our table. They don't want you at theirs."

"They didn't say that," Celeste argued.

"We don't want you at our table," Hunter supplied. "Go."

Celeste's lower lip poked out. "Well, you don't need to be grumpy."

She slunk back to her table, leaving Monica at the edge of ours to offer up an apologetic shrug.

"She can't read a room," Monica explained. "At first I thought it was some weird game, but she really can't pick up on nuance. You have to be ruthlessly blunt with her."

"That's good to know," Hunter said. "I'll make sure to be as mean as possible the next time I see her."

Monica's lips swished. Then something over my shoulder caught her

attention. When I angled to look, I found Florence lobbing hate aster-
oids in our direction with her eyes.

"You clearly have a fan," she said in a low voice. "What's up with
that?"

"She's angry about the Edmund situation," Hunter replied. "They
were all sleeping with him, and one of them probably killed him."

I was impressed he would just lay it out there for her.

"We're still figuring out which one of them it was."

"When you say all..." Monica trailed off.

"All the single women over sixty in that neighborhood were apparently enjoying the fruits of Edmund's loom," Hunter replied. "It's
freaky, but that's where we stand."

"Yeah, I wish I hadn't known that." Monica wrinkled her nose. "I
heard they were all hanging out with Pete the other night. This was
before he showed up at Phoebe's house, intent on rekindling their relationship."

"Pete wasn't well the other day," Hunter replied. "He's better now.
As for the Golden Mean Girls, we're not sure what is happening with
them yet. We'll figure it out."

"Well, good luck with that." Monica offered me a half-hearted wave
before returning to their table.

"Is Florence still glaring at the back of my head?" I asked Hunter as I
sipped my coffee.

"Yup." He grinned. "Is Gwen still glaring at the back of mine?"

I checked. "She is."

"Ah, who doesn't love being popular?"

I laughed, as I'm sure he'd intended, then froze with my mug
pressed to my lips. The restaurant door had opened to allow Deke
Kingman entrance. He was a local contractor who liked his liquor the
same way he liked his women. Hard. He wasn't a regular face at the
restaurant. Oddly enough, however, he didn't seem to be interested in
sitting.

Slowly, I tracked his gaze as it bounced around the café. It landed on
four people in turn. Blanche. Iris. Gwen. Florence. Then, without
another word, he turned on his heel and exited through the same door
he'd used to enter only seconds before.

"What was that?" I asked.

My stomach twisted when I realized the four women were on their feet and heading toward the door. They weren't exactly in trances, but something about their movements seemed meek.

"Seriously, what is that?"

Hunter looked as flabbergasted as I felt. "I have no idea." He slid out of the booth. "I think we need to find out, though."

We only had one chance to follow them, and though I was hungry, some things were more important. "Yeah, let's see where they're going. I bet whatever is about to go down isn't good."

"I bet you're right."

TWENTY-SIX

Hunter drove without debate from me. Each of the women took separate cars when leaving the restaurant parking lot, but they all headed in the same direction.

"Where do you think they're going?" I was understandably confused.

"I'm not sure." Hunter allowed two cars to pull in front of him while keeping an eye on Iris's red coupe—the last in their line. "They're clearly going to the same place, though."

"And Deke? I don't remember a lot about him. Nothing I do remember is good."

"He's an ass." Hunter's lips curved down. "Like, a huge freaking ass. He's been in trouble for a bunch of stuff over the years."

"Like what?"

"Like he was hiring people off the books for his crews. Some people in town had sympathy for him—times get tough in small towns, and he was hiring locals instead of illegals—but most people were smart enough to steer clear of him. Some big sting happened, about four years ago I want to say. The state boys did it, so I don't have all the details. He had to pay monster fines, and a lot of people in town started hiring other contractors to do their house renovations after that."

It made sense. Shadow Hills residents loved a good conspiracy theory. If they thought the Michigan State Police were watching Deke, they would steer clear of him.

"But what's his connection to those women?" I couldn't wrap my head around that part. "How would he even know them?"

"Just off the top of my head, I think he redid Blanche's kitchen about five years ago or so. I only remember because I saw his truck there when I was at one of your family's barbecues."

"That's right. You went to the barbecues without me."

"Let's not go there," he said sternly. "I can't see how any of them would have a relationship with Deke. None of them are related to him as far as I know."

That was when another option smacked me in the face. "Maybe he's not Deke."

It took Hunter a moment to catch up. "Oh, geez. You think he's Edmund."

"It makes sense, right? Does Deke have a girlfriend?"

"No." Hunter shook his head as the caravan of drivers made a right. "I don't think Deke has had a regular girlfriend in years. Sometimes, you can find him up at the bar looking for a bit of fun, but he's not the relationship type. He likes one-night stands."

"He doesn't have any kids, either, does he?"

"No. He's never been married, and as far as I know, he's never knocked anybody up. He's rumored to be sterile, but that could be the guys at the bar having a good time at his expense, even if it's not funny."

"So, he would make a prime target for Edmund," I surmised. "He lives alone. He probably has some money stashed. Nobody would question his activities because he's a loner by nature."

"It does make sense. Also, Edmund's hunting cabin is out this way."

I froze when I realized we were at the edge of town. I'd spent my fair share of time in the woods as a kid—people couldn't be afraid of nature and survive in Shadow Hills—but I wasn't as familiar with that side of town.

"This is where you lived." The words escaped before I thought better of them.

Hunter nodded grimly. "The house I grew up in is over here, a couple of streets over."

"And your father."

"I don't see him, Stormy. I don't want to see him."

I let it drop. Hunter's father had been emotionally abusive to the nth degree when we were growing up. Sometimes—Hunter swore it was rare—he would get physically violent. I was convinced the incidents of physical violence were more prevalent than Hunter let on. I hadn't ever pushed him on it, though.

"I guess I didn't realize Edmund had a hunting cabin," I admitted. "It seems weird to me when you have a house fifteen minutes away."

"I think 'cabin' would be a loose term. It's more like a shack. It's a place for him to warm up when he's cold or hang a deer before cutting it up. I know it's out here, though. A few years ago, Pete and I were hunting and saw him out here."

"Well then, that has to be where they're going, right?" It made sense.

"I think so, but we'll have to wait and see."

THE DRIVE WAS FINE WHEN IT WAS A PAVED road. When we pulled off onto a two-track—Hunter had fallen way behind Iris's vehicle to avoid being seen—I was a little leerier about the trek.

"This is pleasant," I muttered as I gripped the handle above the door to keep myself from bouncing.

"Sorry." Hunter gritted his teeth. "We have to keep going, but I didn't want to risk them seeing us, so we can't drive all the way there. It's not much farther. We'll have to park on this side of the curve up ahead, then hoof it in."

I looked forward to the walk. The bouncing was causing my stomach unnecessary—and unwanted—fluttering. "Okay. Let's do that."

Two minutes later, we were out of the truck, and in the ditch, I bent at the waist to collect my breath.

"Sorry." Hunter rubbed his hand up and down my back. "I forgot how soft you've gotten since high school."

I shot him a dirty look. "I most certainly have not gotten soft. Why would you even say that?"

"Because we used to go two-tracking all the time, and you never once reacted like this. Don't you remember all those times I took you to shine deer when we were kids?" He grinned at the memory. "You never once lost your stomach."

"Oh, please." He was full of it. "We weren't there for the deer. You just went into the woods far enough that we wouldn't risk getting caught making out."

"You still held it together better than this."

"I just didn't expect it."

Hunter rubbed my back for another two minutes, then held out his hand. "Come on. I want to get to that cabin, figure out what they're doing, and leave before they realize we followed them."

I felt better, so I simply nodded and followed him into the woods.

Hunter deftly cut through the trees. I, on the other hand, lost all sense of direction three minutes into our adventure. When we emerged at the back of a single-room cabin, I was in shock because I thought for sure we'd overshot our mark. "Man, remind me to keep you close in the zombie apocalypse. You'll make sure we never get lost."

Hunter smirked. "I thought you planned to keep me close forever regardless."

"That too." I pressed myself against Hunter's back as we edged closer to the cabin. Five vehicles sat parked in front of it, but the back side of the structure didn't have a single window.

Hunter lifted his finger to his lips, signaling to keep quiet—as if I hadn't figured that out myself—then he proceeded to creep around to the side of the cabin, which boasted one small window. He dropped to his knees and drew me down with him, then we got comfortable with our backs against the shack. He'd been right about the cabin being old and rundown. It also had thin walls and a poorly insulated window. If we were quiet, we could make out the conversation inside.

"Why, Deke?" Iris asked. I couldn't see her face, but I could imagine her delicate nose wrinkling. "Why would we possibly want to be seen with him?"

"Hey, I had to go with someone less noticeable," Deke—or rather

Edmund in Deke's body—shot back. "I did the best I could. Stormy Morgan has been onto me."

"Is that why you gave up Pete's body?" Blanche asked. "Did she force you to do it?"

"More or less. She lured me out of Phoebe's house and had some thug with her. He was strong—way stronger than he should've been—and he had vampire teeth."

"Oh, geez." Florence made a throaty, disgusted sound. "Now you're blaming your failure to secure a good body on a vampire? That's so you, Edmund."

"You know, since you're the one who stabbed me, you might want to watch your tongue, Florence," Edmund shot back, disdain positively dripping from his voice. "Death was not part of the deal, you trollops."

I pressed my eyes closed as my eyebrows took flight. Their entire conversation was unbelievable.

"We told you that you couldn't stay in your body for the spell to work," Gwen shot back. "You were the one who said your body wasn't working the correct way. Just because you thought there would be a way around it—and ran like a little girl when we came for you—doesn't mean that we made the mistake."

"Hey!" Edmund sounded on the verge of melting down. "Nobody told me I would have a letter opener plunged into my chest."

"We told you we had to separate your soul from your body so you could take over a better body," Iris argued. "How did you think we would do it?"

"I don't know." Edmund sounded petulant. "I thought it would be like those movies with the killer doll. You know, how he puts his hand on the forehead of the body he wants to take over and chants? I thought it would be like that. No muss. No fuss."

"Well, that's not how it works." Iris was blasé. "We tried to make it easy for you. I brought you spaghetti for dinner. If you'd just eaten it instead of complaining about wanting steak, even though you couldn't chew it with your dentures, we wouldn't be in this mess."

"What do you mean?" Edmund asked dumbly.

"The spaghetti was meant to take you out and make it look as if you'd died of a heart attack at the table. Could you follow instructions, though? No!"

"The spaghetti was poisoned?" Edmund sounded genuinely wounded. "Why wouldn't you tell me that you planned to poison me so I could make preparations?"

"Probably because we didn't want to hear you whine," Blanche replied. "You have no idea how much we hate listening to you whine."

"Probably as much as I hate listening to you complain about doing it doggy style," Edmund shot back. "*Oh, my knees. Oh, my back.*" He mocked her voice. "Not everything is about you."

"No, apparently, it's about you," Iris snapped. "You were the one who volunteered to be first. We planned to follow suit once we were certain we could make it work. You wanted to be the guinea pig."

"I didn't want a letter opener plunged into my chest, especially in the middle of the street."

"Yes, well, that was a mistake," Iris conceded. "That's why you should've eaten the spaghetti."

"You should've told me the plan," Edmund snarled. "I needed a few days to get everything in order. I wasn't supposed to die before I was ready."

"We thought you would chicken out if we didn't take control of the situation," Gwen admitted. "I mean, let's face it, you're not what anybody could call courageous. The only reason you even agreed to the body swap in the first place is because your penis stopped working and you wanted an upgrade."

"My penis worked fine!" Edmund sounded like a crying toddler. "You guys just refused to do things my way. You wanted foreplay and stuff. I got bored when it went on too long. It was all your fault."

"Oh, whatever." Gwen sounded bored with the conversation. "What's done is done. You're dead."

"Yes, but my son has to sort through everything in my house," Edmund complained. "I wanted to do that myself. I wanted to shift some things over from my old life to my new one. You made that impossible."

"You'd better not be talking about those ridiculous movies," Florence warned. "We don't ever want to see them again."

"*Blown in 60 Seconds* was a classic!"

"They were stupid is what they were," Florence argued. "It doesn't matter now anyway. You can't go back. I'm not even certain how smart it is for us to be hanging out here. We need to come up with a plan. Stormy Morgan has become a menace. Now that we know the spell works and you're young ... if still dumb, we need to prepare ourselves to join you."

"We have to kill Stormy," Iris agreed. "She's too great of a threat."

I froze, only allowing a breath to escape when Hunter's hand rested on my knee. He didn't look happy. He also didn't appear ready to depart just yet.

"So, how do we do it?" Blanche asked. "We can't very well get to her inside the restaurant. Charlie isn't much for exerting energy, but he won't just stand there while we kill his granddaughter."

"We can't kill her at the restaurant anyway," Gwen said. "That's too risky. We're lucky we weren't caught when Florence stabbed Edmund in the middle of the street."

"He wouldn't stop running!" Florence snapped.

"We have to isolate Stormy, somehow," Gwen continued. "I think we should fake that Hunter had an emergency. Like ... make her think he's down by the river. It's too cold for anybody to be down there any night but bonfire party night."

"I think that's tonight," Iris pointed out.

"Even better." Gwen was clearly warming to her idea. "We'll lure her out there and kill her before the others arrive. Everybody will think that she was on her way to the party, and they won't be able to prove otherwise."

"How do we kill her, though?" Iris queried. "If she's murdered, Hunter will come looking for us. He's not an idiot."

"We'll have to make it look like an accident." Gwen was thoughtful. "We can bash her in the head with a rock and make it look like a fall."

Hearing them plot my death made me distinctly uncomfortable. When I shifted my eyes to Hunter, I found him fuming.

No, I mouthed when he caught my eye. *We need to go back.* I gestured in the direction we'd come from.

He nodded and followed on his hands and knees until we were at the back of the cabin and far enough away that they couldn't hear us. "I can take them in right now," he whispered. "We can end this."

"Except we're woefully outnumbered, and I wouldn't put it past some of those women to be armed." I did my best to appear calm, but it wasn't easy. "We need help. They might have magic we don't know about."

"You want to get the Winchesters," he deduced.

"Maybe a few."

"What happens when they spring their trap? I can't just sit back and do nothing when they come for you with a rock."

"You're not going to do nothing. I won't sit back and let them kill me either. We'll have our own team in place before they can act."

"I guess that's a good idea." Hunter rubbed his chin. "I won't lie, Stormy, this entire thing makes me nervous. We need to come up with a foolproof plan. I refuse to put you at risk."

"I think we can outsmart Edmund and his harem. Come on."

"Can we do it without killing Deke? He might not be the best guy in the world, but he's not actually responsible for this one."

"We'll do it and save Deke at the same time," I promised. "That's why we need Bay. While we're handling the harem, Bay needs to get rid of Edmund's ghost. She's the only one strong enough. I can get him out of the body, but I can't force the ghost over to the other side."

A muscle worked in Hunter's jaw. He nodded. "I want a solid plan."

"We need to get out of here first. I would prefer they not know we followed them."

"Yeah." He cast another look toward the cabin and then grabbed my hand. "Let's get out of here. I'm ready to end this."

He wasn't the only one.

TWENTY-SEVEN

The Winchesters arrived with little fanfare. Well, except for Tillie, who showed herself into the kitchen and explained to Grandpa—who was finishing his morning shift—that he was doing anything and everything wrong.

"You should have the eggs over there." She pointed toward the left side of the grill. "Why do you have them where they look so lonely? It makes no sense."

Grandpa glowered at her. "Because the left side of the grill is set to a higher heat," he replied through clenched teeth. "That's where the sausage, bacon, and hash browns go. You don't put the eggs over there because they'll turn black, and the yolks will harden."

Tillie worked her jaw, then flicked her eyes to me. "Is that true? That sounds made up to me."

"Get her out of here," Grandpa growled.

"Upstairs." I tugged Tillie away from Grandpa. "We have to come up with a plan. I need that dastardly brain of yours."

"I am good when it comes to smiting enemies," she readily agreed and cast Grandpa one more look. "I'll research that grill thing and get back to you."

"I can't wait." Grandpa glared at Tillie's retreating form, then pinned me with a hard look. "Do I even want to know what you're doing?"

"Probably not, but you need to prepare yourself." I forced myself to remain calm. "Something is going to happen today that involves your neighbors."

I could tell I had Grandpa's full attention when his eyebrows hopped. He didn't speak, though.

"It will probably be a big deal when we're done," I continued. "Just keep Grandma away from Gwen, Iris, Blanche, and Florence until the end of the day, okay?"

Grandpa's forehead creased. "Did they have something to do with Edmund's death?"

"Yes."

"All of them?" He looked flabbergasted.

"It seems so. They had a plan, and they're not done. We're putting an end to it today."

"How?" Grandpa shifted to face me head-on. "You aren't killing them, are you?"

"I'm not sure how it might play out." That was the truth. "I just want you to be prepared."

"That the nut from Hemlock Cove is with you suggests you're about to do something loopy, Stormy. You need to think about this before you do it."

"I have thought about it. I don't see where we have another choice. They're plotting my death even as we speak. They think I've gotten too close for them to safely carry out their plan. It's either them or me."

"Seriously?" Grandpa seemed like he might start throwing loaves of bread. "I can't believe we're in a position to have a conversation like this."

"I know, but it is what it is. Hunter will be with me, so I'll be covered. I just want you to be careful. I happen to know that they plan to lure me out of this restaurant at some point today. If they call you and want you to do something—say, give me a message that Hunter is out by the river, and I need to go to him—I would appreciate it if you'll play along."

Grandpa's expression was impossible to read. Ultimately, he

nodded. "They're setting a trap, but they don't know that you're setting a counter trap."

"That's it in a nutshell."

"Well, I'll do what I can, but you need to be careful. Though you think you've outsmarted them, they could still throw you curveball. They're wily."

"I'm not alone," I reminded him. "And as much as Tillie irritates you, she's surprisingly good at this stuff."

"Oh, I can see it." Grandpa managed a smile. "She's wily too. She's the most feared woman in Hemlock Cove for a reason."

"Indeed."

I left Grandpa to finish his shift and headed upstairs. Bay and Tillie were with Hunter in the kitchen, drinking coffee as he caught them up. Evan, however, stood in the doorway to the second bedroom. He looked thoughtful.

"What's up?" I moved beside him.

"The cat is gone," he said blankly.

"You mean the man. He was gone when we woke up this morning. The chain for the inside door was still in place. That means he left via the balcony. We have no idea if he's still a man or if he changed back to cat form after he left, though."

"You don't seem upset."

I hesitated. "I don't know how to feel about it. Am I angry that he took off without providing us with answers again? Absolutely. I feel a bit betrayed, honestly. I let him off easy last night because he looked so exhausted. He said everything hurt from the transformation. I felt bad for him. Now, though, it's obvious he manipulated me."

"He did," Evan confirmed. "It might not be for the reasons you think, though. Remember when I saw the guy outside Phoebe's house? When I said he was magical, but I couldn't figure out what he was?"

I nodded.

"Well, I sensed it yesterday," he continued. "Once the cat turned into a man, I sensed the same thing."

My shoulders went rigid. "Are you saying Kyle is a gnome shifter too?"

"I think they're more than gnome shifters, Stormy. I can't be certain

—I've never run into another creature claiming to be a gnome shifter, after all—but I sense that they're somehow different. All the plane shifting Scout has done lately drove me to do some research. Krankle said he came from another plane, right?" He continued without waiting for an answer. "He knew what life was like on this plane, though. I think that whatever order he's in—like, whatever group he aligns himself with —was on this plane at one time and left."

I absorbed the information. "Why?"

"I can only theorize about that," he warned. "From everything that Tillie has told me, though, hellcats are something special. You're not a fire elemental. You're not even strictly a fire witch. Your fire magic is rare in that it's not just external. It's internal too. Your great-grandmother was a hellcat from my understanding, but her magic was never as strong as yours.

"If you read up on hellcats, which I have because I like to research stuff when I'm antsy or agitated, it seems they were prevalent a thousand years ago. They were the predominant witch on top of the magical hill, so to speak. Then, when they were gone, the witches switched to being more air and earthbound.

"Now, I don't know why the hellcats lost their standing on this plane, but they started to die out," he continued. "The old guard actually died, and fewer and fewer hellcats were born. By the time your great-grandmother was born with hellcat magic, the entire line was almost completely dormant."

"Then I came along," I surmised.

"Then you came along." He grinned. "You threw everything out of whack. I mean that in a good way. I don't know how the gnomes play into it, but they obviously do. Maybe they were minions of sorts. Or maybe—and I tend to lean toward this theory—they were familiars."

"Cats are often witch familiars in literature," I mused.

"They are, and for all we know, the stories could say that because the gnome shifters chose that form however many years ago. You know, art imitating life and running with it. I'm not sure that part matters, at least for now. What does matter is that Krankle didn't show up until you were back in town. Your return to Shadow Hills plays into whatever this is."

I chewed on my bottom lip as I took in his words. "Do you think Easton is an enemy?"

"Is that his name?" Evan asked.

I nodded.

"Well, I don't know." He held his hands palm out. "I don't want you to trust him only to have him turn on you. The thing is, I don't sense that he wants to hurt you. I think he's trying to help you."

"He could help me by telling the truth."

"He could, but we don't know what other pressures he's dealing with. For now, I think we should give him the benefit of the doubt."

"Hunter blocked the cat door."

"I think that's wise. If Easton wants to come back, he has to pay the toll. Just don't write him off yet." Evan laid a hand on my shoulder. "I don't think he's anywhere near done."

"We have to focus on the dark-magic harem anyway." I offered a rueful smile. "I can't worry about Easton when they're running around, plotting my death."

"Yes, let's focus on one enemy at a time."

Tillie was animated when we joined them in the kitchen. She seemed excited for what was to come.

"I can't believe they plan to do it as a group," she complained. "I mean, I can't decide if it's ingenious or heinous."

"Since they're stealing bodies, I'll say heinous," Bay replied. "If I understand correctly, they want to lure you out to the river before the bonfire party tonight, right, Stormy?"

I nodded. "The bonfire party starts at seven o'clock most nights. They'll want to make sure they have an hour to tie up loose ends, so I expect them to try manipulating me into place about half past five."

Bay nodded. I could practically hear the gears in her mind working. "How will they do it?"

"I don't know." That was the part I grappled with too. "They need to lure Hunter out because, otherwise, I wouldn't believe whatever they're selling."

"So, basically, we need to be on the lookout for a police call coming in," Bay surmised. "They'll lure him out on a false call then arrange for you to hear Hunter is in trouble after he's gone."

"Could they want to kill Hunter too?" Evan queried.

"Maybe," I hedged. "The thing is, if Hunter dies, the town will be up in arms. The reaction will be swift, and the people will join together to solve the case. If I die, they won't care."

Hunter growled low in his throat. "Don't ever say that again."

I couldn't help smiling. "I didn't mean that in a disparaging way," I assured him. "It's just, people love you. They don't feel the same way about me."

"I love you," Hunter barked. "Me!" His eyes flashed. "Don't you even think of being a martyr."

I forced myself to respond calmly. "Nobody is going to be a martyr. Take a breath."

"Take ten breaths," Tillie ordered. "And get a grip on yourself. We're here to make sure this goes down smoothly. No need to freak out now. We've got this. We're way ahead of the curve."

Hunter looked unconvinced, but he nodded all the same. "Sorry," he said softly. "I just don't like the idea of Stormy using herself as bait."

"Nobody likes that," Bay assured him. "It's our only option, though. We need to get ahead of these women. They think they have the upper hand. That will make our victory all the sweeter."

"Yes, we're going to pummel them into paste," Tillie readily agreed. "We need to have a contingency plan for when Hunter is called out, though. He can't just ignore a call—because what if it's a real call?—but it has to look like he's leaving."

"I have an idea for that," Bay assured her. "We'll call Landon and Chief Terry. Whatever call comes in, Chief Terry can check if it's real or fake. Hunter will have to make a big show of leaving because I guarantee they'll be watching. So, Hunter will leave, and Landon will pick him up in a different vehicle," she continued. "Chief Terry will take the call, which I assume will be nothing, but they won't know if Hunter showed up. They'll just be watching for him to leave. They won't pay attention to where he goes."

"So, once I'm with Landon, then what?" Hunter queried.

"We'll keep you updated on the phone," Bay replied. "You guys need to circle around and be in the woods. Can you do that without being noticed, find a different entrance route?"

Hunter smirked. "Nobody knows those woods like we do. I know how to get in there. The problem is, it's a long stretch. How will we know where they plan to spring their trap?"

"I don't know that we can answer that." Bay held out her hands. "Sorry. I know that's not what you want to hear, but we'll have to play it by ear."

"What about Stormy?" Evan queried. "She can't go out there alone, but if they see she's not alone, they'll throw in the towel on their plan."

"That's another issue," Bay acknowledged. "Once they do whatever it is they plan to do—and if I were doing it, I would enchant one of Hunter's fellow officers to call Stormy—then we have to adjust.

"They'll give her a specific location," she continued. "I bet it'll be close to wherever you throw the bonfire parties. They will spring their trap before reaching that location because, otherwise, they run the risk of an early bird catching them. So, they'll set up their trap close but not on top of that location, then try to lure her into the woods."

Evan, his face thoughtful, nodded. "Then I should be in the woods. I can move faster. They won't realize that. I can even be up in the trees, so they won't see me."

"You're a very important piece of our puzzle," Bay agreed. "I'm the other important piece."

"Hey!" Tillie was obviously offended. "I'm always an important piece."

Bay smirked. "You are, but I'm the one who has to handle the Edmund situation. We need to remember, Deke is innocent in this. So, while we have to take out the women, we also need to save Deke. I need to force Edmund out of Deke's body and order him to cross over."

"Basically, while you're doing that, I need to face off with the harem," I surmised.

Bay nodded with a sad smile. "Yeah. I'm sorry. I think that'll fall to you, Evan, and Aunt Tillie. We don't know how it could play out either. We need to be fluid and ready for anything. We can't commit to one plan."

"I don't like this," Hunter groused. "Basically, you're saying I'll be bringing up the rear, and Stormy will be out there by herself."

"Not by herself," Bay countered. "We'll be with her. They just won't know that."

Hunter nodded, but he didn't look happy. "I can't wait until this is over."

He wasn't the only one.

WE WENT OVER OUR PLAN MULTIPLE times, and when the call came in shortly before five o'clock, we knew it was time.

"They're saying a kid went missing from the pageant rehearsal in the town square," Hunter announced as he hung up his phone. "That's a good distraction. We can't ignore a missing kid, and so many other kids are there, it will take time to sort it out."

Bay bobbed her head. "This is it. You need to leave in your truck. You're meeting Landon at the funeral home parking lot. He's already there. Chief Terry will cross the street to handle the missing kid. Once you're in Landon's vehicle, you'll head to the woods."

"Okay." Hunter moved to me and tapped my chin so I would lift it. He covered my mouth with his. "You be careful, okay?"

"I will," I promised. "It'll be fine." I wasn't just saying that for his benefit. I believed it.

"Okay." Hunter grabbed his keys and moved toward the door. "I'll see you soon."

Once he was gone, we waited. The call for me came fifteen minutes later, and it played out just as Bay had expected. Jared called me. He sounded dazed, as if he wasn't quite in control of his faculties, but I played along. When I hung up, I was grim.

"That was Jared. He said Hunter is heading out to the river to look for the missing kid and asked for me to join him. It makes no sense, because Hunter would call me if he needed help, but this is obviously their plan."

"Then let's get to it." Bay darted her eyes to Evan. "You know what to do."

He nodded and started for the balcony. "I'll leave this way. You guys need to give Stormy a full five-minute head start before following. I'll be watching her, so she'll be safe."

"We know." Bay moved in front of me. "We've got this. Don't freak out."

"I'm not freaked out. I'm more resigned than anything. Those women won't come quietly. I'm worried we'll have to kill them."

"It's impossible to say how they'll react just yet," Bay confirmed. "It is what it is. We have to protect the town and the people here. This is the only thing we can do."

Knowing that didn't make it easier. Still, I moved toward the door. "Let's do this."

Twenty-Eight

The walk into the woods was nerve racking. The sun had almost completely set by the time I got to the path that would lead me to the enemies I knew lay in wait. I felt multiple sets of eyes on me from every direction—or perhaps I imagined that—but I did my best to remain calm. I wasn't far into the woods when I heard soft humming. It took everything I had not to jerk my head in that direction. I already knew it was Evan sticking close.

My feet made noise on the barren landscape as I walked. We had no snow yet, but it would come, and soon. Snow was one of the few things I had missed when living in warmer climates. Sure, I hated the January to February stretch, but the first few snows of the season were always magical. I looked forward to them. We had no fireplace to snuggle in front of, but if everything went as planned, we would have one next year.

Not long before the first bend in the river, I heard movement in the trees ahead of me. I told myself I should keep walking, but I went ramrod straight and held my ground instead. There were whispers—all female—and sure enough, after several seconds, the four henchmen of the senior citizen apocalypse appeared.

"You made a mistake," Iris announced in a low voice.

She seemed far more menacing than I would've believed possible two weeks before.

"I'm sure I did." Surprisingly, since I could see them—though Edmund was still running around in Deke's body somewhere in the foliage—I felt better about what was to come. "So, this is the plan?" I glanced around. "This is where you're going to do it."

Annoyance glinted in Iris's eyes. *Did she think I would panic? Turn tail and run? Did she think I would flee, screaming?* She was about to see just how wrong that assumption was.

"You don't seem surprised to see us," Florence noted.

Is she smarter than the others or just curious?

"I'm not." I smoothed my coat. "We knew you were setting a trap. I honestly thought you would let me get farther into the woods before you sprang it, but I guess this is more convenient."

"The walk was too much in this cold," Gwen replied on a grimace. "Arthritis is a bitch."

"That must be why you guys are lining up to kill yourselves and take over younger bodies."

A gasp rippled through the women. *Did they really think I was so far behind the eight ball that I didn't know at least a little of their plan?*

"What are you talking about?" Iris demanded.

I could've dragged things out, given Hunter and Landon time to hike into the woods and join the party. It didn't seem necessary, though. I wanted to end it. "Hunter and I followed you to Edmund's hunting cabin," I replied easily. "We eavesdropped and figured out your plan. We know Edmund is inside of Deke. We know that your goal was to lure me out here so you could kill me and make it look like an accident."

"And yet you're still here," Iris noted.

"I'm not alone."

As if on cue, Bay stepped out from the trees directly behind me. She scanned the faces keenly. "So, this is the crew, huh?" She didn't sound impressed.

"This is them," I confirmed.

"Who are you?" Blanche demanded.

"Oh, I'm the wickedest witch in the Midwest." Bay grinned.

"Hey!" Tillie barked from somewhere in the trees. She sounded as if she were traipsing through cymbals, she was so loud. "That's my line. You can't just steal my line."

When she emerged, she had a mark on her cheek. That told me the walk through the woods hadn't been as seamless for her.

"Tillie Winchester," Florence said darkly, recognition dawning. "What are you doing here?"

"I'm about to smite your ass," Tillie replied, not missing a beat. "You should cower in fear."

Rather than run, which would've been smart, if futile, the four women stood shoulder to shoulder.

"You're in our way," Iris volunteered. "We didn't want it to come to this, but we have no choice."

"If you'd just minded your own business, we would've let you live," Gwen added.

I tried to stifle a laugh, but it didn't work. "You guys sound like *Scooby-Doo* villains. Seriously. You would've let me live? What a bunch of nonsense."

Gwen's expression turned dark. "In case you haven't noticed, you're outnumbered."

"And yet we have more firepower," Bay countered. "I'm sure you've heard about my family. All those rumors that people whisper about Hemlock Cove? Yeah, they're true."

"So true." As if to prove it, Tillie waved her hand and cast a magical net over our heads. It illuminated the area, which was a great relief. I didn't want to accidentally hurt somebody on our side when the magic started flying fast and furious.

"Nice parlor trick." Iris's expression was bold, but a hint of fear lurked in her eyes.

"I'll break this down succinctly for you guys because it's cold and nobody wants to spend any unnecessary time out here," Bay started. "We're born witches. That means we have actual power. You guys have done surprisingly well for individuals who stole power—I'm guessing from talismans and potions—but you're no match for us."

"That's right," Tillie agreed. "I'm the witch your mothers warned you about. I can control the weather. I can drop a mountain on you. I can even turn you into fluffy woodland creatures and feed you to bears."

"She's also responsible for the last *Star Wars* screenplay," Bay added. "So you know she's evil."

The situation wasn't funny, and yet I swallowed the absurd urge to laugh.

"We're not afraid of you," Florence fired back. "We're the power in this area. Do you have any idea what we've done?"

"Yes, you managed to cast a spell that anchored Edmund's soul to this plane," Bay replied. "Then you stabbed him with a letter opener when he wasn't looking."

"Why a letter opener?" Tillie asked. "Those things are dull. You would've really had to put some *oomph* into it to get it through the breastbone."

"How do you even know all of this?" Out of all the women, Gwen looked the most fearful.

"I just told you that Hunter and I were eavesdropping at the cabin," I reminded her.

"If that's true, where is Hunter?" Iris asked. "He wouldn't leave you if he thought you were in danger."

"He wasn't keen on the idea," I admitted. "We needed you to believe we'd fallen for your ruse, though. Right now, I'm certain he's cursing under his breath and traipsing through the woods to find us. He should be here shortly."

Genuine worry clouded Blanche's features. "Maybe we should leave."

"We can't leave," Iris fired back. "We have to put an end to this. Right now. It's our only chance. We can't let her muck up our plans."

"Do you want to keep being old?" Florence added. "We joined forces so we could start over. She'll stop us if she gets the chance. We can't allow that. We've fought too long and hard to get here."

Blanche gnawed on her bottom lip. "I know, but how good will youth be if we're in jail? Hunter won't sit back and do nothing if he knows we killed her."

"Then we'll kill him too," Iris said breezily. "In fact, we can send Edmund to do it right now." She raised her hand and snapped her fingers. "Edmund!"

When he didn't respond or emerge from the trees, she rolled her eyes impatiently. "Hey, Edmund! Stop being a moron. We need you out here."

Still nothing.

When I risked a glance at Bay, I found her smirking. Much like me, she'd already figured out Evan had Edmund. It was the only thing that made sense.

"I think you lost your henchman," I noted.

"I don't care how powerful you think you are," Florence hissed. "You can't force him out of every single body. Once he finds one that works, and we've all got new bodies, we're leaving this place, and there's nothing you can do about it."

"You might be surprised," Bay said dryly. She looked toward the trees again. "You can bring him out, Evan. I think a little display might be in order."

Evan didn't drag things out. He appeared almost immediately, his arm locked around Edmund's neck. Evan dragged him forward as the old man in the younger man's body kicked up a fuss.

"Let me go!" Edmund screeched. "You have no right to put your hands on me. I'm a US citizen. That means I have rights."

"Oh, shut up," Tillie barked, clucking her tongue as she took in Edmund's resentful eyes. "This is the guy you chose? He's already got a bald spot." She checked again for good measure. "If you're going to steal a body, at least make it a good one."

Bay shot her great-aunt a quelling look. "Don't add to this insanity." She gravely looked Edmund in the eye. "I have to hand it to you—no, really—this was a fairly ingenious plan. I don't know what spell you used to anchor his soul to this plane, but obviously, it worked like a charm."

"We have more than one spell at our disposal," Iris warned. "You need to let him go."

"You do," Gwen echoed. "He's our man. You can't have him."

Florence shot Gwen a withering look. "Let's not make ourselves look quite that pathetic, huh? Have a little pride. It's not as if we're with him because he's some great prize. He was just the only one we knew we could manipulate."

"We needed a sacrificial lamb in case the spell didn't work," Iris agreed. "It's not as if he's Chuck Norris or something."

I blinked hard. "Chuck Norris?" I sputtered, unable to control myself.

"He's quite the hunk." Iris gave a demented smile. "Maybe we should see if we can track him down and steal his body."

"He's too old," Blanche complained. "We need someone who doesn't have to pop Viagra. We already talked about this."

"As fascinating as I find this discussion—and I do—it doesn't matter," Bay interjected. "Edmund is about to say his goodbyes."

Iris turned haughty. "Even if you kill Deke, that won't stop Edmund. He'll just find another body to inhabit."

"Hunter's body," Gwen volunteered out of nowhere. "If he's out here in the woods, we could turn things to our benefit. We'll kill Stormy and take over Hunter. People won't even notice once she's gone, and any discrepancies in his behavior can be chalked up to his grief."

My blood ran cold. "You're not going anywhere near Hunter."

"I like this idea." Iris bobbed her head. "Hunter is hot. He's also in a prime position to protect us until we have all our ducks in a row. Once Stormy is out of the way, we'll have a clear shot. This is good."

Panic licked my insides, but I held it together and snagged gazes with Bay. "Do it. Put an end to this now."

"Yeah, I think that's for the best." Bay reached over and slapped Deke's forehead. "Out," she ordered in her darkly magical voice.

I'd only seen her use it once or twice, but each instance fascinated me. Once she engaged her magic, there was no delay. Edmund's ghostly form slithered out of Deke's prone body. The ghost looked positively furious.

"I've had it with you people interfering!" he shrieked. "Can't a man just get a little peace? Stop ruining things for me!"

"You're about to get your peace," Bay promised. She held out her glowing right hand. "*Glacio,*" she intoned, her voice echoing in the cold darkness.

Edmund, whose mouth opened to argue again, froze in place as the magic washed over him. I watched with overt curiosity as the ghost recognized the playing field was no longer level. Bay dominated every position.

"What are you doing?" Iris stepped forward. "Just what do you think you're doing?"

"Ending this." Bay focused on a furious Edmund. "Your tether to this world is gone. It's time for you to follow suit. You can go now."

Edmund's face twisted in fury. "You're not the boss. You don't get a say. This is my life."

"*Go,*" Bay repeated with deadly calm, her magic blowing back her flaxen hair.

That was all it took. Edmund dissipated right in front of our eyes.

"What did you do?" Gwen shrieked when Edmund let loose a final mournful howl.

"I set things right," Bay replied. "All that leaves is dealing with you."

"I could snap their necks," Evan offered helpfully. "I'm not sure I want to drink from them, but we could throw them in the river or something and make it look like an accident. In this cold, I don't think it would take long for them to go hypothermic and die."

Gwen looked horrified. "I want a deal." She jolted her hand into the air, as if waiting for the teacher to call on her in class. "I'll testify against these other terrible people in exchange for a deal. I didn't want to be a part of this anyway."

"We're not the police," I reminded her.

"No, but we are," a booming male voice announced as Hunter and Landon joined the party. They were winded, hair standing up in various directions, but they had arrived. "I don't remember that hike being so hard," Hunter complained as he rested his hands on his knees. "I'm getting old, Stormy. We have to start working out because I'm determined to have a very long life with you."

I grinned. Just his presence made me feel lighter. "We'll talk about it when we're not so keyed up. I don't want working out to get in the way of all the snuggling under a blanket I plan to do this winter."

He cocked his head, considering. "Good point." When he turned to face the women, he looked grim. "Where do we stand?"

"We're about to kill you," Iris replied, raising her hands. "I'm sorry, but that's simply the way it has to be."

I reacted without thinking, letting a wisp of fire magic race in her direction. The magic wasn't designed to destroy, however—well, not a person. It was meant to seek out and destroy the borrowed magic in her blood. The spell, which I'd never tried before, worked surprisingly well despite that I made it up on the spot.

"What is that?" Florence screeched.

She seemed ready to make a run for it, but Evan stopped her with a single look.

"If I have to chase you, I'm going to be really mean," he warned.

"And I'll be even meaner when I catch up," Tillie added.

The magical fire wisp jumped from Iris to Gwen and carried out the same mission. Then it hopped to Blanche. Florence was the last in line, and she looked resigned when the magic made a beeline for her.

"We just wanted to be young again," Florence complained morosely. "We weren't trying to be evil or anything. We just wanted to be young."

"We planned to do it better this time," Gwen added.

"Well, now you'll be living out your final years in jail," Hunter volunteered.

"Jail?" Unmitigated shock rippled across Iris's face. "How do you figure that?"

"You killed Edmund," Hunter replied. "We heard you."

"Yes, but that was so he could move to another body."

"Yes, well, we won't include that part in the report. If you want your attorneys to use it, go ahead. We won't be acknowledging any part of ... this." He gestured toward the swirling magic, which rapidly dissipated.

"If you take us in, we'll tell everybody about you and your friends," Florence warned. "We'll ruin your lives."

"No, you won't." Tillie tsked as she stepped forward. "We're going to make you forget our part in this. Your part you'll remember for the rest of your lives, however long that may be. We, on the other hand, won't even be a memory."

Florence balked. "How will you explain all of this?"

"We've come up with our fair share of stories over the years," Bay replied. "I think we can manage one more." She moved closer to Iris. "Let's get this memory charm going. Then Landon and Hunter can take them into custody."

"And I guess I'm responsible for getting Deke home and into bed," Evan surmised.

"Are you okay with that?" I asked. "If not, we can drag him to my car and take him home that way."

"No, I've got it." Resigned, Evan puffed a breath. "It's best he's not seen with any of you. Hopefully, when he wakes up, he'll believe he tied one on and let it go."

"That would be best for all of us." Hunter grimly turned back to the harem. "Make them forget. Then let's get them out of here." He winked at me. "I have some snuggling to do under a blanket."

The tension I'd carried for days disappeared, if only momentarily. After all, we still had Easton and Kyle to deal with. Still, the harem fight had gone exactly our way, and with minimal bloodshed to boot.

"I think that sounds like Heaven," I said. "Let's do that."

He grinned. "I thought you would see things my way."

TWENTY-NINE

Watching Bay and Tillie perform memory charms was interesting. Briefly, I wondered if I would be capable of that one day. Ultimately, I knew it was a question for another time. Fire magic seemed to be my brand—and I'd managed something entirely new—so that was where my focus had to be.

Once back at the restaurant, Hunter called for backup, and they loaded the four women into two vehicles. The rapidly dissolving harem fought the entire way, blaming each other for their predicament and clamoring for deals.

"That's the prosecutor's problem," Hunter said as he dropped a kiss on my lips. He looked reticent to leave me, but he had a job to do. "Keep my spot under the blanket warm, huh?"

I nodded.

Once they were gone and Evan had returned—he promised he'd tucked Deke into bed and that he was fine to wake up on his own—the Winchesters took off with the vampire. That left me to fret alone in the apartment. Technically, things had gone much better than we'd anticipated—nobody had died—but the bigger problem still loomed.

Hunter brought pizza when he returned, and as promised, we snuggled under the same blanket and ate it while watching old television episodes. I was close to passing out from sheer exhaustion when some-body knocked on the door.

"Are you expecting anybody?" Hunter shot me a curious look.

I shook my head.

"Stay here." He didn't grab his gun from the kitchen table before moving to the door. When he opened it, however, his shoulders and back went rigid.

"Who is it?" I asked, instantly alert.

"The happy wanderer." Hunter opened the door wide to let Easton enter.

The gnome—*is he a gnome or a man at this point?* I couldn't tell—managed a smile as he entered. "I understand congratulations are in order." He glanced around the room, his gaze ultimately falling on the pizza. "Is any left? I haven't eaten all day."

"Oh, so now you want us to feed you, huh?" Hunter was surly as he made his way back to the couch. "If you wanted food, perhaps you should've hung around for the breakfast we talked about last night. You know, the breakfast where you were supposed to spill your guts."

"I had to do something first." Easton flipped open the pizza box and grabbed a slice before settling into the chair across from the couch. When he spoke again, his mouth was full. "Word has spread about what you did with the harem tonight, Stormy. People are impressed."

Agitation gripped my throat. "Are you impressed?"

He bobbed his head. "You managed to pull off an advanced bit of magic. Everything you've done before now has been by brute force. This was nuanced. You burned stolen magic out of those women, and you didn't even break a sweat."

"Well, you can forego the applause and deliver some answers."

I didn't expect him to concede. When he nodded, I narrowed my eyes shrewdly. "Just like that?"

"Just like that," he confirmed.

I waited as he inhaled.

"I'm part of an ancient order," he explained. "Hellcats were once prevalent in this world. Before they died out, they ruled the magical world for several centuries. My order worked with them."

"Serving as familiars," I surmised.

Easton nodded. "That was long before my time. When the hellcats died out on this plane, my people moved to another. It was supposed to be a quiet life. We remembered the old ways, but nobody thought we would go back to them. Then you came along."

I waited. *Really, what else was I supposed to do?*

"Your magic was like a beacon in the darkness," he continued. "It woke my people, and they sent me to investigate."

"As a cat."

"That was the form we often took when serving. It seemed the best way to get close to you without making you suspicious. Unfortunately, I didn't keep my mouth shut. I was not supposed to reveal myself to you so soon."

"Why did you?"

"Because you weren't following the timeline they'd provided me." He offered a rueful smile. "You were advanced right from the start. The Winchesters helped you along, so much so that you're even farther on your journey than I would've expected a year out."

"What does that mean?" Hunter asked.

"It means you're coveted." Easton's answer was simple. "It means nobody knows what to expect. Are you just a fluke? Are you the start of something new? We'll all be figuring that out together."

I couldn't wrap my head around his words. Sure, the basics were straightforward enough. He was still holding back, though.

"What's your part in this?" I demanded.

"I was supposed to be your guide, but you don't need one. You're figuring it out on your own. I guess that means I'm a sidekick of sorts. I'll answer whatever questions you have and wait to see what powers you manifest next."

"And your friend? Kyle? What part does he play in this?"

"You mean Weston, or West as he's apparently going by on this plane. He's also of my order, though he's more of a traditionalist. He wants to control your magic."

"Easton and Weston?" Hunter demanded. "That can't be a coincidence."

"It's not. He's my cousin. Our fathers were born to the same family but grew to be enemies." Easton adjusted in his chair. "You have to understand, my family is interested in a hellcat resurgence, but we don't want to return to the days of old, when your witches dominated all the other paranormals. We're interested in balance. West doesn't want that. He wants you to embrace the old ways. He won't be subtle when trying to motivate you. He will make an enemy of himself if he thinks he can prompt certain reactions from you."

"What does that mean?"

Easton shrugged one shoulder. "I don't know. I don't have a means to contact my people right now and get answers either. I wasn't supposed to need them for at least another year. I'm unsure what to do. West's appearance doesn't help matters. I didn't know him growing up. I only knew *of* him. I wasn't even sure who he was when he first showed himself to me."

The shadow behind the storage building, I realized. *That was him.* "And how long have you been talking to him behind my back?"

"Not long." Easton looked sad. "You must know, I wasn't working against you. I tried to get him to back off. That's not his way, though."

There was more to the story—much more, if I had to guess. Still, he'd opened up at least a little, which was more than he'd done before.

"And what do you want from me?" I asked.

"I just want to see how it plays out." He held out his hands. "You haven't followed the timeline I was told was a certainty. You don't kowtow to outside influences. The Winchesters will have a big hand in molding you."

"Meaning?"

"Meaning that nothing is set in stone. For right now, we just have to wait it out."

I narrowed my eyes. "We? Does that mean you're staying here?"

"I was hoping to." He flashed a charming smile. "If you kick me out, though, I understand. I'll have to romance somebody in town to find a place to bunk, but that's never been a problem for me. I mean ... look at this face." He pointed toward his dimple, which made me want to punch him.

"You can stay here for tonight at least." I shot Hunter an apologetic look. "I'm not offering you a forever home. I need to think, though. I'll have more questions for you."

He bobbed his head. "Of course."

"Will you actually be around to answer them this time?"

"Of course."

Hunter stirred. "What about this West guy? Should we assume he'll keep coming around?"

"Yes, but you've thwarted him for now. You took his vehicle and his job. He has to regroup." Easton looked smug. "We have time. I expect your powers will continue to grow in the interim."

"What if they grow to the point where I become a danger?" I demanded. "Is that a possibility?"

"I honestly don't know." Easton was rueful. "I look forward to finding out, though." With that, he stood and stripped off his shirt. "Thanks for the pizza, but I'm used to sleeping eighteen hours a day. I need a nap."

I watched him head toward the second bedroom. "That's it?"

"For tonight." His charming grin was back. "You need to process, and I need rest. In the coming days, you'll have more questions, and hopefully, I'll be able to come up with more answers. For now, though, we seem to be at an impasse."

I wanted to say so much. I didn't say any of it. "I guess we'll see you in the morning."

"You certainly will." Easton beamed. "I would like to try eggs and hash browns tomorrow. They look delicious."

"Yeah, I'll get right on that."

He offered a saucy salute. "Then I'll see you on the flip side."

Once he was secured in the other bedroom, I shifted my eyes to Hunter. "What do you think?"

"I think he's going to be a problem."

"I know that. What about the hellcat stuff?"

"I have no idea. I guess we'll have to watch it play out, like he said."

"I'm afraid." It was hard to admit. "I don't want to screw up our lives."

"Oh, Stormy, you won't screw up our lives." He tugged me tight against his side. "We'll be happy regardless. Will it take time to figure this out? Yes. We can do it, though. Together. Always together."

I wished for his faith. "I'm really tired," I said finally.

"Yeah. Do you want to head to bed early?"

"Definitely. We need to start locking the bedroom door. You know, just in case. I don't want any unexpected guests, especially now that he's not a cat."

"See, now you're thinking." He gave me a soft kiss. "It really will be okay," he whispered.

"From your lips to the goddess's ears."

Made in the USA
Las Vegas, NV
10 February 2024

85588437R00156